One Leaf Too Many

Julie B Cosgrove

Write Integrity Press

One Leaf Too Many
© 2018 Julie Cosgrove

ISBN-13: 978-1-944120-71-9

Published by Write Integrity Press
PO Box 702852
Dallas, TX 75370
Find out more about the author, **Julie Cosgrove,** at her website: **www.JulieCosgrove.com**
or on her author page at **www.WriteIntegrity.com**

Printed in the United States of America.

Dedication

To my brother and sister.

I am glad we've stayed in touch after our parents died.
You both mean the world to me.

Chapter 1

Bailey Matteson paused in the entry.

"What is it?" Her best friend, Shannon Johnson, halted to keep from running into Bailey's back.

"It's too quiet. And cold." Bailey rubbed her arms as she stepped across the marbled foyer.

"I'd say they have the AC set on seventy-two. Not exactly energy-conscious but comfortable to me, girl."

Bailey scrunched her mouth to the side. "I didn't mean the room temperature. It's not how home usually feels for Sunday dinner." She peered into the formal living room. "Mom? Dad?"

From deeper in the house, high heels clicked across the floor. Her mother, Emily Matteson, appeared, wiping her hands on a dish towel.

"Hi, Mom." Bailey shuffled to meet her.

Before she got within hugging distance, she noticed

the wrinkles on her mother's brow, furrowed underneath her department store foundation and blush.

"I didn't feel like cooking. Sorry. Instead, I ordered from Chang Wong's." Her mother flashed a hostess smile. "Can I get y'all some iced tea?"

Bailey eyed Shannon, who arched an eyebrow. Emily Matteson's Sunday dinners were renowned, and her recipes had been featured in the local paper numerous times. She loved to cook and usually put out a spread for ten—even though her family now consisted of three— leaving leftovers for Bailey to cart home and devour for lunch the following week.

"Um, sure, Mom. That's fine." Bailey glanced around as she followed her mother into the parlor. "Where is Dad?"

Her voice cracked. "In his den, I imagine. Pouting." She slumped into the down cushions of the davenport. "He refuses to go to our college alumni banquet during homecoming… again. Every year we get an invite and each time he firmly says no. But this year is a milestone. His fiftieth. I only mentioned it and boom!" She waved her hands in the air.

Shannon leaned into Bailey's ear. "Perhaps I should leave?"

Bailey widened her eyes "Yeah. I'll get a ride back. I think there is more to this…"

Her mother jolted from the sofa. "Shannon, dear. Please don't leave. My husband is being stubborn. He'll come around. Come help me set the table, ladies."

The two thirty-year-old friends traipsed behind the woman's matronly swishing hips, reminding Bailey of ducklings following a mallard to a reflection pond.

Throughout dinner, the four adults barely spoke. Each forked their vegetable fried rice, Mongolian beef, or cashew chicken. Her father finally pushed his chair from the table.

"Bailey, Shannon, please excuse me. I have a lot on my mind." He bent to air-kiss his daughter's cheek, nodded to her friend, ignored his wife, and plodded down the hall.

Her mother rose and went into the kitchen.

Bailey nodded to Shannon. They gathered up the take-out containers, placing them into the plastic sacks they'd arrived in, then stacked the china plates, sterling silverware, and crystal water goblets onto a silver tray resting on the sideboard. Then Bailey mouthed for them to leave.

As they drove out of the older, established neighborhood toward their newly built apartment complex, Shannon broached the subject, her ebony hands tightly gripping the steering wheel. "Are they going to be okay?"

Bailey swatted her concern away. "Sure. Dad's probably feeling his age, that's all. Doesn't want his peers to see him with a paunch and white hair, as if they all don't look like that by now." She gave her head a small shake. "Still, it's weird."

"What?"

She swirled a lock of her auburn hair. "Dad rarely talks about his college years. I wonder why?" She turned to her friend and gazed into her chocolate eyes. "And Mom never mentions her side of the family. It's like they contracted amnesia right before Travis was born."

"Your older brother?" Shannon chuckled. "Text him. Maybe he has a clue."

"Perhaps I will." She squinted into the sun as it traveled in an arc toward the western hills.

The two rode in silence the rest of the way.

Shannon pulled into their complex and parked in her designated spot. "See ya for choir."

Bailey closed the car door. "Sure. See ya."

She flashed Shannon a quick grin and plodded down the corridor to her unit. When she heard the faint mew on the other side, her world became better. As she shoved the key in the lock, she sloughed off the angst of the afternoon.

Surely her parents' solid marriage remained crack-free.

"What's taking Jessica so long in there?" Shannon eyed the wooden door with the silhouette of a woman on it.

Bailey clenched her jaw to stifle a yawn and shrugged. "I don't know. But we promised we'd wait." She pulled up her sleeve and stared at her watch. "Nine-fifteen? Wow, choir practice ran late tonight."

Shannon pressed her shoulder against the wall of the corridor connecting church's classrooms and the choral room as she ran a hand through her black, wiry hair. "And I still have two pets to look in on before I can go home."

"Pampered Plants and Pets is booming, then?"

"It's September. Kids are back in school, so the cruise lines offer huge discounts. I have eighteen empty-nesters and retirees on vacation who've booked my services. Had to hire a new part-time assistant."

"Very nice..." Bailey smiled back despite a headache inching into her temples.

"Except when she calls in with a sick kid on her third day." Shannon thumped her head onto the wall. "Think we should check on Jessica?"

"Maybe she has an idea for a new article and is scribbling it on the toilet paper."

Shannon snickered.

The yawn finally escaped. Bailey clasped her hand to her mouth. "Oh, excuse me. It's not the company... well, I take it back. It's *the company* I work for. They're running me ragged. This week has been a killer so far, and it's only Tuesday. Hours poring over cash receipts to discover a $5.93 discrepancy have left my brain frazzled."

"Well, that explains things." Shannon winked. "I thought maybe you were going for the smoky look with those dark circles under your eyes."

"Are they that bad?" She turned to view her pasty reflection in the glassed case displaying a poster for the upcoming sermon series on spiritual gifts.

"Still worried about your parents?"

"Not in the least." Bailey raised her chin.

"Uh, huh. Whatever you say."

A piercing shriek echoed from inside the ladies' room. Bailey spun toward Shannon. "Did you hear that?"

The two pushed open the door and rushed inside.

Jessica White, wide-eyed and flushed, thumped a flier near the hand dryer as she danced on her toes. Her blond ponytail swished back and forth like a pendulum wound too tight. She beckoned Shannon and Bailey with her other hand. "Look. Look."

"What now, Jess?" Bailey slumped from relief her friend didn't lie bleeding on the bathroom floor with a knife-wielding madman hovering over her.

"Read." Jessica tapped the paper again.

Bailey inched forward and squinted to decipher the blurred letters, caused by water splatters from numerous wet hands reaching for the dryer button. "The Gospel of Matthew. Led by Grace Perkins." She scrunched her brows. "So?"

"This is our answer." Jessica's head bobbed rapidly as her blue eyes grew even larger.

"To…?" The throbbing headache frizzled Bailey's patience. She wanted to go home.

"Oh!" Shannon's face illuminated. "To what we discussed last Saturday over our momentary indulgence of pizza. Wanting to get into a good Bible study."

"Exactly." Jessica bounced again, her eyes shimmering under golden bangs. "Mrs. Perkins knows everything about the Bible. *Eve-ry-thing.*"

Shannon shifted her weight to her left foot. "True. She's been leading Bible studies and Vacation Bible School as long as I can remember, and I've been going here since second grade."

Jessica's hand, still tanned from summer, patted Shannon's darker arm. "With a brain still sharp as a pin, I hear. Even though she's at least eighty."

"Very well. I'm game." Shannon turned to Bailey. "You?"

"Sure. Why not?" Bailey stifled another yawn. "Let's go sign up."

"Goodie. This will be so much fun." Jessica danced out of the ladies' room and down the hall to a sign-up clipboard hanging outside a classroom.

"I need her energy." Bailey dragged her feet.

Shannon scoffed. "You need sleep."

"That, too." Bailey scuffled down the corridor, putting a reminder in her phone to purchase a new study Bible, a college-lined tablet, and a pink highlighter.

For the next two weeks, Bailey reconsidered taking on this weekly class. She had enough on her plate. But Jessica had been so enthusiastic, Bailey had been swept up in the moment. Besides, signing her name to the clipboard meant she had committed to the course. And Mattesons never went back on their word.

So, she changed from her work outfit into a casual pair of slacks, grabbed her Bible and supplies, and headed out. Shannon and Jessica waited at the front door of the building for her and waved as she pulled her car into the parking lot.

Several other women walked toward the entrance ahead of them. Strolling down the hall with her friends, all clutching books, reminded Bailey of her first day in high school. So did the ripples in her gut. Why did her nerves tap her mind as if tonight would somehow change her whole life?

"Wow, there are a lot of others here." Jessica's petite frame strained to peer over the heads in front of them. "I hope we can sit together."

As they entered the room, Baily noticed three vacant chairs in the circle, all next to each other. "See? Prayer answered. Come on."

The three scurried to claim their seats. After a few minutes of conversational hums, the room quieted when an elderly woman cleared her throat.

"Welcome, ladies." Mrs. Perkins gazed around the room over her readers, perched half-way down the bridge of her nose. The earpieces were supported by two rhinestone-covered strings around her neck. The fake jewels twinkled in the harsh fluorescent light as she pivoted her head to count each face staring back at her.

I'm going to become hypnotized for sure. Bailey squinted from the prisms' twinkling glare.

"This year we are going to be studying the Gospel of Matthew. We will take one chapter per week." She nodded as several hands rose. "Yes, that comes out to twenty-eight weeks, which I know leads us right up to Easter. Minus two weeks for Christmas break of course. It will be so meaningful to study the events leading up to His crucifixion and resurrection as we prepare for Easter, agreed?"

Bailey rubbed her eyes.

"Are you okay?" Jessica leaned in, drowning out Mrs. Perkin's attempt to answer Amanda's question about how many times they were allowed to be absent.

"Yeah, just tired. Work." She rolled her eyes. "I love equation solving and researching economic ways to manage restaurants, but eye strain is the pits."

Jessica and Shannon gave her a sympathetic shrug. Bailey wiggled in her seat to try to find a better position while balancing her Bible and notebook on her knees. Her parents' continued iciness toward each other caused her the tossing and turning through the nights even more than work stress. So uncharacteristic for them. She shot up a silent prayer to God, confessing her worry again and asking for clarity.

After they went around the room telling their names and why they had signed up, the sixteen ladies, ranging from twenty-two to sixty-something, settled in to begin the study.

"Let's turn to the first chapter that explains the genealogy of Jesus." Mrs. Perkins cleared her throat, shoved her readers further up onto the bridge of her nose, and began to read. "Matthew, chapter one, beginning at the first verse. 'This is the genealogy of Jesus the Messiah, the son of David, the son of Abraham: Abraham was the father of Isaac, Isaac the father of Jacob, Jacob the father of Judah and his brothers…'"

As Bailey focused on the passage, her brain perked. Jesus could be traced all the way back to Abraham? Wow. She recalled God's promise to Abraham that he would be the father of many nations, and then how the Bible said believers were all children of God. Now it made sense. A new energy shot through her mundane workaday world. *How cool is this! God had it all planned out.*

That encouraged her that He had plans for her situation. She inched a bit closer in her chair as Mrs. Perkins went down the list of names, letting the ladies find the passages in the Bible that related to each ancestor and allowing a few of them to read.

Bailey wrote copious notes. By the end of the session, her hand cramped. She shook it, which sent her pen rolling across the floor.

Shannon retrieved it. "Girlfriend. Were you writing a novel? I thought that was Jessica's thing."

Bailey chuckled. "Practically."

"I texted almost everything Mrs. Perkins said into my

tablet. She is interesting, right?" Jessica sucked on her finger. "I think I sprained my left thumb."

"You were right, Jess." Bailey lifted her New Testament and notebook to her chest as she stood. "Mrs. Perkins does know everything about the Bible. I could barely keep up. It's got me wondering…" Bailey peered off into space.

Jessica came around to her side. "Uh, oh. The wheels are churning again."

Her friends began singing the chorus to *Rolling on the River* about the wheel of the riverboat, *the Proud Mary*, churning up the Mississippi.

Bailey chuckled. "All right, y'all. Listen up. How much do you know about your past? Who begat who in your families? Anyone famous back in the day?"

Jessica frowned. "I'm adopted, remember?"

"Oops, yeah. Sorry."

"It's fine." She pushed through the door into the courtyard of the church.

Bailey grimaced and quickened her step to catch up to Jessica. "Really, Jess. I sometimes speak before I think."

Shannon scurried to catch up and laughed. "Sometimes?"

The three nudged each other as they walked to the parking lot. Bailey glanced at each of their faces. "We know each other well, don't we?"

"Sure." Jessica bobbed her head. "Which is why we can razz each other."

"And share secrets." Shannon winked at them

"True." A warmth swept over her as she realized how her two good friends blessed her life. Bailey halted at the curb. She clicked the keyless fob. Her hatchback blinked in response. "I have a sneaky suspicion my family may have a few secrets I don't know about. Mom never really talks about her life growing up. I mean, I know she had three brothers, but…"

"You never met your grandparents, right?" Shannon shaded her eyes from the setting sun gleaming over their town before it slipped behind the lush mounds of the Texas Hill Country.

"Nope. Not on either my Dad's or Mom's side. Dad's father died in action and his mother committed suicide several years later."

"That's awful." Shannon laid a hand on Bailey's shoulder.

"Hmm. And my mom's parents died in a car accident during her freshman year in college. An aunt helped raise her youngest brother." She scrunched her mouth to one side. "At least I think that's right."

"No wonder they don't talk about their youth."

"It does make sense, Shannon. Maybe that's why Dad doesn't want to go to the reunion. Bad memories." She shrugged. "But that doesn't mean I can't learn more about their parents' lives."

Jessica's eyes lit with sudden revelation. "I get it. Studying all this begetting has you curious about your family history?"

"I guess it does, Jess. To be honest, I've been a bit concerned about their standoffishness. I prayed to God for an answer. Maybe this is it."

Shannon chuckled. "Bailey, I haven't seen you this excited in months."

Bailey's face warmed. Work really had been getting to her, zapping her of her normal go-get-'em attitude. Along with her parents' bizarre behavior. "It's like a kiwi seed stuck in my gums. The idea won't let loose of my brain cells."

Jessica cocked her head and ran her tongue over her teeth at the idea. "So...?"

"I want to study my family genealogy." Bailey set her shoulders back with purpose. "Starting next weekend."

"Seriously?" Shannon knitted her brows.

"Yep. See y'all for the special choir practice on Thursday." She grinned and waved as she stepped off the curb.

"Don't remind us!"

Her girlfriends giggled at their response in unison.

Bailey slid into her front seat, started the ignition, and turned on the radio. A peppy DJ announced, "And now a blast from the past. All the way back to Christmas, 1968, recorded by Credence Clearwater Revival. Get yo' grandparents and jack up the volume. They'll remember this one fo' sure."

I don't have any. She reached her hand to punch in

another station, then halted. The men's voices started blaring out the story of the Proud Mary steamer on the Mississippi River.

"That's what Shannon and Jess were singing. Humph." Bailey shrugged her shoulders, threw back her head, and sang along.

Halfway through the chorus, chill bumps coated her arms. Could this be a sign?

She knew her mother's mother, Mary Beth Holston, came from Louisiana. *Proud Mary*. Lived all her life on the Mississippi bayou until she moved to San Antonio after WWII. Both are known for their rivers. *Kept rollin' on the river*. She and her husband were killed in—wow, 1968! The year they recorded this song— leaving behind four children ranging from fifteen to twenty-two.

Had to be a sign. She didn't believe in coincidences. But why would God want her to delve into her family history?

Bailey turned the radio off as she edged into her neighborhood. In the distance, the big city lights twinkled. Pretty, but it meant that urban sprawl threatened to encroach on their cozy town like spilled ginger ale seeping toward the remote control on a coffee table. Not that she could do anything about it, so why worry?

With a shrug, she turned the corner as the song replayed in her brain. Hmm. She calculated the year span in her head. 1968. Fifty years ago. Mind-boggling how long songs remained a part of their culture. Which ones would *her* grandchildren know in fifty years? If she ever married, that is.

Bailey waited at the traffic light. If her grandmother Mary had died while in her mid-forties, it meant she would have been born around 1922 or so. Is that where she should begin?

Unanswerable questions danced in her head. What had it been like to live through the Depression and World War II? The Civil Rights Movement and all those assassinations? What had her grandparents been like? Did they have a great marriage?

A pang hit her chest as Jacob's dear face passed across her memory. If he hadn't found that land mine in Afghanistan four years ago, would they have had a great marriage? Bailey never had the chance to walk down the aisle to find out.

Sniffling back a lump in her throat, she returned her thoughts to the 1960s. So much to learn about that era. Why wait until the weekend when she could begin tonight? Bailey made a sharp right and headed to the edge of town where her parent's acreage lay.

She should check on them anyway. Besides, her mother always served her mouth-watering King Ranch Chicken casserole on Tuesdays. Surely there would be leftovers. Better than downing a salad or yogurt again. Her stomach grumbled at the thought.

She'd run an extra two miles tomorrow morning to make up for it. Settled. She exited the expressway.

As her headlights bounced off their four-car garage, a thought tickled her mind. Perhaps her mother never talked about her kin for a reason. Open that door, ask the questions, and nothing might be the same again.

"Don't be silly," she scolded her reflection in the rearview mirror. "Drama is Jessica's thing, not yours."

Chapter 2

Bailey tapped her turquoise-polished nails on the steering wheel as she pulled into her parent's circular driveway. Then she froze and spread her hand in front of her. "Oh, my gosh. I forgot."

She rolled her eyes and began to peel the vibrant color from her fingertips. Her mother's taste consisted of blush, clear French-manicure or slightly frosted polish *only*. Anything else? Gauche or tacky. If Bailey showed up sporting bright aqua, the conversation would never segue from her mother's chatter about Bailey's lack of fashion sense. Bailey could hear it now. How did she ever expect to attract a decent man, blah, blah, blah… wa-wa.

Forgetting to apply a clear coat first made the stripping-away task nearly impossible. With a deep exhale through her mouth, she backed out and drove to the pharmacy on Main Street, two miles away. Snatching polish remover, a blush crème polish, and cotton balls, she stopped to retrieve a tin of the imported ginger cookies her mother loved from the emporium next door. That way, in case Mom had been peering out the window, Bailey had an excuse for her quick retreat.

She rehearsed her line as she returned to her parents' street. "I forgot to bring a gift, and you always told me to never arrive any place without a present for the hostess." Yep, that'll make her mother's mouth turn into that tight-lipped, eyebrow-cocked smirk. Bailey imitated her voice as she drove back to the house. "See? You raised your daughter right, after all, Emily Sue Holston Matteson."

Sure enough, as soon as she pulled to the curb, the front door flew open and her mother traipsed down the illuminated walk to greet her. As Bailey emerged from her sub-compact, her mom leaned in for the usual daughter to mother air-kiss on the cheek. "What a pleasant surprise."

"Here, Mom. For you." Bailey presented the treat as if seeking an audience with the queen. In fact, she stifled the urge to curtsy since her mother had been raised old-school. To be fair, Bailey had to admit that underneath the Southern high society pomp lay a God-fearing, honest woman who dearly loved her family and would do anything for them—well, almost. As long as it didn't start tongues waggling, go against the social grain of decency, or smudge the Matteson family's reputation in the community. Heaven forbid.

"Oh, Bailey. You remembered the emporium down the way carried them. How thoughtful of you to bring me a hostess gift, even if I am only your mother." She pivoted on her heels and headed toward the house. "Obviously I did raise you correctly."

Bailey pressed her lips. So, her mother had been watching. She wouldn't put it past her to know the sound of both of her children's car engines, much less most of her neighbor's vehicles. Texas families practiced neighborhood watching long before it became a civilian safety program.

"So, what brings you by this evening? Not my King Ranch Chicken, is it?"

Bailey inched through the door, held open by her mother. "I can never fool you, Mom. I had a hankering for your cooking. Sometimes I have to go off the diet and splurge, you know."

"Hmm. Well, you have a nice, slim figure. So, I am sure it won't be too devastating. Besides," her voice lowered. "I now use fat-free cream, lean chicken, sea salt, and veggie cheese anyway." She leaned in to whisper in her daughter's ear. "Don't tell your father I've altered the recipe, though."

Bailey winked. "Of course not."

"Bailey. My favorite daughter." Her father's booming Texas drawl echoed from the dining room. His boots thunked across the hardwoods to greet her.

She bear-hugged him, drinking in his scent of Stetson cologne and leather. "Daddy. I'm your *only* daughter."

He chuckled. "That's my story and I'm stickin' to it."

"Jonathan Matteson. Really." Her mother swatted at his shoulder.

For a moment their eyes locked in a playful, adoring embrace. It made Bailey's heart hollow and warm at the same time. Whatever angst had existed between them over the college reunion had dissipated. If only she could find a lasting love like that. Maybe she should think about dating again.

"Come, daughter. Sit. Tell us what is happening in your life." Her father pulled out one of the mahogany chairs in the formal dining room as her mother slid in a placemat, brass charger, and linen napkin. "I'll dish you up some casserole and bring you a salad. Do you want a Porterhouse roll?"

A blush rushed into Bailey's cheeks. She felt like a guest of honor in her own familial home. That didn't seem right. She hopped up like a gopher from whack-a-mole. "Oh, Mom. Let me help."

Her father nodded his approval, pulled her chair back out for her, and then rounded the table to finish his pie and coffee.

Twenty minutes later, Bailey dabbed the napkin to her mouth, sated and full. Her mother truly earned the title of best cook in the county. "Mom, as tasty as your culinary skills are, it isn't the only reason I dropped by."

Her parents darted a brow-knitted expression between them.

"Oh, no. Nothing major." Bailey waved her hands in

front of her. "Sorry, didn't mean to freak you out."

She waited as their shoulders drooped back to a normal, relaxed position. "We've been studying Jesus's genealogy in our Bible group, and it prodded me to begin to study mine. I hoped y'all could help."

"Oh, of course, my dear." Her father pushed his sleeve back. "But I have an important phone call to make and then some papers to review. On Sunday, after dinner, we can chat in my study."

He rose and came over to help her, then her mother, from their chairs. As she rose, she brushed her lips to his cheek. "I'd love that, Daddy. Thank you."

His face reddened as he pecked both of "his gals" on their foreheads and plodded down the hall.

"I can lend you my photo albums until then if you like." Her mother grabbed some of the dishes from the table.

"That would be great, Mom." Bailey gathered her empty plates and followed into the kitchen.

Her mother clanked the dirty items in the sink. "Oh, my. I forgot. I have a beautification committee meeting in twenty minutes. Oh, Bailey, I am sorry." She began to untie her apron strings. "Go look in the cedar chest in my craft room. In there you will find the albums my mother kept. She always wrote on the back of each photo where they were taken and who appeared in them. I was never that diligent, I'm afraid."

"Thanks, Mom. I'll load the dishwasher for you first.

Go freshen up and I'll see you on Sunday."

Her mother's slightly wrinkled, but still velvety hand stroked Bailey's cheek. "Good girl."

A little while later, Bailey crouched on the area rug and creaked open the chest. Musty aromas of history, mingled with a lingering whiff of jasmine and cedar, assaulted her nose. Under folds of fabric lay three leather, albums with brass buttons along each spine. The kind with thick paper and the little back triangular corners to slip in square black and white photos.

Bailey lifted out the first one and nestled it into her lap. With her lower lip tucked into her teeth, she gingerly opened the binding. Many of the ancient pictures had yellowed and faded with age. Even so, she could clearly view the images. Inside the cover, written in a very neat penmanship, the date *1957—*. In an obviously different handwriting had been added in black ink, *1968*. The year they had…

Bailey flipped through the pages as unrecognizable faces stared back at her through time. A flutter tumbled in her stomach. She rubbed her finger over the photo of two scrawny teens and a dog standing on a porch. "You're my family. And I know so little about you. Did the dog have a name? Did you own it for long?" She slipped it out of the page and turned the photo over. Pale blue ink revealed a partial answer. *Edmond and Eugene with Brutus*.

It would take time to log in the names, try to connect the dots, and begin to decipher the timelines. More than she could do tonight. Besides, her knees cramped. Feeling older than her thirty years, Bailey eased up from the rug-covered floor and began to stack the three photo books in her arms. She quietly closed the lid to the chest and tiptoed down the stairs.

"Night, Daddy."

From somewhere in the depths of the house echoed his muffled reply.

Bailey glanced around the foyer, the silence etched only by the ticks of the grandmother clock. Home, yet not anymore. Bailey dangled in limbo, not knowing exactly where to belong. The plight of a single adult. She envied Shannon. Wives made a house a home, even if their husbands were absent a lot for their jobs.

With a deep sigh, Bailey repositioned the albums and her purse in her arms and exited. A bizarre, almost instinctual whisper flowed over her as she walked to her car. She turned to gaze back at the house one more time.

In the dark, illuminated only by the porch light, her childhood home almost spoke through the rustling leaves of the oak in the front yard. "Tonight, Bailey Matteson, your life has changed."

Chapter 3

The decades splayed before her on the apartment carpet as the mantle clock chimed eleven. Bailey unwound herself from the semi-lotus position she'd been in for eons. Her left leg tingled. Wiggling the circulation back into it, she padded to the kitchen and plopped another pod of chai tea into the machine. As it whirred and groaned to brew, she mentally went over what she had deciphered. Her mother, nee Emily Sue, had three brothers named Edmond Lewis, Edgar Eugene, and Elliott Douglas.

As her gray tabby, Bower the Meower, wove a figure eight between her feet, Bailey analyzed out loud what she had discovered. She found speaking her thoughts often made things gel. "So, Elliott had to be the one that Mom's aunt raised after their parents died in the car accident. He would have still been in—" She mentally counted the years, "—ah, ninth grade. Way too young to be out on his own."

As she poured milk into Bower's bowl, she recalled meeting Uncle Elliott about fifteen years ago. Her high school team traveled to Beaumont to battle his alma mater in the state football playoffs, and he happened to be there for the thirty-year homecoming of his graduating class. That would put him now in his early sixties, four or five years younger than her mother. Uncle Elliott occasionally sent cards around Christmas, but Bailey assumed they had never been close.

What about her mom's two older brothers, Edmond and Eugene? They never wrote. Never visited as far as she knew. Did they have a falling out with her mom?

Bailey looped her thumb through the teacup and sipped it as she wandered back to the living room. Her muscles begged her not to crouch down on the living room floor any longer. Apartments never had great padding underneath the industrial-knapped carpet.

She set her tea on the bistro table and picked up the legal pad. Settling onto the dinette chair with one foot tucked under her, she began to draw the family tree.

She calculated her mother's siblings' ages from birthday party photos and baby pictures. Back then, the photoshops date-stamped each one on the edge of the squiggly border, serving as a make-shift frame. Along a straight line, she wrote: *Edmond–b. 1942, age 75. Eugene– b. 1943, age 74. Emily–b. 1950, age 68. Elliott–b. 1953, age 64.*

Cute, all their kids' names began with an "e." Must

have been the style back then. Above her mom and uncles' names, she scrawled her maternal grandparents' names—Colonel Edgar A. Holston and Mary Beth Dupree Holston. He must have served in World War II and settled in San Antonio afterward. Many of the soldiers from Texas did.

But why the seven-year gap between Eugene and her mom? Not due to her grandfather being in World War II, which ended in 1945. Then what? She shrugged and wrote in the margin to explore that later. Back to what she knew.

When Mom edged into her teens, Edmond and Eugene would have been in college. Too wide a spread for them to be really close growing up. Bailey's and her older brother by three years, Travis, seemed worlds apart at times growing up. Well, right now he lived in Beijing with his wife and two girls, so… yes, he still did.

Bailey shook her head at her own pun and took another gulp of tea.

Hmmm. So, her mom's eldest brothers had been—or still were, she didn't know—at least seven or eight years older. Perhaps that is why Bailey never met them. If her mom had been nineteen when her parents passed in 1968, then both Edmond and Eugene were probably married with children by then. Maybe they'd served in the Vietnam War. Or participated in the peace rallies. How she'd love to hear their life stories.

Bailey retrieved the latest of the albums and thumbed through it. The photos confirmed it. It contained the brothers' weddings in 1964 and 1966. Edmond wore a military uniform in his pictures. Then there were baby pictures. Three of them. Two sons born to Edmond by the names of Michael and Taylor, and one to Eugene named Robert. She scribbled down the names and dates provided by her grandmother's handwriting on the back of each.

She retrieved the oldest album from the floor, flipped back to the first page, and gazed again in wonder. They contained several pre-marital photos of Mary Beth, then Dupree. Bailey scanned her memory banks for what she recalled about her mother's ancestry. She flashed back to sitting on her mother's four poster bed, watching a figurine twirling inside a glass globe of a music box from France. Her mother said it had belonged to her grandmother, Claire. Bailey snapped her fingers and wrote it down.

She recalled a conversation with her mother in the car on the way to one of the Daughters of the Texas Revolution meetings. It adhered in her mind as if dipped in that wonder glue they advertised on TV because her mother so rarely mentioned anything about her family.

The Duprees emigrated from France and settled in Louisiana, owning a tobacco plantation. The Holston clan originated from Tennessee, if Bailey recalled correctly, but settled in Texas in the 1840s before it became a state. Why hadn't her genealogy curiosity perked up then? Probably because she'd found the occasions boring. Indoor high teas kept her from wandering the hills and riding horses. Even so, the honor, along with the Dupree wealth, solidified her mother's place in Texas high society.

According to the photos and her grandmother's handwriting, Mary Dupree met her future husband, Edgar, when they both had attended college in Austin. Ah, so that is why they referred to Edgar Eugene by his middle name. To avoid the "junior" thing, no doubt.

Bailey wondered who her maternal great-grandparents had been—the ones who had migrated from France. Did she still have distant relatives living there? How many kids did her mother's grandparents have? Obviously, another girl, since her mother's aunt had raised Elliott.

She picked up the last album again, which contained photos from the time her mother turned seven until her parents' death in 1968. It remained more than half empty. A clump of sadness lodged in Bailey's throat as she flipped through the empty construction paper pages, faded lighter around the edges like ghostly shadows of what never came to be. Blank years never lived out on earth. Missed events… like her mom's wedding, Travis's and her births, their graduations. Did those who went before watch from heaven?

Bailey sat back down. Swiping her finger over the now-muted handwriting, she pondered the what-ifs swirling in her mind. "Had you lived, what would I have called you? Grandmama? Gran? Something formal like Grandmother Holston?"

When she put it aside on the chair, Bower immediately hopped up and deemed it the best place to take a bath. She chuckled and scanned through the second album dating from 1940 to 1956. Her mother had been born in 1950. There, ah. Her mother's christening pictures. She gingerly lifted the photo of everyone gathered around the baptismal font and turned it over to read the names left to right. She stroked Bower and told him, "Mom wasn't kidding. Her mother did keep great records."

She lifted a silent prayer, thanking God for giving her a grandmother's meticulous habits. The old-fashioned cursive handwriting connected Bailey to her across the decades, even though they'd never met.

In the photo, two younger women stood next to her grandmother. Agnes Dupree. Juliana Dupree. Her great aunts, no doubt. Elizabeth, her grandfather's sister, according to the legend on the reverse side, clustered with her grandfather, Edgar, along with the two boys, evidently her uncles, Edmond and Eugene. Some lady named Johanna Mansfield and another man, Joseph Jamison, stood next to her grandmother, who cradled her mom in a long white gown. Both were listed as godparents. Agnes Dupree acted as the second godparent.

Bailey reached for her phone and typed in "godparents" in the search engine. Per the digital encyclopedia, these people made a confession of faith on the baby's behalf, promising to help the parents raise the child in a godly manner and to learn the creeds and the Bible until the child came of age to make her own confession of faith, usually around the age of twelve.

Typically, the baby had three godparents, two of the same sex as the child. In lieu of the parents' death, the website reference stated the godparents would be in charge of raising the child. Ah-ha!

She flipped forward to 1954. Elliott's christening. Godmother listed on the back as Juliana Dupree. She must be the great aunt who took him to Beaumont to live with her, where he later graduated from high school. It began to make sense. Bailey wondered why Juliana never married. "Did you lose your fiancé to war, too?"

Bailey rubbed a stray tear from the corner of her eye. Her phone screen blared 12:05.

"Ugh." Bailey yawned. She had to be up in six hours to get ready for work. Her accounting department had a breakfast pow-wow at the diner at 7:15 to finish compiling their report for the quarterly corporate budget meeting in San Antonio. "So much for my morning jog, Bower. Okay, so I'll not order the pecan waffles."

He stretched and repositioned his body in response.

She made a mental note as she patted her belly, still partially full of King Ranch Chicken, and shuffled down the hall to her bedroom.

All night long the photos of her ancestors whirled in and out of her dreams.

Chapter 4

The next day Bailey hardly had time to think, much less ponder over her family tree, as sparse as it was so far. The corporate meeting flew everyone in accounting into a tailspin. Find a thirty percent reduction in costs per store without affecting payroll. Easy. Ha.

She finally dragged home at ten-thirty at night after hours of poring over the numbers with two coworkers.

On Thursday, she met Shannon and Jessica at a local deli for a quick salad before choir. After they ordered, Shannon chose a table for four. As she placed her napkin in her lap, she picked the topic for them to discuss. "Any news of the genealogy quest, Bailey?"

"Since you asked… Mom lent me her mother's old photo albums. They date from the late sixties all the way back to the roaring twenties."

"Oh, how cool." Jessica set down her drink and scooted into a chair next to her friend. "I'd love to see them."

"Me, too. I adore old pictures. How they dressed, their big hair." Shannon raised her hands in an arch over her head, making Bailey and Jessica chuckle.

"Okay. Come by after choir tonight and you can gawk to your heart's content. I'll introduce you to the ancestors I now know. Well, their names and pictures that is."

"Great." Jessica winked as the waitress set down her wild greens and strawberry salad with pecans and avocado drizzled with raspberry balsamic dressing. "You better have Rocky Road in the freezer. I've been way too good."

Bailey scrunched her nose. "No, sorry. Only low-fat vanilla. But I do have sugar-free chocolate syrup."

"Blechhh." Jessica stuck her finger on her tongue.

"Sounds like a trip to the ice cream parlor first." Shannon rubbed her hands. "Waffle cone for me."

The three giggled and proceeded to crunch their dinners.

"Wow. How old was your mom when she married your dad?" Jessica held up a wedding picture.

Bailey pointed to each face. "No, that's my uncle Edmond and his bride. My mom is the shortest bridesmaid."

"Oh. Yeah." Jessica peered closer at the photo and followed Bailey's finger.

"But to answer your question, Mom was 29. She begat my brother, Travis, two years later."

Shannon chuckled. "Begat, huh? This Bible study has really affected you."

Bailey gave her a ha-ha head tilt. "Anyway… after two miscarriages, I came along two months prior to her thirty-seventh birthday." Bailey scraped the bottom of her sundae cup. "Growing up, many of my friends, whose parents were in their mid to late twenties, thought my grandparents raised me."

"I get that. My parents adopted me when they were almost forty." Jessica lifted one shoulder. "I didn't mind too much though. At least I got adopted."

Shannon swallowed the final piece of her waffle cone as she pointed to the photo. "Wow, look at your mom's hair. What did they call that hairdo?" She flipped her hand by her ear. "It's all brushed out and curled away from her face."

"Must have taken lots of hairspray." Bailey pushed her legal pad into their line of vision. "Here is what I have so far."

They went over the timeline and the blank spaces.

Shannon's expression became more somber. "So you want to fill in the blanks, right? Are you going to use that online search?"

"The one that gives you a leaf every time you find information on an ancestor? I guess so. It seems like a good place to start. Especially if I can get a few more names.

Luckily, my grandmother, Mary Beth, wrote on the back of most of the photos. See?" She pulled one from its pocket corners and flipped it over.

"Oh, wow. So cool." Shannon's eyes widened. "She had gorgeous handwriting. Almost calligraphy, yeah?"

Jessica re-tucked her legs under her. "They stressed penmanship big time in school back then. Typewriters were expensive and, of course, there were no computers. So, writing was the best way to communicate. People had to read what you wrote, so everyone took print and cursive handwriting in elementary school."

"Thank you, madam-journalist-turned-author." Bailey bowed with a giggle.

"Not yet. Still working on my first novel." Jessica clapped her hands. "Maybe you can find some letters your grandparents wrote to each other. I hear those genealogy sites contain all sorts of stuff like that."

Bailey scrunched her forehead. "I wonder how? I mean who scans them all in?"

"I think people volunteer to do that as they connect with each other." Shannon reached for another photo. "So perhaps someone from your grandfather's side of the family runs across them in an old trunk and enters them into the site. You could do the same with some of these photographs, Bailey. That way, you could meet some distant cousins."

"I hadn't thought of that. Hmm."

Shannon sat straighter. "Also, I have heard there are

links, like to public records and things."

"Well, then." Bailey stretched. "It appears I have my work cut out for me. Any help you two want to offer would be amazing. I could sure use it."

Jessica side-hugged her. "Of course. I envy you because you have such a rich heritage." She released her arm. "No, that's wrong. We are not supposed to envy. Sorry."

Bailey squeezed her hand. "It's okay. And if you don't want to help, I'd understand."

Her face brightened. "No, I do. I find this fascinating."

Shannon glanced at them both. "Me, too."

Jessica frowned. "But what if we find out something you don't want to know?"

Bailey chuckled. "Like what? I doubt if I have any mass murderers hanging from my family tree."

"I know, still…" She stood and shook herself. "Forget it. I'm being fanciful again. You know me."

Bailey and Shannon laughed out loud, causing Bower to scurry under the sofa.

"It's late. We better go." Jessica grabbed her sweater from the back of the chair.

"Yeah, I have to get up before sunrise tomorrow to walk five dogs in three neighborhoods. And feed two hamsters, four cats… and a bull-nosed grass snake. It eats dead mice. Yuck." Shannon stuck out her tongue.

Bailey and Jessica shuddered. "Ew."

After they all said good night, Bailey watched her

friends walk down the corridor. Uneasiness wisped over her shoulders, almost like... she swiped away the silly notion. Ghosts were only in fairytales. Still, Jessica's comment about finding any skeletons in her family closet tickled Bailey's imagination.

Did she really want to delve into her past? Could there be something ugly she'd uncover, which explained why her mother rarely talked about her kinfolk?

That idea seemed a tad melodramatic, like a black and white shadowy movie from the 1930s on the cable channel. Seriously, what could it hurt to do a little research? After all, her mom had loaned her the albums.

Bailey sloughed it off as being overtired.

Bailey made herself some low-fat cheese nachos, using sweet potato tortilla chips from the health food store. She fine-chopped some avocado—proud of herself for picking one at the peak of ripeness with no brown spots—added some drained black beans, sprinkled on the veggie cheese shreds and tomato chunks, and nuked it. Then she pinched off several cilantro leaves from the bunch and pulled them apart into small pieces, scattering them on top of the sizzling goo. Perfect. A glass of iced herbal tea fortified her to tackle the photos again.

What a way to spend a Friday evening. Oh, well. She didn't want to date anyone right now, and genealogy sounded better than zoning out on a romantic comedy. Most of them were getting too suggestive anyway, and the ones that weren't had saccharin and sappy dialog. And plots way too predictable. They needed Jessica's imaginative touch.

Anyway, she needed to get the photos back to her mom on Sunday, so she had better get at it. She decided to begin with her mom's teenage years and work backward. Go through birthdays, family events, and Christmas photos one more time, writing down any new names. Then later she'd try to graph them into the family branches.

Bailey smirked at her mother's lankiness in her pre-teen years and felt an awakened simpatico between them. She, too, had suffered that plight before her body finally decided to grow curves. Her father's wise words echoed in her brain. "Your inside beauty will shine through to the outside, Bailey. That's what people will be attracted to."

She ciphered through the years, recording the various names in group-gathering pictures. Time disappeared into the ages gone by as she tumbled down the ancestral rabbit hole into her past lineage.

The tomorrow song from Little Orphan Annie played on her cell phone, jolting her back to the present. Jessica. She'd picked the identifying tune not so much because Jessica was adopted, but because of her optimistic outlook on life.

"Hey, Jess."

"Hi. Whatcha doing tonight? Watching a movie?"

"Nope. Going over these old photos. And chomping on nachos."

"Both stellar ideas. Can I join you? I don't have to babysit my cousins after all."

"Your aunt and uncle aren't going to the opening show? Those tickets were her birthday present, right?"

"He's come down with the flu."

"Aw, that's a shame." Bailey wiped her fingers on a paper napkin. "Sure. Come over. I have enough to make another batch."

"Great. I'll swing by El Caldo and get some tamales. Beef or pork?"

"Hmm, how about chicken?"

"Done. See ya in twenty."

Bailey clicked off and scanned some more pages. Her mother's sweet sixteen birthday party. She ran her finger over a few of the captured moments. One felt thicker than the others. She threaded her fingernail underneath the photo and heard the sound of paper separating. Sure enough, another picture had been hidden underneath the first, adhered together by time. She gingerly pried the two apart, careful not to pull away much of the second one's image. A bit of it tore, unwilling to release from the back of the first. She stomped her foot. "Drat. Go slower, Bailey."

Maybe if she steamed it? They opened letters that way in the movies. She microwaved a cup of water and dangled the two photos over the rising heat droplets. Then she shook them back and forth and blew in between the layers. Returning to her seat, she bit her lower lip as she gently peeled the two from each other. There.

She held the piggy-backed one to the light. Splotches of white, from where the developed picture had been too stubborn to let loose, obscured part of it. But from the rest, Bailey could detect some sort of birthday party in a backyard. Yes, through time her mother's teenage face glowed.

And next to her mother stood a girl Bailey had not seen in any other photos. In a bizarre way, Bailey could have easily been gazing into her own gray-blue eyes. A shiver fluttered through her. Who was she?

Chapter 5

"Who is that?" Jessica's fingernail tapped the face of the older teenage girl, the photo stamp dated 1966. "Your mom only had brothers, right?"

"Yeah."

"Hmm." Jessica cocked her head. "Maybe it's a cousin?"

"I don't know. Everyone else on Mom's side had dark brown hair. I know it's a black and white photo, but her hair looks lighter."

"Perhaps auburn. Like yours?"

She pulled a strand of hers toward her eyes. "Maybe."

"She definitely has your eyes, though. Perhaps she favored her father's side of the family and the others favored your mom's side. Then you got those genes, too."

"Perhaps. If she is related. We don't know that."

Jessica took it in both hands, bringing it closer to her

face. "She really resembles your mother in the face, and you, too. She has to be a relative."

"Wait, now that you've held it to the light I can see writing on the back. It's faint but..." Bailey squinted to read it. "It says Edwina 18, with Emily 16."

Jessica slid the photo album to her. "Let's see if we can find any other pictures of her."

Together they huddled over the faded photos and flipped through them. No other pictures revealed the mystery girl. Jessica rubbed her temples. "I think my eyes are crossing."

"Why don't you fix us some more iced tea while I look through this one?" Bailey retrieved one of the other volumes. As she thumbed through the Christmas holidays, vacations at the beach, and Thanksgiving dinners, she scanned the faces. Then, in a cluster of pages from 1951, she found another one tucked behind the top photo. "Jess. Here's another hidden one."

Jessica leaned in as Bailey gingerly lifted the photo from behind. It showed a small, toddler peering at a baby in a perambulator. On the back, barely visible through the faded ink, she read aloud the words, "Edwina meets Emily."

"You found her again?" Jessica scooted closer to have a glance.

"Yeah. On Sunday I'm definitely asking Mom who she is." Bailey slipped the photos into her purse.

All day Saturday, Bailey flipped through the family pictures, searching for this mysterious Edwina. To be around eighteen in 1966, she had to have been born in 1947 or 1948. She peeked behind every photo, but no others held a hidden one. She browsed back until 1947, just in case. Surely a baby picture or something would exist if this girl was related.

Then again, why would there be any? Perhaps Jessica surmised incorrectly. She could have been a next-door neighbor and playmate of her mother's. And yet, there had been that other one of her as a small child peering onto Bailey's mom's bassinet. Neighbors did remain neighbors for longer periods of time back then. But it seemed more likely the mystery girl would be a visiting cousin. But from which side of the family? Dupree or Holston?

Bailey stared at the camera image again. A peeled-away white patch covered most of her torso. Curiosity got the best of Bailey. She grabbed the first two photos that had been adhered together and dashed down the hall to retrieve the tweezers from her manicure set in the bathroom. With her tongue protruding from her mouth a tiny bit, Bailey steadied her hand.

Gently she dabbed her finger under a trickle of water to moisten the bits secured to the back of the front photo for over fifty years. Minuscule progress gave her hope. She dampened it again and slipped the sharper edge of the tweezers underneath, lifting a small jagged corner. It peeled away. Hurray.

She placed it on her fingertip and pressed it to the mystery girl's body in the photo which had been hidden behind it. Then she spread out the tiny wrinkles and peered at what it revealed. The girl wore a peasant blouse over some cut-off jeans. Beads hung from her neck. The flowery embroidery on the sleeves and neckline became visible now. Yes, very late 1960's fashion. But wait.

Bending closer to the counter, Bailey used her magnifying makeup mirror. She squinted to focus in on the girl's clothing. Black and white photos often played shadow tricks, but there appeared to be… no way. A baby bump?

Bailey could barely make it through the service. It seemed the pastor's sermon went on forever. When her father caught her glancing at his watch for the third time, he covered it with his hand and flashed a parental glare. She slunk a little in her pew and concentrated on the worship program.

She followed her parents to their house and busied herself in the kitchen, helping her mom put the finishing touches on the meal. Travis planned to internet-call at two, so they wanted to be finished eating by then.

As Bailey entered the dining room with the bowl of

peas and carrots, her father rustled the newspaper held to his face. From behind the sports section, she heard, "The way you kept glaring at my timepiece, you must be anxious to talk to your brother."

"Sorry, Dad."

He folded the paper and laid it next to him. "It's okay. It'll be good to chat with him and the girls."

"And Liza." Her mother added with an arched brow as she placed the platter of sliced ham on the trivet.

"Yes, dear. And Liza, too. Our son married a fine woman."

Bailey felt the thud of an unfinished thought. And yet she remained single. Still. Please don't ask if I am seeing anyone. She spoke up. "Are we ready to eat, then?"

Her mother nodded. "As soon as your father blesses the food."

They all bowed their heads. After thanking God for their bounty, Bailey passed the rolls. "Mom, I appreciate your letting me look through the albums. I'd like to keep them for another week or so… if that's okay."

Her father frowned. "You didn't tell me that, dear."

"I imagine so, Bailey. May I ask why?" Her mother handed her the vegetable bowl.

Had her mom's cheeks paled for some reason? Bailey scooped some peas and carrots onto her plate. "Grandmother Holston habitually recorded dates and events, thank goodness. I am still trying to piece it all together, but it really helps. I'd like to learn more so I can go online and trace the family tree."

Her father pointed with his knife. "Ah, like those commercials. Scrounging for leaves, right?"

Bailey giggled. "Yes, Dad."

He winked. "I'll *leave* you to it, then."

They all groaned.

She turned to her mother. "But maybe you can solve one mystery for me."

"And that would be?" Her mother cocked her head as she carved a bite-sized piece off her slice of ham.

"Who was Edwina?"

The clatter of the knife to the china plate echoed throughout the room like the gong of an iron bell in a steeple. Her mom's hand shook and all the color drained from her face. Wide-eyed, she stared at her husband.

He leaned in and covered her hand in his. "Emily, darling, I knew giving her those albums was a bad idea."

"I thought they'd all been destroyed." Her mother's fingers clasped her strand of pearls.

Bailey's gaze flashed between her parents. "What do you mean?" Her voice wobbled over the clump in her throat. "Mom? Dad?"

Her mother stared at her father, her mouth partially open.

Her father's eyes narrowed. "Emily. What have you done?"

"It's time Bailey knew, dear."

"Knew what?" Bailey's eyes continued to dart

between her parents. "That she became pregnant at a young age in 1966?"

Her mother let out a whimper. Her hand covered her mouth as she dashed from the dining room.

"Mom?" Bailey's eyes began to tear up.

Her mother's hastened footsteps sounded on the stairs, then over their heads on the second floor. A door slammed. Probably the one to the master bathroom. Her mother's place of retreat.

She whipped around. "Dad?"

Her father remained stone-faced, but his eyes wouldn't focus on Bailey. He wiped his mouth and slapped the linen napkin down. "I better go to see to her. Your brother is calling in twenty minutes."

"But..." Bailey clamped her mouth at her father's stern glare.

He stomped from the dining room.

As his footfall faded, Bailey closed her eyes and slammed her back into the Edwardian chair spindles. Shannon's premonition vibrated through her skull. "What if you find out something you don't want to know?"

Her mind swirled. She recalled only one time she'd witness her mother on the verge of losing control. Travis had hugged her goodbye at the airport, bound for China for his career move.

She sniffled and stared at the chandelier. "Yes. I guess I have. Do I keep digging, or cover it back up with the family dirt and let it lie?"

Chapter 6

Bailey scraped the mostly untouched food from the dishes, rinsed the plates and utensils, and then loaded them into the dishwasher. She spooned the rest of the meal from the platter and bowls into plastic containers and put them in the fridge. Then she returned to the dining room to fold the napkins and remove the lace cloth. The whole time she tried to swallow past the lump lodged near her tonsil scars. How did she know what she'd discovered in those photo albums would upset her mother like that?

As Bailey placed the crystal salt and pepper shakers back in the china cabinet, her father's steps thunked down the stairs. However, they didn't turn toward the dining room. Rather, they clunked in the direction of his office. A few minutes later, her mother's high-heeled step sounded across the hardwood floors then became muffled by the Oriental rug. "Oh, you cleared the table. Thank you, dear."

"Sure thing, Mom." Bailey turned to face her and

immediately determined from her mother's expression that pursuing their previous conversation was not a good option. Her face resembled the fine bone china from her great-grandmother Claire Dupree, now displayed in the china cabinet—pale, fragile, aged… ready to crack. Her makeup seemed impeccably applied, as always, but redness still rimmed her eyelids.

Her mother cleared her throat. "Travis should be calling. Perhaps we should join your father in the office."

Bailey closed the cabinet doors. "Yes'm."

Head lowered, she followed her mom down the hall to the den. Her father already broadcasted the computer screen's display to the flat screen TV over the fireplace for better viewing.

She settled in one of the side chairs. Steeling her eyes, she sent a vibe through the cyberspace image coming into focus.

Please, brother, dear. Let's make this a happy conversation, filled with good news and fun conversation with your little girls. We kinda need it now. Your little sis has pulled a whopper.

"Hey, little sis. This is a pleasure. How's it going?"

Bailey told Travis about her new hobby, the Bible study, and life in general. Her sister-in-law, Liza, gave her some direction in how to use the internet for her genealogy hunt. She had researched a branch of her family tree for a history project while in college. It seems her long-ago ancestor went on the Lewis and Clark Expedition.

"Be careful, because this hobby can get quite expensive. Don't be tempted to purchase information. Most libraries now have online access to their records. So do city halls, if they are large enough. Check for death certificates first."

"Hey, thanks." Bailey rose, grabbed a pen and some paper from her father's desk, and began to write. She glanced at her mother's pursed lips and her father's icy stare. She mouthed the word sorry.

"Oh, and check obituaries. They usually list the surviving kin. You can fill in a lot of blanks that way."

"Wow, that's great, Liza. This helps a lot."

Bailey's mom rested her hip on the winged-back chair's upholstered arm, toying with her necklace. Her face resembled a stone statue.

"I think you have hogged the conversation long enough, my dear." Her father's stern tone stopped Bailey from objecting. "Let's let you mother catch up on the news."

Bailey turned on a bright smile. "Of course. Travis, Liza, take care. We will chat again soon. PM me, okay?"

Her father scowled.

Travis laughed. "That means private message, Dad. It's a social media thing. Don't worry about it. Let me get the girls."

As soon as the grandkids squeezed into the lens' range from their computer, they were all squiggles and giggles. Bailey saw a twinkle reappear in her mother's eyes. Good.

Bailey took the opportunity to slip out of the room, now that her parents were focused on happy things. She'd upset her mom—and her dad—enough for one night. Prudence told her the conversation should not be picked up where they left off. Edwina, whoever she was, remained a sore spot on her mother's heart. With Liza's suggestions, Bailey could find out about her in other ways.

She found a grocery list pad in the kitchen and scrawled a see-you-later note, explaining she had a ton of things to do. She thanked them for Sunday dinner and promised to call soon. Then her pen hovered over the paper. Taking in a long breath, she apologized for upsetting her mother and promised it wouldn't happen again.

Next, she rummaged through the junk drawer to find the tape dispenser and secured the note to the door frame leading into the office. Her mother's melodic laughter flowed from inside. Good to hear.

Bailey tiptoed through the foyer and out the front door, gently closing it until she heard the lock softly click into place. The late afternoon sun filtered through the trees, casting long skinny shadows over the street. What a visit. Not the average, bordering-on-boring Sunday meal with the parents lately. In a way, she missed those.

With a residual mixture of sadness and excitement, she started the car and drove away.

Hunger pangs began to prick her torso. Due to her Sunday dinner debacle, she hadn't really eaten since the protein shake for breakfast. She pulled over, did a search for her favorite soup and sandwich chain nearest to her location, and then placed an order for a cup of cashew and carrot ginger soup, along with a kale and Brussels sprouts salad. Then on a whim, she squinted as she punched the request for a chocolate chip muffin. With butter. Oh, well.

By the time she pulled in the to-go line, her order had been filled. She waved her phone app over the reader. It beeped that her debit had been accepted, so the teenage server handed her the sacked meal with a monotone thank you.

"Rough day so far?" Bailey glanced at his name tag. "Shafer, is it?"

He blinked, and then his eyes focused when he realized a customer actually spoke to him and called him by name. "Huh? Um, yeah. Two people called in sick. I'm on overtime. Guess it'll be a twelve-hour shift."

She grimaced. "Sorry. Hope it goes better."

He handed her the receipt. "Thanks. And you? How's your day?"

Bailey tapped the steering wheel. "I just made my mom cry."

"Ouch."

"Yep. This muffin will make it better, though."

His face broke into a smile.

She winked and raised her car window.

As she drove away, her heart became bit lighter because she'd gotten him to grin.

"Well, Lord. I guess I did something right, today."

Two miles later, she pulled into her complex, clicked the fob to open the gates, and pulled into her carport spot. Gripping her sack of food in her mouth, she slipped her purse strap onto her shoulder and, in a half-contorted twist to peer into the side pocket, dug out her house keys.

She entered the quiet apartment—her footsteps didn't disturb Bower's afternoon catnap—and set her food on the small dinette table. Unpacking her order, she put the salad in the refrigerator for lunch tomorrow and grabbed a spoon from the drawer, shutting it with her hip. Soup eaten with plastic spoons never tasted good.

After three slurps, she decided she only wanted the muffin. Lathering each half with a pat of butter, Bailey took a bite, rolled her eyes back in delight, and opened her laptop to begin her surfing. Look for obituaries. She searched for the San Antonio *Light*, dated May 11, 1968. She scrolled through the local news section. Third article down read, "Couple Tragically Killed in Accident Outside of San Marcos." Her grandparents? But they were from San Antonio. No pictures gave her a clue. Might as well read it. She clicked to enlarge it onto her screen.

The events surrounding her grandparents' demise

came to life. She read how it had been their thirtieth wedding anniversary. "According to their eldest son, Edmond Lewis Holston, from Austin…"

Bailey scribbled down his full name and the fact he lived in Austin in 1968.

"… the couple was returning to their residence in north San Antonio after seeing the performance of *Swan Lake* by the Austin Ballet, a gift from his father to his mother. As they pulled off onto the access road to stop for gas, another driver veered into their lane and hit them head-on. The driver left the scene on foot before police arrived. Authorities are in search for a young male, possibly college age, as of this printing. Alcohol is suspected to have played a part in the accident. Several beer bottles were found on the floorboards of the oncoming vehicle."

She sat back. A drunk driver killed her grandparents. How tragic. No wonder her mother never consumed alcohol. Not even a glass of wine during the holidays.

Determined to discover more, Bailey searched through the next few days. She found it, dated May 15th. The Obituary, along with a picture, obviously taken many years prior, of her grandparents. She rubbed over the pixilated photo on the screen, tracing their faces with her fingertips. "Hi, grandmother, grandfather."

Throughout her childhood, Bailey always felt a bit cheated that she had never known them. All of her close friends talked of summers with their grandparents or a bundle of gifts received at Christmas.

Her college roommate's grandmother sent her a dollar for every year she had been alive every birthday. When her roommate turned twenty-one, she received a black velvet box filled with twenty-one silver dollars and a pair of diamond stud earrings.

When she turned sixteen, Bailey's Aunt Susan, on her father's side, told Bailey about their parents, Maxwell and Joanna Matteson. Both long deceased before Bailey's birth, Maxwell Matteson died in Vietnam in 1964, and Joanna never quite recovered from grief. Bailey's father, Chester, and Susan shuffled between relatives while his mother floated in and out of rehab hospitals for depression. When her dad turned eighteen, the age to be drafted, she overdosed on her anti-anxiety medication.

Perhaps tragically losing parents so young formed the initial bond between her mom and dad. Whatever the glue, it stuck firmly. Unlike many of her school pals, her parents never divorced, nor even considered it as far as Bailey knew.

Bailey searched a bit further to discover if the drunk driver had ever been apprehended. None of the articles mentioned his name. That seemed weird unless he'd been underage. She vaguely recalled a law about that and made a note to look it up later. Nothing further appeared in the newspaper for the rest of the year.

She started over, this time bringing up the police report section. Back then San Antonio, where her parents both grew up, listed arrests daily. She'd once recalled her dad talking about that. "We never got in trouble because it would appear in the paper and everyone would know."

Her search came up empty. She thunked the palm of her hand against her head. Well, duh. The wreck didn't happen in San Antonio. She searched the San Marcos paper, a weekly edition back then. An article on the wreck appeared on the front page. She scanned through the sketchy details to the first sentence in the last paragraph. *Police may have a lead on the identity of the other driver. The car matches the description of a rental vehicle, which may have been stolen.*

The article stated a driver in a similar white vehicle had stopped off at a convenience store on the highway and attempted to buy beer. The store clerk asked for ID and recognized a fake one. *He stated, "His eyes were bloodshot and he wasn't steady on his feet. I guess he'd already had several that night."*

The report went on to describe the driver as in his late teens or early twenties with black hair and blue eyes. Tall, lanky, wearing a t-shirt with "Roll Over Beethoven" on the front. The partial name the clerk recalled could not later be confirmed. Ah.

The next week, a two-line report appeared on the back page. *Police drop investigation on drunken driver wreck. Store clerk admits he lied. Rental company withdraws claim.*

What? Why? How would she ever find out? The convenience store may not be in existence now, and even if it was, would they have employee records back that far? Doubtful.

She stifled a yawn and rubbed her eyes. Too much drama for one day. Maneuvering her mouse to click on the print icon, she waited for the whir of her copier in the bedroom to churn out the obituary and the newspaper articles.

After the week she'd had, she needed to zone out. Maybe she'd go over it again tomorrow. She bookmarked the internet page for the small-town newspaper and closed the lid of her laptop. Besides, her favorite mystery series started in an hour, and if she researched anymore, she might delve too deeply into it and lose track of time.

Until then, maybe she'd throw in a load of laundry and clean her bathroom. Scrubbing could be therapeutic.

Chapter 7

Monday morning raced in rudely with the high-pitched beep of the alarm on her cell phone. Bailey slapped the screen, threw the pillow over her head, and groaned. She really had to choose another tone. But then again, this one did wake her from a deep dream. Her mind tried to recapture it, but only fuzzy, half-images remained. Something about her diving into a photo album, sort of like Alice tumbling down a hole to Wonderland, only to be trampled by dead relatives screaming for her to go home.

"Oh well, Bower. Time to get up." She tossed off the covers, which sent her feline companion sailing off the mattress to the carpet. He dashed toward the kitchen belting out a series of urgent meows.

"Yes, yes. I'm coming. You won't starve. Promise."

One of those days. Everything she touched in the kitchen broke, malfunctioned, or shorted out. Except the fridge and microwave. She sent a prayer of thanksgiving for the small reprieve.

As she slipped her leg into her slacks, her freshly manicured nail broke. She flopped back onto the comforter, hands held to the ceiling. "Please. Lord. Enough."

Fanning her eyes so she didn't run her mascara, Bailey rolled off the bed, padded down the hall in her more comfortable sandals, and grabbed her purse. Not once did she think of the obituary in her printer tray beginning to curl from the Texas humidity.

God must have heard her plea because her car started, she hit every green light on her commute, and a parking space on the first level of the garage appeared as she entered. She turned off the engine and lifted her eyes. "Thanks, Abba. You know what this girl needs."

For a Monday, things plodded along fairly smoothly. The Sunday tills balanced, and the morning shift ones. She decided to splurge and ordered a macchiato latte with her salad at the coffeehouse one block over.

Jane, who worked in accounts payable, joined her. She unwrapped a juicy chili cheeseburger from the roach coach that often parked across the street from their office.

"How do you do it?"

"What?" Jane wiped the corner of her mouth.

"Never gain weight?"

Her coworker shrugged. "Fast metabolism. My whole family looks like beanpoles."

"And she jogs five miles a day." Becky slid in with her sack lunch. "*Every* day."

"Actually, I'm up to seven."

Bailey flashed Jane a smile, squelching a sudden pang of jealousy, and forked her lettuce and tomato, sans dressing. She made a mental note to jog more than once or twice a week.

At five-thirty she dashed out the office door to make it to Bible study on time. Tonight, they'd go over Matthew, chapter two.

Jessica met her on the curb. "Hey, Bailey? Good weekend?"

"Until I made my mother leave the table in tears during Sunday dinner."

"Oh, no. Over what?"

"The mysterious Edwina." Bailey wiggled her fingers in air quotes as she balanced her notebook against her chest with her arms.

"Ouch. Why?"

"Dunno. Didn't dare ask."

They walked in silence a few paces. Then Bailey halted. "But, my sister-in-law, Liza—"

"The one in China?" Shannon came up behind them.

"Yeah." Bailey half-turned to greet her. "We chatted with them on Skype. Anyway, she did a genealogy search in college for a course and gave me all kinds of tips."

"Game-changer stuff?"

"Maybe." Bailey shifted the notebook to her other hand and yanked her purse strap back onto her shoulder. "It's the best way to discover why the mention of Edwina's name sent my mother into orbit."

Shannon started walking backward to view her face. "It did?"

Jessica bobbed her head and traced a finger from her eye down her cheek.

"*Your* mom, Bailey? Stoic, proper-at-all-times Mrs. Matteson had a meltdown?"

Bailey took in a shaky breath. "Not pretty."

The three walked in silence the rest of the way to their classroom. They found their seats nanoseconds before Mrs. Perkins began the prayer.

"Today we will review Matthew 1:18 through 2:12." She waited as some of the students flipped pages and others punched up the verses on their phones or tablets. "All right, ladies. Let's start. Tell me, why do you think an angel came to speak to Joseph?"

For the next hour and a half, a lively discussion ensued. Mrs. Perkins showed them several places in the Bible that foretold the events surrounding the birth of Jesus.

As the three walked out of the classroom, Bailey puffed out a sigh. "My heavens, she is a walking Biblical encyclopedia! I had no idea the Old Testament held so many clues to Jesus' coming. Why didn't they get it?"

Shannon laid a hand on her shoulder. "Are we so different? I mean there are times we don't either."

Bailey rubbed her temple. "True, but I have had enough deep thinking for one day. My brain is mushy."

"You need food, girl."

"You're right. My salad didn't stick with me." Bailey clutched her midsection.

Jessica caught up with them. "Let's split a pizza."

The three walked down one block to the pizza parlor. They chatted about their day and life in general as they waited for the piping hot pies to be brought to their table.

As they chomped their wedges, Jessica picked up the genealogy thread. "What did Liza suggest?"

"Start with obituaries. They list the next of kin. From there you do name searches in public records, death indexes, and newspaper archives."

"And have you?"

Bailey put down her food and wiped her fingers. "Sort, of, Jess. I found the obit on my mom's parents and printed it out. Then I found some articles on the wreck itself. Seems the clerk who identified the driver later recanted his story."

"Wow. I wonder why?" Jessica slurped the last of her iced tea through a straw.

"I didn't research further. I still reeled from the Matteson family drama."

Jessica pouted sympathetically. Then she perked up. "Listen, Bailey. I'm not doing anything tomorrow night. I could bring over my laptop and help you search."

"Hey, and I could bring mine. You have WIFI. We'd save a good bit of time if all three of us searched." Shannon glanced downward. "It gets kinda lonely for me at night sometimes when the hubs is on the road for weeks on end."

"You need a dog, girlfriend. A good-sized one for protection as well as companionship." Jessica shook more parmesan onto her slice.

"I don't know…"

Bailey sat back in her booth. "Really? Y'all would do that for me? Come over and help search?"

Her two friends answered in unison. "Sure."

The residual tightness in her chest eased, and warmth spread instead. "Thanks. You two are the best ever. Say about seven?"

Shannon swirled her napkin. "Just like the Three Musketeers. All for one…"

"And one for all." The other two sang out.

The three slapped palms and broke into uncontrollable giggles.

The lady in the next booth spouted a little too loudly to her husband. "I didn't know they allowed such rowdiness in here? Did you, George?"

Shannon slid down in her seat as Jessica's face reddened from now silent laughter.

Bailey smiled. She loved her friends.

The next evening the three gathered around Bailey's small dinette table, laptops open and a large bowl of popcorn in the center. Bailey had copied the obit for each one of her fellow sleuths and highlighted a name. She claimed Edmond, assigned Eugene to Jessica and Elliott to Shannon.

"What about the mystery driver?" Jessica wiggled her eyebrows.

"That would entail a drive to San Marcus to learn more. Even then it might be a dead end after a half-century. So, let's concentrate on learning more about my family."

"Sounds good to me." Shannon opened her computer.

"It's weird that no Edwina is listed. Perhaps she'd been a best friend, and they had a falling out?" Jessica plopped a half-handful of popcorn in her mouth.

Bailey's chest tightened again at the mention of the name. "I'm guessing a cousin on my grandfather's side. Though it doesn't explain my mother's reaction."

"Maybe she stole a boyfriend from your mother, and she never forgave her?" Shannon shrugged.

Jessica looked at the wall, obviously processing the information. "Could be. You know what they say? 'Old wounds never heal.'" She shifted her attention back to Bailey. "How did your mom get all the family albums anyway? Or did she? Maybe the mysterious Edwina is in one you don't have."

"I doubt it. They are all synchronized. My guess is the brothers weren't interested in them."

Shannon nodded. "Guys often aren't. Jayden couldn't figure out why I cried when his mom handed me his baby milestone album on our first anniversary."

"She did? Ahhh." Bailey drew her hands to her heart.

"I know. Right?"

"How is Jayden? I know you miss him when he's on the road so long."

"I do. Being a long-hauler's wife is hard sometimes." Shannon grinned. "But when he gets home we make up for it."

Jessica rolled her eyes. "Too much info, Shannon."

"Ahem. Speaking of information. Have you two located any on my uncles?"

Her friends shrank behind their screens.

For the next half hour, only the clock ticking and an occasional crunch of popcorn broke the silence. Then Shannon yelled, "Oh."

"What?" Bailey leaned to view her friend's screen.

"I found Elliot's high school graduation picture. It's a bit grainy, but it's not too bad. I see your mom, but not your dad."

"She may not have been serious about him yet. They met in college, but she made him wait until she graduated to get married in June 1972." Bailey scooted her chair around to get a better angle.

Jessica came and stood behind them. "What year is this?"

"1971. Oh my gosh." Bailey threw her hand to her mouth. "Is that Uncle Eugene with long hair and a beard?"

Jessica giggled and made a peace sign with her fingers.

"I'm going to copy it, paste it into my photo app, and make it larger. There." Shannon clicked print.

Bailey swiveled out of her chair and loped down the hall to the bedroom to retrieve it from the laserjet. Halfway back, she stopped and gasped.

In the background behind her mother, half out of sight stood Edwina. It had to be. And she held a small child on her hip.

Chapter 8

Bailey had no idea how long she had stood in the hall with a gaping mouth, gawking at the photo. Long enough for her friends to wonder what had happened to her. Soon they huddled around her.

"Bailey, what is it? You are as white as a marshmallow."

Shannon clucked her tongue. "Jessica, must you always relate everything to food?"

"I don't. Do I?"

"Well, you are the one who always brings it up. Now I have a craving for s'mores."

Jessica hung her head. "I'm sorry, Shannon. I know you want to lose a few pounds."

Bailey blinked. What were those two discussing? Food? Didn't they eat before they came over? "I'm sorry. I blanked out there. Are you all ordering take-out or something?"

Shannon sighed. "No. But you look like you need smelling salts." She slung her arm through Bailey's. "Come, let's sit down."

Bailey shuffled down the hallway and plopped in the dinette chair, her right hand clasping the picture. "It's Edwina. She's in the background."

"Are you sure?" Jessica edged closer.

"I think so. Let me get her other photos. I have them in my purse." She rose and went to the balcony door where her bag hung on the knob. After a few rustles, she pulled out a cellophane sandwich bag containing the old pictures. "Here, you tell me."

The girls stared at each one back and forth for several minutes. Finally, Shannon scratched her eyebrow. "It's possible. I wonder if there is a way to get this blown up even further. Do you have a better photo program on your desktop computer?"

"No. But good idea."

Jessica snapped her fingers. "We could take it to the drug store and ask them to do it. They have a digital machine there. It does amazing things."

"How do you know that?" Shannon gathered the photos together.

"I had them reproduce my adopted parent's engagement photo and framed it for their 50th wedding anniversary last year."

"It would probably be better to put it on a thumb drive, right? I have one in my desk drawer." Bailey scooted her chair back. "I'll go get it."

In a few minutes, she returned and handed it to Shannon who stuck it in the computer port. "Do you think they're still open?" She squinted at the screen.

Bailey and Jess gazed at the wall clock over the kitchen door. Eight fifty-five. Their shoulders stooped.

"I know the pharmacy closes at nine. Bet the photo department does, too." Bailey took the flash drive from Shannon and shrugged.

Jessica rested her chin on her hand. "Drat."

Bailey slipped it in the baggie along with the pictures. "No worries. I can drop it off during my lunch break tomorrow. It's only two blocks down from the office."

Jessica straightened her spine. "I know. Let's search for more photos online. Lots of kids graduated from Beaumont High that day. Maybe we will catch another shot of this mystery woman in the background."

Bailey laughed. "Way to go, Jessica."

The three high-fived each other and returned to gazing at their screens.

However, at nine-thirty they gave up. After scanning numerous articles, and even a few throw-back Thursday posts, no one came up with a clearer photo.

"We've earned a treat." Bailey went to the freezer and pulled out her low-fat, sugar-free, vanilla frozen yogurt. "Who wants some?"

Shannon and Jessica groaned.

Bailey combed her hair as Bower sat on her dressing table and switched his tail off the edge. "I had no idea genealogy tracing could take so long. Lots of dead ends." She stroked her pet. "Still, it is a bit addictive. I see why people really get into it."

As she slurped her protein shake, she reread her notes and make-shift timeline. So many holes, but a few more filled in. Perhaps she should concentrate on finding out what she knew about the people she'd identified and quit chasing after this Edwina person.

"I won't spend more than two hours a day researching, though. I do have a life." Bailey frowned. Did she?

Nearly four years after Jacob died in Afghanistan, she still possessed little desire to date. But that didn't mean her life wasn't full, right? She had choir, and Bible study, and her volunteer work. She went out to eat with her friends. She shoved the thought aside and returned to the task at hand.

The enhancement didn't lend much more detail, other than the fact the child on the woman's hip appeared to be a boy of about four. Hard to determine if her facial features matched the earlier picture of the pregnant Edwina. How could she be certain?

Then Bailey remembered one guy she dated briefly, the son of a Bridge partner of her mother's. Chase Montgomery. They hadn't really hit it off, but he did work at the county sheriff's department. Didn't they have computer programs to determine what runaways might look like years later? All of the CSI programs on TV showed them.

Bailey flipped through her contacts. Yep, she hadn't deleted him for some reason. Maybe because his eyes had mesmerized her. Her finger hovered over the receiver icon. *Should I do it?*

"Bailey. Do you have the totals for last week's sale on salted caramel milkshakes? Corporate wants a tally."

"Um, yes." She slipped her phone into her lap and swiveled to her screen. "I emailed it to corporate yesterday. Here it is." She hit print, then returned to balancing the till counts, hoping he didn't notice the warmth oozing over her cheeks.

Chapter 9

"You should do it." Jessica elbowed Bailey as they changed in the gym locker room.

"Really? I mean calling out of the blue after almost six months." Bailey bent to tie her shoe. "And to ask a favor?" Somehow it sounded even more wrong after it left her mouth.

"You liked him, though."

"I know. Which is why I never went out with him again."

Jessica nodded. "I get it. Honestly, I do. It's almost as if you are betraying Jacob, right?"

"Does that sound stupid?" Bailey leaned against the locker. "I can hear my mother now hounding me about how Jacob would never want me to pine over him."

"She has a point."

"I know." Bailey swatted the comment away. "But, I'd

also known Chase as a kid, and it felt weird. Literally the boy next door."

"Ah, well. Yeah, I could see that being a tad awkward." Jessica moved her fingers barely apart to gesture her point. "But since your families know each other, what harm would it be to contact him now?"

"True. I'm calling Chase for professional advice after all. That. Is. All."

"So, you are calling him?"

"Maybe. Yes, I guess." She pushed off. "Let's hit the elliptical machines."

"Whatever you say..." Jessica snickered as she followed Bailey through the women's changing room door to the gym floor.

The subject didn't surface again until they met Shannon for Chinese food. She had already ordered the Happy Family dish for them all to share by the time they arrived. "So, what did you learn?"

"Not to spend ten minutes on the elliptical at the mountain incline level. Ugh." Bailey rubbed her calf.

"No, I mean the photo, silly."

Bailey slid into the booth after Jessica. "Not much." She put her napkin in her lap, but then shifted her gaze as the waitress placed water glasses in front of them. "Thank you, ma'am."

The Oriental woman bowed and backed away.

"She didn't get a clear view in the blow-up. So, she is dredging up an old boyfriend..."

"Date, Jessica. One date. And our families have known each other forever. He grew up next door."

Jessica waved her hands back and forth in an erasing motion. "Okay, okay. Anyway, she is going to call him because he works in police forensics. Maybe he can tell her if it is Edwina in the photo."

Shannon snapped her fingers. "Oh, Chase, right? Dark curly locks. Icy blue eyes. Three-piece charcoal suit."

Bailey's mouth dropped open. "How did you know?"

Jessica slid down a bit in her seat. "We sort of spied on you that night."

"You did not!"

Shannon scrunched her shoulders to her earlobes. "Only because we care. It was your first time out with a guy since…" She stopped and pressed her lips.

Bailey scooted out of the booth. She waved down their waitress. "Excuse me. Can I have mine to-go?"

"Bailey, sit. Don't be silly." Shannon tugged on her blouse.

"Silly, Shannon? Ever hear of privacy? I don't sneak a peek through your window when Jayden comes home." She could feel the heat rising up her neck. Her nostrils flared. The faces of her friends blurred. With a stomp of her foot, Bailey pivoted and dashed to the ladies' room at the back of the restaurant.

She paced back and forth in the small restroom with two stalls. Why had the mention of Chase hit her angry button? Because she was jealous. Oh, my. That was it.

Shannon had a husband, even though he spent most of the time on the road as a long-haul truck driver. Her happiness turned her into a matchmaker at times because she probably wanted Bailey to find it, too. And Jess, after her disastrous choice of a husband, who got Jessica's then best friend pregnant and left Jessica for her, probably wanted to make sure Bailey wasn't making a similar mistake.

Shannon said they did it only because they cared. Okay, so her friends had her best interests at heart. A sudden contriteness washed over her as she splashed water on her cheeks. Bailey dabbed a paper towel to her face, sucked in a deep breath, and waltzed out to apologize for her outburst. She picked up on their conversation as she approached their booth.

I know, right? She almost fell out of it. Cut down to her navel. Gross."

"Beyond tacky."

"Who is?" Bailey stood over them.

"That pop-star on the Emmy's last night. The one in the chartreuse, sequined, slinky mini-dress."

"Oh. I didn't watch."

"You didn't miss much, honestly." Jessica scooted back over a bit and patted the bench seat. "Come. Sit. Eat."

Bailey chuckled as she slid in. "You sound either like an eastern European grandmother or a movie title, I'm not sure which."

All three sputtered a laugh.

"I'm sorry I exploded, y'all. You hit a nerve, I guess."

"We know." Jessica laid her hand over Bailey's, "But we shouldn't have done it. We're sorry, too."

"Apology accepted." Bailey smiled. "Truth is, even though we'd lost contact when we went off to college years ago, at the time I thought going out with an old friend would be a safe way to ease back into the dating scene, you know?" She glanced at them both. "And appease my mother."

Her friends rolled their eyes at the same time.

"But an hour in, I knew I'd made a big mistake. I got the feeling he saw me as something more and it freaked me out." She flipped her fork. "I guess I bruised his ego big time."

"So that's why you're iffy about contacting him." Jessica nodded. "I get that."

"Yeah, I can see it. Even so, I think it could be wise to get in touch with him, given his profession." Shannon gave her a thumbs up gesture.

"You do?"

"Sure. You should call him. Be professional, polite, and humble." Shannon lifted her chin. "I bet he says okay."

"That's what I'm afraid of." Bailey grimaced. Either way, this would be a tough phone call.

Chapter 10

Bailey sucked in a long breath and pushed on the revolving door leading into the sheriff's department. As she marched the flight of stairs to the second floor, she gazed up. He waited at the landing, handsome as ever. Darn.

Chase extended a hand in greeting. "Right on time. My office is the third on the right."

Bailey shook it firmly, hoping her palm didn't feel cold. "I appreciate you taking the time to look at these. I didn't know who else to turn to." Oh great, now she sounded like a damsel tied to a railroad track.

His silver-blue eyes twinkled as his jaw worked ever so slightly. "My pleasure. This way."

He let her go first. Gentlemanly maneuver or to check out her backside? She fought the urge to tug on her pencil skirt. Did she have to choose one so tight, even though it matched her jacket and accented her blouse?

"In here?"

"That's it. Have a seat." He edged around her and pulled out a metal armchair upholstered in industrial blue fabric.

As he rounded the desk, she scanned the small room. A lateral filing cabinet rested against one wall with a small copier on top, along with potted ivy trailing down the side. A picture of the Alamo at night hung on the wall. A bulletin board littered with notices, mug shots and notes hung on the other side over a three-shelf bookcase jammed with more folders, a few books, and loose papers. His desk held a computer screen, several folder trays, a flip-over calendar with Bible verses on it, a stapler—and a stuffed frog playing a guitar?

He pulled his desk chair forward. "What do you have for me?"

"Huh?" She blinked. "Oh, the photos." She dug in her purse, pulled out the baggie with the old photos and the flash drive, and handed it across the desktop. Their fingers brushed. The emotional electricity between them made her jolt a bit, so she returned her hand to her lap.

His expression remained unchanged. Professional. Maybe he hadn't been as into her as she thought. Maybe he'd gotten married. She glanced at his left hand. Nope, still bare.

The corner of his mouth curled slightly. Had he noticed her looking at his hand? Oh, great.

He lifted the flash drive out of the baggie. "May I?"

She felt a blush cover her cheeks and coughed into her fist. "Um, yes. Of course. It's the file marked Edwina." Her memory scanned what else might be on that disk. Surely nothing she would be embarrassed about.

He squinted at his screen. "Ah. Here it is." He maneuvered his mouse, as the cross ring on his right hand gleamed from a ray of sunlight streaming through the slats in the window blinds behind him.

"Nice view."

His eyes narrowed. "Excuse me?"

Her cheeks grew hotter. "From your window. Of the park across the street."

Chase half-turned. "Oh, yeah. I guess so."

Bailey felt the formal thickness hanging between them where a lifelong friendship had once been. She rose. "Look, Chase. I am so sorry—"

"About what, Bailey? Giving me the cold shoulder six months ago or asking for my help now?"

She gulped at his bluntness. "Um, both?"

They stared at each other a moment. She couldn't tell if his comment held residual hurt or if he wanted to be upfront and get the uneasiness out of the way.

He motioned for her to sit back down. "I'm sorry, too. I acted inappropriately the last time we were together."

"No, it's okay. Really. You acted like the perfect gentleman. I never considered you date material, that's all. I should never have accepted the invitation. It's just that my mother…"

"Ah, well. That makes sense." He clucked his tongue. "Mine, too. They want grandchildren too badly, right?"

A nervous chuckle escaped her lips.

His face softened. "Tell you what, Bailey Matteson. Let's leave the past where it belongs. After all, our families have known each other a very long time."

Relief flooded her heart as she eased back into the chair. "Sounds good to me. Clean slate?"

"Absolutely." He grinned. "So, then. Tell me how the forensic department can be of assistance to you today."

"Thank you. I guess I need to start at the beginning."

He leaned back. "Always a good plan."

"It began with Matthew, Chapter One…"

One dark eyebrow arched as he tented his fingers under his chin.

Twenty minutes later, after she'd over-explained her reason for contacting him, she figured she'd taken up enough of his time. "So, can you help me find out more about her?"

He held up one of the photographs. "May I keep these? I promise not to ruin them."

"Sure." She stood and extended her hand. "Thanks."

He stood also and took it in his free hand, giving it a firm, yet soft shake. "I'll run the photos through the identification program and also do a background check. We might turn up something. They had this developed in San Antonio, I see." He still gripped her hand as he spoke. "Too bad the photo lab is no longer in business. At least they are date stamped. That helps."

She slipped her hand out of his grasp and pointed. "Yes, that and the names are scrawled on the back."

He flipped it over." Ah, yeah. So they are. My grandmother used to do that, too." Chase laid it on the desk with the others. He grabbed a fresh file folder and slipped them inside.

"I appreciate it, Chase." She flashed him a sweet smile. "But don't waste too much time on it. I mean I know your job is important and you must have a ton of other cases…"

He perched his hip on the edge of his desk, the badge clipped to his belt catching the light. "Actually, it's slower than usual. So, your timing is impeccable."

When he crossed his arms, she noticed his biceps bulge. Of course, he worked out. All cops do these days, right?

"Oh, good." She lowered her eyes and grabbed her purse strap.

He pushed off from the desk and motioned the way out with his arm. "I'll call you next week. I will probably have something by then."

"Right." She slipped her handbag onto her shoulder. "There is one other thing."

"And that is?"

"My grandparents died in a car accident on I-35 near San Marcos in 1968. A hit-and-run. I did an online search of the newspaper, and a short article said the police had a suspect, thanks to a convenience store clerk's testimony. But they dropped it because he later recanted his story. Is that common?"

"Happens more than you think. People want their fifteen-minute claim to fame. Then they get caught in a lie and get a guilty conscience."

"But the police dropped the case awfully quickly." Bailey felt annoyance gurgling inside her.

Chase gave her a sympathetic smile. "I know. The family rarely understands. But if all leads are dead ends, well…" He returned to his side of the desk. "Give me the date again and their names and I'll see what I can discover. Not that I'll find anything from almost fifty years ago."

She parroted off the facts as he scribbled them on a notepad.

"I might turn up something, but no guarantees."

She couldn't ask for more. "Thanks, again. Give my greetings to your mom."

His eyes scanned her. "And mine to yours."

Bailey sucked in a breath, pivoted on her heel, and scuttled out of the office. She took the stair steps two at a time back to the lobby. As she went through the turnstile, she glanced back up the stairwell. No Chase. He hadn't followed to watch her leave.

Good… I guess.

As she drove back to the office, she decided to pursue other avenues in her family tree search as she waited for the results from Chase's investigation. Then a cold lump plopped into her abdomen. Tonight, they had another special choir rehearsal. Bailey groaned. Jessica and Shannon would assault her with twenty questions.

How did they get along?

Is he still single?

Maybe she could skip choir altogether? No, they were to rehearse for the upcoming fall festival program. And she had a small solo. Nix that idea.

To her surprise and relief, neither of her friends asked any questions. Instead, they discussed what went on at work and if they had finished their lessons for Matthew, Chapter Three. No mention of genealogy, mystery women, or good-looking policemen.

What had gotten into them?

On Saturday morning, Bailey tackled her timeline again as her laundry churned in the washer. An idea had sprung into her mind during the middle of Thursday night. Trace the family forward and plan a family reunion to be held in San Antonio. Then she'd find out what the rest of the siblings recalled about their ancestry. She spent all of Friday evening at the task, finally clicking off her laptop at 11:45 p.m.

So far, she had located Edmond and the names of his two children. Edmond married in 1973, the year after her mom, after serving ten years in the Navy. A Vietnam veteran, he retired from the auto repair business in 2010 and now helped his wife run a bed and breakfast in Nicaragua. The youngest of his children, Taylor, was Travis' age, single, and lived in Chicago. The eldest, Mitchell, had married in 1994 and his wife birthed twin girls, Madison and Megan, in 1999. They lived in Colorado.

Eugene, whom she'd discovered was really Edgar Eugene, married in 1966, moved to Chicago, had one son, Robert, and then lost his wife to cancer twelve years ago. He remarried in 2006 to Autumn Simpson, eleven years younger with no children. Bailey did a search and located an article about his retirement chronicled in the Texas Association of Lawyers Newsletter, dated 2015.

Elliott, politely described as a bit slow by the family, never married. He lived in Houston and worked in an oil refinery. Closest to her mom in age and location, it made sense that they semi-stayed in touch. But she still didn't understand why her mother's older brothers lost contact with her. Perhaps due to their parent's demise? Death, especially a tragic one, can unwind family ties. Maybe she could ask her dad tomorrow if she could get some time alone with him. Possibly at church during the social hour after worship. Still, his icy stress when she talked to Liza made her question that idea. On the other hand, he could be an ally and knew how to persuade her mother.

Eventually, she would have to run her theories by her mom, but before she proceeded much further, she wanted her dad's opinion. Even if their generation had severed communication, why did hers have to? She'd love to meet her cousins, their kids, and spouses. What would be wrong with that?

Yet, like a ghostly decoration in the October wind, the mysterious Edwina floated through the corners of her mind. Would her mother's siblings know anything about her? Could discovering her identity be the true motive behind her plotting out this soiree?

Bailey bit the end of her pen. Yes, she admitted to herself. Partially.

So why did admitting it send a shiver over her backbone?

Chapter 11

After Sunday services, Bailey located her father and hooked him by the elbow. "Dad, may I speak with you for a moment?"

"Sounds serious. Is everything all right?"

She tilted her head. "Yes, I do have a few questions about Mom's past. And I am afraid if I ask her it will upset her again."

"You are referring to this cockamamie genealogy thing?"

She bobbed her head. "I am hoping to get in contact with my uncles."

"I wouldn't get my hopes up, daughter. They were never close. In fact, Elliott was the only one who showed up at our wedding."

"Why, Dad?"

Her father placed his foot on the concrete bench in the meditation garden. Birdsong flitted above them and a soft breeze spritzed their arms from the softly trickling water fountain. "Well, if I recall, one was in the Navy overseas and couldn't get leave. The other lived too far away and told us he couldn't afford the trip."

"So, it's not as if they were mad or something?"

He scratched the back of his balding head. "Well, I'm not certain. I didn't really get to know your mom until after her parents died. Her brothers had scattered to the winds by then, including Elliot who lived with her aunt. Up until then, even though we traveled in the same social circles, she wouldn't give me the time of day." He chuckled at the memory of their long off-and-on courtship. "But, you know all that."

"Verbatim. You escorted her to a Fiesta ball, but she dumped you and joined her friends as soon as you arrived? Dad, pardon me, but that sounds horrid."

He chuckled. "Not really. That's the way it was back then. All of the dates to these types of things were socially coordinated. All part of the debutante's coming out to expose her to as many eligible bachelors as possible. Rather archaic, but there you are. Tradition." He rolled his eyes. "No one ever took it seriously. People rarely left with the one they came with."

Bailey nodded. "I see. That makes a bit more sense, I guess."

He shrugged.

"So, you met her again at a college frat party and decided to woo her?" She air quoted the old-fashioned term.

"Not that archaic, my dear. But, yes." He winked. "We'd both grown up a bit, I guess. In fact, we didn't connect the dots until months later."

"It's a nice story. Kind of like God gave you two a second chance because He knew you were meant for each other." She smiled warmly. He did as well.

"Dad, I sincerely want to locate her brothers and find out why they fell out of touch. Trouble is I don't want to upset Mom. After the Edwina incident—"

His face became concrete as he waggled a finger in front of her nose. "Don't mention that name, Bailey. Ever. Understand?"

She cowered. He rarely used that disciplinary tone with her. The few times in high school when her actions warranted it, it made her quiver. Still did. "Okay, Daddy."

"That's not why you want to delve into the past, is it?"

She half-glanced at his face. "Perhaps. A little." She hurried through the rest of her thoughts. "But, it's mostly pure curiosity. I'm related to all these fascinating folks, and I have no idea who they are."

"Harrumph." He straightened, residual sternness set in his jaw, but his eyes held a daddy's little girl love. "It's been nearly fifty years, honey. That's a lot of time with little or no contact. I'd forget the whole thing if I were you."

"Yes, Daddy."

Why had she reverted to calling him that today? She

hadn't referred to him as "daddy" since elementary school.

But she couldn't drop her family leaf gathering. Not when a name search on Facebook yielded results. Once she got home she searched again.

Bailey found Edmond's wife, Eugene's new one, and their various offspring. She asked to friend each of them. Would they know who she is? She pulled up her profile and listed "Daughter of Emily Sue Holston Matteson." Then she sent up a small prayer.

Off and on over the next day, she checked her phone. By the next afternoon, five of them had accepted her friendship. Two—Eugene's new wife named Clara, and Edmond's son, Mitchell, who lived in Chicago—had sent her a private message hello. She clicked off a question to each of them in PM. *Would you be interested in a family reunion?* By the time she arrived at the gym, her phone had pinged five times.

Yes.

I guess.

Sure.

Where?

I'm game.

Bailey pumped her fist. Her thumbs danced over the tiny qwerty board. *Okay - get back to you soon.*

She slammed her back into her car seat and closed her

eyes. Now her dad would change his tune. And her mom.

Then her eyes flew open. Boy, did she have oodles of planning to do. And, she shuddered, it probably would be a good idea to clue her mother in. She could use her mom's well-bred, party-planner help. But when to ask? Dropping another bomb during Sunday dinner would not be a good move. She'd call her tonight when she got home.

Ugh. No, she wouldn't. She'd talk herself out of it, conveniently forgetting until it was too late or pulling some other procrastinating stunt. All right, all right. She texted Jessica that she would be a bit late. Then Bailey counted to three and dialed her mom's cell phone.

"Mom, it's Bailey. Do you have a second?" More like fifteen minutes…

God must have shined His favor. After the initial dead silence, her mother had been almost reasonable. Though she didn't approve and doubted anyone would actually show up, she understood Bailey's desire to reconnect with family.

"Then you'll help me plan it?"

"I imagine. We may as well have it here. The house is large enough, I think, and we do have two guest rooms and the pull-out sofa in the den. That should house a few who may not want to get a hotel."

Her mother's suggestion took her back a bit. Had her father talked with her? "Wow, Mom. That would be a big help. But when?"

"We'll be getting into the holidays soon. We'd better

wait until next year."

"One lives in Chicago and another Colorado. It'll be snowing then and hard for them to travel."

"True, then we'll have it after the weather warms. Before it gets too ghastly hot. Summertime the kids are out of school, but I'm not sure a pool party would be appropriate, do you? People may be shy meeting for the first time wearing bathing suits."

Actually, Bailey liked the idea. Grilling burgers around the pool sounded like her style. But hardly her mom's. "Late spring, then? After Easter. People love to come to Texas in late April or early May when the wildflowers are in bloom."

Silence.

"Mom?" Bailey's heart beat a bit harder. Had she said something to upset her again?

"May 10, 2018, is a Saturday. The fiftieth anniversary of…" Her whispered voice cracked.

"Of your parent's accident."

"That can't be a coincidence, can it?"

The emotion in her mother's voice twisted her heart. Tears clouded Bailey's windshield view. She sniffled and wiped one from her cheek. "No, Mom. It isn't. That's the day, then."

"Yes. That's the day."

Her phone's day stamp flashed October 12. It allowed seven months to plan the biggest family party ever. Bailey clicked off and added May tenth to her calendar.

As she typed the event in, a thought flashed, which took her breath.

Golden anniversary.

Gold leaf.

Family is golden. And so are memories.

That would be the theme. She'd make gold foil leaves with each person's name on it and dangle them from the oak tree in the backyard. All the decorations would be in gold and white. Happy 50th anniversary decorations would be easy to find. Well, maybe not "happy" happy. They would be commemorating their patriarchs' death.

Lord, I hope it is a sort of a happy one, though. She snatched her gym bag and locked her car door with a punch of her fob.

Bailey's phone rang as she entered the gym. Chase. Great. "Hi. Can you wait a sec?" Too noisy to hear anything with all the clanking of weights, whir of machines, chatter, and background yoga music, she slipped into the locker room. "There, that's better. I can hear you now."

His baritone voice tickled her ear. "Where are you?"

"At the gym, but I haven't started working out yet."

"Really? Where do you train?"

"Family Fortitude. It's on the highway, halfway between work and home."

"Ah, yeah. I've seen it. It appears clean."

"It is. Where do you work out?" She cringed. Why had she asked that?

"Um, at home. I turned one of the spare bedrooms into a gym. Nothing fancy. Weights, a couple of machines."

"Oh." The man must make some dough. As a law enforcement investigator? Well, his parents were wealthy, so...

His voice jolted her back to the present. "Do you have a moment?"

"Um, yeah, sure. What's up?"

He cleared his throat. "So, about this long-lost friend or relative, Edwina."

Bailey's knees weakened at his voice's change in tone. She edged onto a bench. "Yes?"

"I have some information for you. But I don't think you'll want to hear it over the phone. Maybe we should meet. I get off in an hour. Can I join you for dinner?"

A warning siren blared in her brain. An attempt to date her again? Well, if they met up, she'd have her own vehicle. The moment it turned personal, she'd leave. "I guess so."

"El Caldo at seven?"

"Sure, Mexican sounds good." She bit the right side of her lower lip. "But, Chase?"

"Yeah?"

"This is Dutch treat."

He chuckled. "Whatever you say. Later."

She sighed. Then out of the corner of her eye, she noticed Jessica standing off to the side, hands in the air and "What?" on her lips.

Bailey pocketed her phone and shuffled over to her. "Oh, do I have news."

He waved to her from across the crowded restaurant. As Bailey approached, Chase stood and pulled out her chair. His jacket hung on the back of his own. He'd removed his business tie and rolled his Oxford shirt sleeves halfway up his forearms. The light blue stripe deepened the same color in his eyes. Why had she noticed that?

"I took the liberty of ordering you some water with lemon."

She scooted in. "Thanks."

He returned to his own chair and handed her a menu. "What do you recommend we order?"

Is he nervous? She smiled gently. "It's a Tex-Mex restaurant. That means ordering anything with chili, beans, rice or cheese on a tortilla works."

"Right." He buried his head in his menu.

She slipped a few strands of auburn hair back over her shoulder. "Sorry. I've had a weird day. I didn't mean to be terse."

"You weren't." He lifted his eyes and gazed at her for a second. Then he took a sip of water and set his glass down. "But, Bailey."

"Yes?"

"I'm about to make it even weirder, I'm afraid."

Chapter 12

Bailey lost her appetite. Not even the warm tortillas chips with fresh cilantro salsa called her name. "What do you mean?"

Chase set his menu on the tabletop. "I planned this wrong. We should have chitchatted through the meal. Caught up, kept it light."

"I'm not a chitchat kind of girl."

A smile etched the corners of his lips. "True. I do recall that." He placed his napkin in his lap.

Bailey waited. He then rearranged the condiments on the table. Why did he seem to stall?

"Well, what did you discover? You're killing me."

He lifted his gaze and met hers. "Edwina is your aunt."

"My what?" Her heart thumped against her chest. Several patrons turned their direction. She must have belted it out in a squeal. She cleared her throat. "That's impossible."

109

"Afraid not. She's your mother's sister." Chase leaned forward and lowered his voice. "Or was. I haven't found any evidence whether she is alive or dead. I did find some information on her, though but I don't think you'll like it."

She sucked in a shaky breath. "I don't care. Tell me."

"I hate to be the bearer of bad news. But your aunt hasn't always lived a very nice life. She has several warrants, starting with possession of an illegal substance and then the kidnapping of a child. There's more."

"More?" The room suddenly felt frigid. She rubbed her arms.

He removed his jacket from the chair and stood to drape it over her shoulders. "Yep. Do you want me to continue?"

She clutched it around her with a small whimper of thanks. "Yes."

"I'm sorry to tell you all of this." He reached for her hand.

She slid it back and grabbed her water glass, taking a long gulp of water.

He waited.

She set the tumbler down and ran her finger down the side, chasing a water droplet. "Are you sure? I mean, that this Edwina is my—?"

"—Aunt? Yes. We ran it through our computer program. It revealed ninety-seven percent accuracy so the pictures are definitely the same person. That's why I did some digging. Your mother's sister, Edwina Jane Holston, born July 15, 1948."

Bailey sat back and turned to gaze out the restaurant window. "So that is why there is such a gap."

"Gap?"

"Between my mother and her elder brothers. She was born in September of 1950, and her brothers during World War II. Edwina came in between." She fingered the cross around her neck. The cool hard surface and the fact it represented her faith helped her stay grounded as her brain processed the information. "I see why you didn't want to tell me over the phone." She shifted her focus back to Chase. "Thank you."

"You weren't sure of my motive for suggesting dinner, were you?" He crossed his hands over his chest and scoffed. "Seriously, Bailey, I find you attractive, but I haven't pined over you. You made your opinion of me loud and clear the last time."

"Oh, no. That's not it at all." She opened her mouth to reply more but saw the waiter come up to them.

"Do you still want to order?"

She glanced at the tabletop and shook her head.

Chase's voice sounded professional, empathetic, and genuine. "I'm sorry. The lady has received some disturbing news. I'm afraid we've changed our mind about dinner. We'll come back soon, though."

She lifted her eyes to catch him slip a ten-dollar bill into the waiter's hand. "Thank you for understanding."

The waiter nodded, flashed Bailey a soft smile, and

walked away.

Chase rose and pulled her chair out for her. "Perhaps we should have had this conversation at my office."

Bailey retrieved her purse and handed him back his jacket. They walked through the restaurant to the foyer. Then, Bailey halted and faced him. "I want to clarify something. You did or said nothing wrong six months ago. You were charming. In fact, you were the perfect gentlemen and escort."

His lips pressed together as one eyebrow arched.

"Well, maybe escort is a poor choice of words."

"In our generation, yes. But thank you, I think." He pushed open the restaurant door. "So why did you ignore my calls?"

She stopped under the small portico covered with a festive, striped awning. "My fiancé was killed in Afghanistan."

"I knew about it. I attended the memorial service with my parents. You were in a fog of grief so you probably don't remember."

"Sorry. I don't."

He gave her a warm smile. "So…?"

"My mom pushed me into getting 'out there' again." She gestured the quote.

"Ah. And I became the lab rat?"

"Sounds horrid, doesn't it. I thought I'd be more comfortable being with an old friend than a stranger. I am so sorry."

Chase swallowed and turned his eyes to the street.

"I don't think I was ready. I... I'm not sure I am even now."

He took her left hand and thumbed the amethyst ring that she always wore on her ring finger. "So that's why you wear this."

"Yes. I returned the engagement ring to his parents. But he gave this one to me for my birthday the last time..." She blinked back old tears.

His facial expression softened. His voice quieted. "I am truly sorry. If I had known..."

She plastered a flat grin on her face. "It's all right. I should've told you, It's just that..."

He let go of her fingers and bobbed his head. "Mothers can be persuasive. No further explanation necessary."

"Thank you, truly." Bailey focused on the sincerity in his face in the dim light coming from the restaurant. Inside a mariachi band began to play. "I really appreciate all of your research, too. And I do want to know more."

"Are you certain?"

She nodded firmly, more to convince herself than him.

"Then let me check my calendar to see when we can meet at work." He reached for his phone.

She held up a hand. "No. I'd rather learn about it now or my imagination will go berserk."

"You sure you're up to it? You still look a bit pale."

"The fresh air has helped. How about we go get something less spicy? Or heavy."

He titled his head. "Very well. You choose. I'll follow."

She glanced down to think, then back to his eyes. "Pocket-A-Pita by the antique shop?"

He took his car fob from his pocket. "Know exactly where it is. Meet you there in ten."

Bailey punched in the speed dial on her phone. She wanted moral support. Shannon answered on the third ring.

"Shannon. I need your help."

"Sure. What?"

"Meet me at the sandwich shop we like."

"Okay?" Her voice trailed off. A pause.

Bailey gulped.

"When, Bailey?"

"Now?"

She heard Shannon exhale. "What's going on?"

Bailey's eyes welled and her voice shook. She spit it out rapid-fire to keep from bursting into sobs. "Oh, Shannon. Chase just told me the most awful news. And there is more information he wants to share. He wants me to meet him for a bite to eat. I'm not sure I can hear this alone."

"About Edwina? He's found something out?"

The tears flooded her cheeks now. "She's my aunt. And a criminal."

"Honey, I am on my way."

Bailey whispered a thank you, hung up, and wiped her eyes. Great. Now, she surely looked like a red-eyed raccoon. Way to impress a guy. She pulled into a gas station and asked for the key to the ladies' room. Staring through the grungy mirror, she dabbed at her eyes, wiped under her lower lids, and fanned her face. She reached in her handbag for her makeup pouch and did a quick repair job. Then she fluffed her hair, took three deep breaths and drove the rest of the way to the pita shop.

Chase stood at the entrance. When she joined him, he slipped his hand to her back. "Are you okay?"

"I think so. Listen, Chase. It's not that I don't trust you. But I have a feeling I am not going to like what you have to tell me. I've invited my best friend to join us."

He gave her middle spine a small rub. "That's cool. And you are right. You probably won't."

She puffed out her cheeks. "Wonderful. I can hardly wait."

He snickered and opened the door for her. They walked to the counter, ordered their food, paid, and found a table in the corner closest to the entrance. "What does she look like?"

"Shannon? Short afro. Coffee-colored skin. High cheekbones. Slim."

Chase pointed with his chin. "There she is." He stretched his hand in a wave.

Shannon weaved through the bistro tables for four and

slid in next to Bailey, across from Chase. She extended her left hand, as the rainbow-colored bangles slid down her arm, making a small tinkling sound. "Shannon Johnson."

He half-rose out of his chair, quickly eyed her wedding set, and then met her face. "Chase Montgomery."

"Oh, I know who you are."

He narrowed his eyes. "Really?"

Bailey felt her cheeks flush.

Shannon stumbled. "Um, Bailey told me she had given you the pictures of Edwina. You're a friend of her mother's or something, right? And a policeman?"

"Yes, something like that." His eyes darted between them as he held back a smile.

Luckily, the server called their number.

"I've got it. Can I get you anything, Shannon?"

"Diet root beer."

"Coming right up." He slid back his chair, rose, and strolled to the counter.

Bailey leaned in and hissed. "Shannon."

She rolled her eyes. "Sorry. But he's even better lookin' close up. You need to rethink this, girl."

"What do you mean?"

Shannon opened her mouth to respond but shut it quickly as Chase's footfall neared the table.

The two fell silent as Chase divvied up the order. He folded his hands onto the table. "I think we need to pray. Agreed?"

Boy, do we ever. Bailey and Shannon glanced at each

other, knowing they both thought the same thing, and silently nodded.

After they said amen, Bailey's elephant no longer sat directly on her stomach. Just nudged it a little, but not enough to keep her from eating. She took a bite of her sandwich and swallowed. "Okay, lay it on us."

He sputtered his drink. Laughing, he wiped his mouth. "You're no-nonsense, Bailey. I like that. It's refreshing."

Shannon's eyes became slits. He glanced at Shannon, cleared his throat, and wiped his mouth. Then he turned his attention back to Bailey. "Very well. You started at the beginning for me. Let me return the favor."

He pulled out his phone and thumbed through it.

Bailey reached for Shannon's warm, reassuring hand.

Shannon grabbed hold and squeezed.

"First off. I haven't heard back from the San Marcus APD on your grandparent's case. But that is not unusual. They will assign someone to it eventually, but it is hardly top priority to them. And since it doesn't apply to any current case, I can't request the file."

Bailey slouched a bit.

Chase repositioned in his chair. "Let me tell you what I did turn up. Edwina is verified to be your mother's older sister. As I said, she was first arrested for possession of an illegal substance. She received a six-month probation as a first offense when she told the judge her boyfriend slipped it into her purse without her knowing it while the police stopped him for speeding. That occurred in April 1966. A

117

year later, she had a warrant issued against her for the kidnapping of an infant from the county hospital in Beaumont."

"Beaumont!?" Bailey dropped her pita into the basket.

"Does that mean something?"

"Yes. After my mother's parents died, her younger brother went there to live with a spinster aunt."

"Interesting." Chase returned his attention to the phone screen. "However, she was never convicted. The charges were eventually dropped. Seems the child was hers." He paused to focus on Bailey's reaction.

She turned to Shannon. "See, she had been pregnant in that photo."

He narrowed his gaze. "She was cited for disorderly conduct and assault to a government official in June of 1969 in El Paso, sentenced to twenty-five hours civic service duty, and placed on probation for a year."

"You did say El Paso?"

"Yes. Trouble is, it seems she left the county. Stopped checking in with her probation officer."

"Could she be arrested for that?"

"Not now. Statute of limitations. But it is a red flag." He took a bite of his sandwich and chewed. After a moment he wiped his mouth. "Let's get back to the kidnapping charge. I called in some favors and thought the details were sketchy. She had placed the newborn for adoption but decided to renege on the deal, so she stole the baby from the hospital. The adoptive parents dropped the charges.

Evidently, someone reimbursed them for their expenses."

"I wonder who? I wouldn't think the baby's father or his parents would. Not when she was an unwed mother."

"Well, that's not true. In May of 1966, she eloped."

Shannon gawked. "While in high school?"

"Legal age of consent for girls in Texas back then was sixteen. Edwina was seventeen, almost eighteen." He tapped the screen. "But get this. She married Arthur Archer."

Bailey sat up straight. "*The* Arthur Aloysius Archer? Who owns five car dealerships and sits on the city council as mayor pro tem?"

Chase slid back in his chair and folded his arms. "And whose son, A.A. Jr., is running for State Comptroller. Yes."

She turned to Shannon, whose mouth could have caught a horsefly, then turned back to Chase. "Was he her druggie boyfriend that slipped the stuff in her purse?"

"That would be speculating. The report doesn't mention the boyfriend's name."

Shannon rubbed her thumb and finger together, holding them up over the table. "Someone paid someone to stay quiet, I bet."

Chase shrugged. "To continue. Arthur Archer's dad, Angus Archer—"

Bailey waved her hands. "Slow down. All these "a" names have my head swirling."

"Well, your mom's family named all their children with an "e"." Shannon sat back with her arms crossed.

"Sounds like the in thing back then."

Bailey waggled her head and focused her attention back to Chase. "True. Sorry. Go on."

"Okay. Angus Archer evidently got steamed when he learned of the elopement between Arthur, his son, and Edwina, your aunt. He hired a private detective, who located them in a rent-by-the-week motel in Las Vegas, Nevada. He hauled Arthur back to town and insisted on annulling the marriage. Order was filed on June 15, 1966."

"And... Aunt Edwina?"

"Signed the papers per my sources. I've requested a copy to make sure she actually did."

He stopped, laid down his phone, and folded his hands.

Bailey sucked in some air. "So, are you saying Arthur Archer and his dad didn't know she was pregnant?"

"Don't know that. It may have been why they eloped. It happens, even in the best of families."

Shannon scoffed. "It would explain why your mother never told you about her."

"No." Bailey shook her head as a damp chill skidded down her spine. "She appeared in the birthday photos with my mom later that year. And she wore a maternity blouse. Obviously, she got pregnant after they'd eloped, but maybe they didn't know it at the time. I think they pressured her into the annulment so she had no choice but to come home. When she started to show, after my mom's sixteenth birthday party, her parents shuffled her off to live with her aunt in Beaumont until time for the birth."

"Plausible. Especially given their social status." Chase pocketed his phone. "Do you know why she would end up in El Paso?"

"Because she did a runner with her child." Shannon shrugged. "That's the only thing that would make sense if both her parents and the Archers had pressured her into giving up the baby."

"By why El Paso? Do any of your relatives live there?" Chase leaned in. "Bailey?"

She blinked. "No. I, um, I don't think so."

Bailey felt the room spinning. She gulped a few ounces of lemonade through a straw, but it jolted back into her throat, along with the few bites of pita. "Excuse me."

She covered her mouth and dashed for the restroom, with Shannon close behind.

When they returned, a to-go box sat at her place and Chase had finished his meal.

"I'm sorry all this upset me so much." She held her stomach.

He shook away her apology. "No need. It's a lot to— pardon the pun—swallow all at once." He handed her the takeout container. "Maybe you can have it for lunch tomorrow."

Bailey ran her hand over the Styrofoam lid. "I usually have control of my emotions."

He squeezed her arm. "I know. You are a Matteson. Your mother taught you well."

She glared at him.

He held his hands up in surrender. "Hey, I'm a Montgomery. Same musty, old society family as yours."

Bailey's scowl broke into a smile. She liked him, darn it.

"Look. I am going to type this all up and email it to you so you can read over it in your own time, all right? I'll also forward you the links I'm allowed to give you. You can send me your email address." He handed her his business card.

"Thank you. Truly. I appreciate your research."

He stood and folded his paper napkin. "You're welcome. Sorry, it couldn't be more pleasant news."

"Not your fault." She extended her hand.

Chase's shoulders relaxed a bit. He switched his glance to her confidant. "Shannon, nice meeting you. Thanks for being here for Bailey." He took Bailey's hand and held it. "If you have any questions after you have gone over my findings, let me know."

He acted with such formality and poise, she almost thought he might bow and kiss her fingers. She would've keeled right then and there. Instead, he slipped his grip out of hers and with a final nod, left the sandwich shop.

Bailey breathed for the first time in two minutes. She steadied herself by grasping the back of the chair. "Oh. My. Word."

Shannon gave her a side hug. "What's got you more flustered, girl? Chase or his report?"

Bailey didn't know how to respond.

Chapter 13

By four in the morning, Bailey gave up. Sleep had been spotty at best. She untwisted herself from the covers, dislodging Bower's body from where her feet should've been. With a huge yawn, she shuffled down the hall to the kitchen for caffeine.

Chase's news shook her. No wonder her mother cried at the mention of her wayward sister's name. Some families could embrace deviant behavior. Not hers. Hers was more of a hide them in the attic type. Or disown them. Is that what had happened after Edwina ran away with her baby? No, a few years later she came to Elliott's graduation. With her child.

Bailey viewed the three photos again. The first one she'd discovered stuck behind another, showed Edwina around four months pregnant in October. She'd eloped in May. The timeline fit. She definitely became pregnant after marriage.

In the graduation photo, Edwina hoisted what appeared to be a little boy on her hip. The time lapse between the two pictures made sense. Edwina had birthed Arthur Archer's heir in 1967, so he'd have been about four years old in 1971, the year Elliott graduated in Beaumont. Had Edwina and her child returned there to live with her aunt after her arrest in El Paso? Did Arthur ever learn he had a son? That would have really ticked off his pompous father.

She clicked on her laptop to check her messages and found one from Chase time-stamped 9:04 pm. The man must have headed back to his office after leaving the pita place. She squinted to adjust her eyes to the monitor's bluish light and opened it.

Bailey, I am sorry the news upset you tonight, or if I handled it all wrong. Attached are my findings. I scanned my handwritten notes, so I hope you can decipher them. If not, please let me know. Or if I can help you further. Best wishes in your research. Chase.

P.S. Be careful. You may ruffle a few feathers in your search. The Archers are a powerful family.

Also attached were two links to the public records on Edwina's disorderly charge. Bailey didn't open them yet, though. Instead, she read through the email several times, searching for some indication that he... but that would be stupid. She'd acted like a wimpy female, told him she was not ready to pursue any type of relationship and ended the evening queasy and knee-wobbly. Not exactly encouraging for any dating in the future.

Fine. She shut the computer. Why would her mind go down that path anyway? The last thing she needed was to chase after Chase.

Her pun brought on a giggle. Enough of this. A better use of her time would be planning the reunion and forgetting about digging up more family dirt.

Even so. Should she try to locate Edwina now? She *was* her kin. At least her son might want to connect. But then again, perhaps not. What if she gave him up for adoption later? Or Child Protective Services put him in foster care? Would he want anything to do with the relatives who shunned him? For all she knew by now, he could either be a thug or a CEO with three kids in a five-bedroom, four-bath house in the 'burbs.

Didn't matter. Water under the bridge. Still, as she rinsed out her cup and padded down the hallway to her bedroom, her conscience nudged her to at least make the effort to locate him, which meant discovering his name. Not a task she wanted to tackle in the wee hours of the morning. She stifled another yawn, stared at the clock, and debated if another two hours of sleep would be beneficial or only make her more sluggish throughout the day.

More sluggish won out. She turned around, went back to the dinette set and decided to catch up on her Bible study reading. She also downed the uneaten sandwich and pickle spear from the pita place. With food in her stomach, life seemed rosier.

125

By the time her phone alarm went off at 6:00 a.m., she had made up a partial guest list, planned the decorations by cruising various party house websites, and figured out the best way to send invitations. He mother would insist on pre-printed ones through the mail. However, she didn't have many of her relatives' addresses other than their social media links.

E-vites wouldn't do. Most of her long-lost family's emails were still a mystery anyway. Bailey decided to design one using a free graphics program and private message them, asking if the ones who responded would contact their family members and forward it. She tacked on an RSVP with her email and phone number. Risky, but it might also be fun to actually hear their voices or email back and forth and build some type of bond.

She texted Shannon. *Got the public records on Edwina. Should I delve into it or let sleeping dogs lie?*

Within a minute she got her response. *Pray about it. God will let you know.*

Of course. Duh. She did as she changed into her jogging outfit and headed to the track.

As she stepped into the parking lot, she wondered if she should be doing this in the predawn hours. Bailey spanned the area. Her neighborhood seemed safe enough. Crime in her small town involved kids toilet-papering a house or a mad girlfriend keying her ex's car. She ventured out and breathed in the crisp, autumn air. Well, autumn for southern Texas meant the temperatures no longer clung to the nineties during the day. A welcome relief to experience weather in the low sixties before sunrise.

Strolling down the sidewalk, Bailey cocked an ear into the stillness. The crickets had gone to bed and the birds had yet to awaken. The very soft rush of a few cars on the nearby highway and the distant bark of a dog seemed to be the only detectable sounds, other than the slap of her running shoes on the pavement. Nice. Peaceful.

Suddenly a car pulled up. Bailey halted. Her heart did as well.

Then she puffed out a sigh when she recognized the vehicle. Chase.

He lowered the passenger side window and leaned across the seat from the driver's side. "Are you all right? What are you doing out here before dawn?"

She leaned into the window. "I could ask you the same thing."

"Got a call an hour ago, only now returning. It's my job. And you?" His police radio chattered in the background.

"I'm going for a morning jog."

"Alone? Is that wise?"

She waved her hands. "This is one of the best neighborhoods in a quiet, small town."

He wagged his head. "True. But the big city crime is encroaching onto our serenity. You didn't see what I saw no more than six miles from here. It's not the same world we grew up in. You take care, all right?"

"I will."

He nodded, raised his car window, and drove off.

She opened the chain link fence to the high school's track and began her leg stretches. The soft glow of a street lamp illuminated most of the field, except for the part shadowed by the buildings. Wagging her neck from side to side, she breathed in and began her jog.

The third turn around the track, Bailey thought she saw movement in the shadows. The thud of her steps on the crushed clay kept their rhythm as her eyes tried to focus on the darkness.

There. It moved again. She slowed her pace.

Should she turn and leave? Whatever it was, it now stood still as a statue, and though she couldn't detect them, Bailey definitely felt a pair of eyes zeroed in on her.

Bailey halted. She held her hands to her hips and took a few deep breaths to ease her nerves. The figure didn't budge. *Is that a person crouched down watching you? Maybe it is a bush and you are being paranoid.*

She didn't recall a bush planted there before and she'd jogged this track for five years. Okay, maybe she'd cut it short today. She began to walk backward and then turned to run for the gate.

Footsteps sounded on the gravel behind her. Faster. Closer. Her lungs began to burn but she pressed on, the gate to freedom looming closer.

She grabbed the latch, swung it open, dashed through, and pulled it closed.

Panting met her, as paws lifted between the links. A huge dog, more like a Shetland pony in height and stature, cocked its ears and whimpered.

Bailey's adrenaline plummeted. Good grief.

"Hey there, boy. Did you get locked in here all night?" Bailey bent down and scratched its fur through the fence. She lifted the latch again and opened the gate for the pooch. It dashed through and lopped down the street, she hoped for its home.

Relief flooded her senses. No boogie man. Only a homesick mutt. She leaned against the fence and watched the wispy, dark clouds outlined by the soft hues of the predawn sky. After her heartbeat returned to normal, she walked down the street to her apartment complex and began the rest of her day.

Halfway to work, it dawned on her. She'd let the dog *out*. Most likely it had gotten tired of trying to find an exit from the enclosed track within the eight-foot security fence and had fallen asleep until she arrived. She'd, in essence, not let sleeping dogs lie.

Did that mean God had responded with an answer? Did she have the celestial go-ahead to pursue Edwina, her son, and reveal his parentage?

Chapter 14

Edwina Jane Holston. The computer search that evening came up with very little. One newspaper article from the society section mentioned her and Arthur Archer's annulment and a comment from his father, Angus Archer. "Kids are stupid. They take puppy love and blow it up into a Great Dane. They never consider breeding, background, how they were raised, or how they are going to make ends meet. Love is the answer to everything according to their music. And these teenagers believe that garbage."

Okay, another reference tying Edwina to a dog seemed a tad too coincidental. Bailey scratched her forehead. She pulled up her Bible app for a reference she recalled someplace in the gospels about a woman and dogs. It popped up a story in Matthew, the book in the Bible she currently studied. Icy chill splashed across her chest. In

Chapter 17, Jesus told the non-Jewish woman that it is not proper to toss the bread, made for the children, to the dogs. And she responded that even dogs can lick the crumbs from the table. He acknowledged her faith.

Bailey sat with her hands resting on her chin and read it again. Even if Edwina got pregnant by the heir to the Archer dynasty and agreed to the annulment, her son lacked a father to raise him. He had the right to be part of the Holston family, like the woman who begged to be a part of the family of God. Bailey should give him that opportunity—and Edwina also if she was still alive.

She needed to offer them crumbs, then see if they wanted bread. Or did she stretch the analogy too far? Neither Edwina nor her son had asked to be included in, nor had made contact with, the rest of the family in fifty years, as far as Bailey knew. Unless Edwina's showing up at Elliot's high school graduation counted.

What had happened before the camera bulb flashed? Had there been a confrontation, or had Edwina attended with good intentions but then become too unsure of the reaction to even approach the rest of the family? Had she been living with Elliott and her aunt in Beaumont? Knowing that much would help a lot.

She asked Jessica and Shannon later that evening at choir practice. "Am I interpreting all of this correctly?"

"I can't say." Shannon shrugged. "If you prayed, and you believe God has spoken, then act on it."

"How does she know for sure?" Jessica focused in on Shannon's face.

"Yes. How do I?"

"Well, why don't we ask Mrs. Perkins?" Shannon gave her friends a shrug and proceeded down the hall of the church building.

Bailey shuffled to catch up. "I guess it can wait until Monday."

Shannon stopped with her hand on the choir room door. "Which gives you more time to reflect and pray."

Jessica huffed into her cheeks. "I hate it when she says something wise."

The three chuckled and went inside to begin practicing their chorale for the festival next weekend. As they pushed open the door, they almost ran into Mr. Hanson and Mr. Garcia, some of the older choir members.

"Oops. Sorry." Bailey lifted her ears to her shoulders.

Mr. Garcia harrumphed. "Young girls these days have no manners. Do they, Albert?"

Mr. Hansen opened his mouth, but not before Shannon spouted a response. "She said she was sorry." Hooking Bailey through the arm, she pulled her away from the grumpy old men.

Through the rehearsal of the first three hymns, Bailey felt as if their eyes were on her. Especially Mr. Hanson's. Maybe he'd wanted to be picked to do the solo?

At the break, Bailey stood with her friends as they gulped down some water.

"Next one's where you have your solo. Excited?" Jessica grinned at her.

"Honestly, I wish I didn't have a solo, then I could bail and spend the evening researching what happened to make my family stop talking to each other. I mean, besides my grandparents being killed in that wreck." She half-twisted to face her friends seated next to her. "Wouldn't that draw them closer?"

"Tragedy does weird things to people, Bailey. Well, getting everyone together might help heal wounds. Maybe they will begin to talk about how they all felt." Jessica tilted her head in a half shrug.

Shannon patted Bailey's hand. "You have plenty of time to contact people."

"But they will have to book flights, hotel rooms, make plans to get off work…"

"Girl, this is October. You're talking May. Plent-y of time."

Jessica tapped Bailey's shoulder. "She's right. Stop stressing. Besides, you know we will help you get it done."

Bailey squeezed their hands. "Thanks, y'all."

Yet all during choir practice, the names and timelines kept tap dancing through Bailey's mind. Had she become obsessed with all of this relative seeking?

"What if Edwina doesn't want to be found? Maybe instead of your family disowning her, she disowned them? I mean, they wanted her to put the baby up for adoption, and obviously, she didn't."

Bailey's eyes and mouth widened. She hadn't considered that angle at all.

"Shannon makes sense... again." Jessica chomped on a carrot from her salad. The three had met for lunch at Bailey's apartment that following Saturday after Bailey's volunteer work.

"Yes, you do, Shan. I hadn't really thought about it like that. I figured with Mom being raised all Southern prim and proper, her parents may have sent the black sheep out of the pasture when she returned home with the baby. Hide the scandal from social tongue wags and all."

"Maybe she joined a commune or something. Subculture back then. Woodstock, Haight Ashbury. I mean she had a drug charge in 1966 before she eloped. I'm just saying..."

Bailey stopped her. "I get your point, even though Woodstock happened a few years after that. But I doubt there were communes in El Paso. Besides, she said her boyfriend slipped it into her purse. Oh!" Bailey slapped both hands to her cheeks. "I remember what Chase said. To be careful of the Archer family and their power. It must have been Arthur who dumped them in her purse. I mean she married him a month later. My, my. The dirt gets thicker."

Shannon held up her palm. "Whoa. He stated the boyfriend's name didn't appear in the report. I agree that someone must have paid to keep it out, but it also may have been because he was a minor."

"Who else would have been her boyfriend?" Bailey wiped the last thought away with her hands. "Anyway, I still want to find out what happened to her and the little boy. And if she had been kicked out of the family, why did she show up at Elliott's graduation?"

"Maybe because he graduated after their parents had died. She thought it would be easier to come back then?" Shannon cocked her head.

"And hang out in the background?"

"Bailey, it's possible no one else knew she came." Jessica tapped the table to make her point. "She never had the gumption to face them but wanted to see him graduate. Kinda sweet, actually."

"Or maybe they had a huge fight when she made her appearance with her child so she backed off. As I recall. Her face didn't appear very happy." Shannon folded her arms.

"I can't believe we are spending a fine afternoon speculating about my wayward aunt." Bailey picked at her meal of broccoli, sprouts, and lettuce. She set down her fork. "I hate dieting, too."

"Whoa. Li'l Miss Pouty." Shannon snickered. "Who told you to put on grumpy pants today?"

"Sorry. Maybe I should forget the whole thing."

Bailey laid her head in her arms.

"Why don't you, then?"

Bailey jolted straight. "What did you say, Shannon?"

"What is driving you to pursue this? Is it really worth it? I mean if any of your family wanted to connect, wouldn't they have done so by now?"

Bailey felt the burn rise from her neck. "Then why did they all say yes to my suggestion?"

"Exactly. Just getting you back on track." Shannon winked. "We are supposed to forgive. Not build walls that shouldn't be there. And from what I can tell, your family has erected a doozy. Time to knock it down."

Bailey turned to Jessica. "She has on her wise hat again."

"Yep." Jessica grinned. "So, let's get to it. Where do we go from here?"

Bailey sent them Chase's email. "Can y'all check the criminal files? I am not sure I am ready to do that yet."

They agreed and pulled out their smartphones.

Bailey retrieved her laptop and searched the San Antonio newspaper archives from 1966-67, especially the neighborhood gossipy ones. Perhaps there she'd find more clues. But the neighborhood paper didn't have digital archives back that far. She wrote down the address and phone number of the newspaper headquarters in the high society area of San Antonio where her mother spent her childhood, folded it and put it in her coin purse. She'd call during her lunch break on Monday.

She gazed at the photo of Edwina with her baby bump. October 1966. "Okay, ladies. Think this out with me. She looks about four months pregnant, right? She had to have gotten pregnant after they eloped."

"How do you know that?" Jessica grabbed the photo and peered at it.

"Well, the annulment happened on June 15th. Per Chase's notes, Angus Archer hired a private detective to locate them. I'm guessing it took him several weeks to find them in Vegas. I'd think it would be the first place to look. Where else do you elope to?"

"I know a couple who went to Laredo." Jessica shrugged.

Shannon and Bailey waggled their heads. "But they didn't if he found them in Vegas."

Jessica glanced down at her lap. "True."

"However, it would make sense for them to disappear right after finals."

"Or, right before. That is my suspicion. Drop out before the end of school and head to Vegas." Shannon smirked. "I know I'd be tempted."

"Of course." Bailey slapped her forehead. "I need to check the marriage records in Las Vegas for May or June 1966."

"Whew. That'll take a while." Shannon shifted her lips to one side. "Las Vegas *is* the wedding chapel city."

"Look who has on the grumpy pants now?"

Shannon smirked. "I need chocolate, girl."

Bailey rose, went to her pantry and reached on tiptoe to the top shelf. She pulled down a bag of Halloween bite-sized candy and tossed it on the dinette table. "Let's take some candy from the babies. No one ever knocks on apartment doors anyway."

"Then why did you buy it?" Jessica tore open the sack.

Bailey looked at the ceiling. "In hopes no one knocked on the door…"

Shannon unwrapped a caramel and peanut nugget coated in chocolate. "Confession is good for the soul." She plopped it in her mouth and rolled back her eyes in satisfaction.

Twenty minutes later Bailey cried, "Ah-ha. Found it!" She swiveled her laptop for her friends to view.

Jessica read the photocopy of the handwritten entry. "Mr. Arthur A. Archer and Ms. Edwina Holston. Married Saturday, May 21, 1966. 4:32 p.m. Chapel of Abiding Love. Las Vegas, NE. Pastor, Joseph Carr, Officiant."

"They were married about three weeks. Long enough." Shannon winked.

Bailey shook her head. "Why did she agree to the annulment if she was pregnant?"

"Probably didn't know."

Shannon slammed her palm down. "Unless that is why they eloped as Chase suggested, remember? Arthur had, um, visited the well and it wasn't dry."

"Which means she'd have been about six weeks along in May. That's when most women are sure they are with child. I mean that's the way it is in the movies." Bailey bit her lip. "That would make her at about…" She counted on her fingers. "… six months along in October. No. The picture doesn't show much of a bump."

"Well the rest of her looked skinny. Some women don't show much." Shannon cocked an eyebrow.

Bailey snatched the photo and eyed it one more time. "I feel in my heart she waited until they got married."

"Which brings us back to your original question, girl. Did they know she was pregnant when she agreed to the annulment?"

The three stared at each other. No one said anything for a few moments. Then Bailey spoke in a whisper. "I don't know."

"There is only one way to know." Shannon crossed her arms. "Ask Arthur Archer."

Chapter 15

The girls found the report about her June 1968 arrest in El Paso—right after her parents' death. Why had she ended up there? And did she have her son with her?

Since the second picture revealed her pregnancy, she had obviously returned to the fold a while after the annulment. It seems Bailey's grandparents had embraced their prodigal daughter after all, but they expected her to give her baby away. And she defied them. Is that why she ran away with the baby and tried to raise him on her own? Who did she know in El Paso?

Too many unanswered questions. Bailey knew the best way to find out meant asking either Arthur or approach her mom. Neither option sounded like an easy task. A root canal would be more fun.

She called her mother Saturday evening, almost hoping to connect to voicemail. No such luck.

"Mom, I need to talk to you about your family and this

shindig in May. When can we do that?"

"Are you coming for Sunday dinner as usual?"

"I am, but I didn't want a repeat—"

Her mother's voice hardened. "This is about Edwina, isn't it?"

"Yes, Mom. I know she is your older sister, that she eloped at seventeen, and then agreed to have the marriage annulled. And that she had a baby boy."

"My, you have been busy snooping, haven't you?"

Bailey shuddered at her mother's icy tone.

"Mom, please. I would have eventually found out somehow."

Silence.

Her throat tightened. Had she crossed the line again?

"Very well. Come over now if you like. Your father is at a golfing awards banquet and I had a weird feeling I shouldn't go, so I stayed home. I guess I know the reason now."

"Be there in fifteen minutes. Have you eaten?"

"As a matter of fact, no."

"Chowder from the organic market?"

"That would be perfect, dear. I'll heat up some baguettes."

Bailey almost heard her smile through the phone. Her father despised chowder, one of her mother's favorites. So, she never ate it around him. She'd get some dark chocolate pecan brownies, too.

With sack in hand, Bailey rang the bell. She lifted a

quick prayer as she listened for her mother's footsteps and the front door's bolt release.

Her mother answered with a terse smile. "Come in. I thought we might eat in the kitchen where it's warmer. This cold front has chilled my bones."

She held up the take-out bag. "I hope this will help."

Her mother took it and her lips stretched further toward her cheeks. "Thank you. I know it will. I love chowder."

The kitchen table had been set with orange and yellow placemats, harvest patterned napkins, and tan soup bowls. A centerpiece of autumn leaves, pine cones, and nuts carefully arranged in a terracotta platter added to the décor. Typical Mom.

As the two unpacked their dinner, they exchanged small talk. Then, after they'd blessed their food, her mother broached the subject. "Well, so you know Edwina eloped and had a baby straight out of high school. What else did you need to know?"

Bailey nearly sputtered out her mouth of soup. Instinctively, she swallowed it way too fast, feeling the heat burn her throat. She gulped some water. "Um, several things. Mainly to satisfy my own curiosity more than anything."

"You always were inquisitive." Her mother set down her spoon.

"Did Edwina and Arthur elope because she became pregnant?"

"No. Of course not. Shame on you for thinking such a thing."

"Then why did she agree to the annulment? Is it because she didn't know she was going to have a baby?"

"Correct. A few days after the annulment the nausea began. At first, mother thought it to a case of nerves."

"So, Arthur Archer didn't know?"

Her mother dabbed her napkin to the corner of her mouth. "The Archers were a powerful family even back then. Angus threatened to cut Arthur off if he didn't annul the marriage, and he gave in, even though I think he truly loved my sister. Mom and Dad made Edwina see that fighting that family would only lead to trouble."

"But surely they noticed in a few months…"

"No. They whisked Arthur away for a European vacation until the society tongues stopped wagging. Mom and Dad sequestered Edwina to keep an eye on her, and when she began to show, she went to live with Aunt Agnes."

"So, this picture…" Bailey lifted it from her handbag.

"Taken before she packed off to Beaumont. She pleaded with Mom and Dad to let her stay through my sixteenth birthday." She set down her spoon. "You were not meant to find it. Dad became so angry when Edwina disappeared with her newborn that he never again wanted her name mentioned. He told Mom to destroy every photo of her. I later discovered Mom kept back two, including that one." She rubbed her forehead. "I'd forgotten or I'd have removed them before I let you take the albums."

"She had the baby in Beaumont?"

"Yes. I'd persuaded her to go see Arthur after they returned to San Antonio, but he refused to acknowledge her. His father gave us hush money to help with her prenatal expenses. We packed her up to wait out the rest of the pregnancy at Aunt Agnes' home. Edwina agreed to give the baby up for adoption. The family had already been chosen through the Catholic Charity in Beaumont. But once she held her baby, Edwina changed her mind and snuck out of the hospital in the wee hours. She never told us where she went." Her mother dug in her pocket. "Here, I don't know why, but I kept this. Her letter telling us all goodbye, dated February 4, 1967. I found it with Mother's things."

Bailey read the note from her aunt telling how she couldn't give up the baby, she'd disappear for now and vowed to find Arthur and marry him again when they turned twenty-one.

"She really loved him, didn't she?"

"I guess she thought she did."

"Your poor parents."

"They searched for her for months." Her mother glanced away. "Mom cascaded deeper into a slump the longer she heard no word. Another year went by and no Edwina or her child. Dad must have spent a small fortune on private investigators." She stopped and took a swig of water.

Bailey waited.

Her mother dabbed her mouth and continued. "Edwina couldn't make it on her own. She returned around Easter in 1968 with little Edwin in hand."

"Edwin?"

"Edwin Arthur." He mother gave her a sad smile. "A combination of their names. I guess her way of hanging on to the young man she loved."

"Where had she been all that time?'

"Out in west Texas somewhere, I think is what she'd said." Her mother's chest heaved. "It hit my mother very hard. Socially, that time of year, daughters were to come out into society, and hers sat at home, annulled, and with a toddler." Her mother fiddled with her pearl necklace. "All of Edwina's schoolmates debuted that year and it rubbed deep. The gossip resurfaced. Dad took Mom to the ballet in order to console her. The doctor suggested it. Change of scenery, that sort of thing." She returned her focus to Bailey's face. "So you see, Edmond, Eugene, Elliott, and I partially blamed Edwina for…" She bit her lip.

"Your parents' death in the auto accident returning from the ballet."

"Yes." The word barely escaped her mouth. Unshed tears glistened in the corners of her eyes.

"I'm sorry, Mom."

"She became a convenient scapegoat for us. The police never found the driver of the other car, a rental paid with cash, at least that is what the police told us. The company didn't keep records back then as they do now."

Bailey felt the blood leave her face. "I had no idea."

Her mom placed her hand over Bailey's. "I know. Not your fault." She patted it. "So you see, trying to track her down and invite her would not be a great idea."

"Were you two ever close?"

"We were. Elliot adored her. She practically raised him. And me. I still recall us playing school in the tree house and she being our teacher. Elliott was a slow learner and socially awkward. I imagine today he'd be diagnosed with Asperger's Syndrome. Edmond and Eugene thought him wimpy and weak. They didn't understand him like Edwina and I did."

"Mom, there is one more picture I need to show you." Bailey pulled out the newspaper photo from the baggie and spread onto the table.

Her mother's hand shook as she brought it to her mouth.

"You didn't know she attended, did you?"

"No." Her finger traced the girl and the child. "No one expected Elliott to ever graduate. I'd always thought Edwina would be so proud of him if she knew." Her mother's lips quivered. One lone tear dripped down her cheek. "Excuse me."

She rose from the table and left the room.

Bailey stared at the soup bowls.

Chapter 16

Bailey decided not to share about her aunt's arrest in El Paso in June 1968. Her mother had rattled down a bumpy memory lane enough for one day. Perhaps alcohol had been Edwina's misjudged way to mourn. Did she blame herself for her parents' death? Was that why she left again?

The rest of the evening, the two women chatted about nothing at all, more as friends than mother and daughter, as they consumed the soup and bread before diving into the decadent brownies. Bailey drove away, warmed by the meal and the rare camaraderie they'd shared. Perhaps God could turn things for the good.

However, she also smiled because she had gleaned some valuable information. When she returned home, she turned on her computer and did a birth certificate search for a male baby named Edwin Arthur, born in early February

149

1967 in Beaumont. Bingo. Edwin Arthur Holston, seven pounds, eleven ounces, born the second of February at 11:52 p.m. A new leaf on her family tree. She bookmarked it.

The mood remained light at Sunday dinner the next day. In fact, several times her mother laughed. Bailey's dad dashed curious glances between them but didn't say a word. As usual, he pecked their foreheads with a kiss and retired to his den after the meal ended. Bailey helped her mother clean up and then hugged her briefly before driving home.

When lunchtime came around on Monday, Bailey left the building, sat in her car, and dialed the neighborhood newspaper headquarters. A woman answered on the fourth ring.

"Good day. I am researching some family history and wondered if you kept editions as far back as 1966."

"Oh, dear. I am sorry. Not many. You see, a fire back in 1981 destroyed most of our records, which of course were not computerized then." Her voice hesitated.

Bailey's heart sunk. She almost hung up but the woman spoke up again. "The high school kept some volumes, though. The issues that contained articles pertaining to them such as football victories, homecomings, prom. They donated them. However, they are fairly fragile"

Bailey thought for a moment. "Do you have volunteers to scan them into digital formats?"

"Well, no. Our staff is rather small."

"I could spare a few hours a week to do that for you and then do some research at the same time."

The lady on the other end of the lined gasped. "That would be wonderful. What did you say your name was?"

"Matteson. Bailey Matteson."

"Emily Sue's daughter?"

Bailey stifled a groan. "Yes'm. Are you open on Saturdays?"

"I will be for you, honey. How about ten? I'll have to leave by eleven-thirty, though."

"Perfect, Ms.?"

"Mrs. Douglas, but you can call me Amelia."

Amelia Douglas? She knew that name, had seen it on something having to do with the Archer family. "Are you Arthur Archer's daughter?" Might as well throw something out there if she was planning to fish for information anyway.

"Oh, heavens no. Sister."

The goosebumps zipped up Bailey's arm again. Wait until Jessica and Shannon hear about this one.

Until Saturday came, Bailey spent her evenings, after gym or church, researching into the relatives she did know about. She found the marriage certificates of Edmond, Eugene, and of her grandparents. She also found the marriage and birth certificates of Edmond's sons and the birth certificate of Eugene's kid.

Plus, she found the website of the B&B in Nicaragua where Edmond retired with his wife. How she'd love to go there! Maybe she, Shannon, and Jessica could save up their pennies. Well, perhaps Shannon would prefer to go with her hubby for a few romantic days. They saw so little of each other.

Saturday morning, Bailey stood in front of the newspaper building with her laptop and portable scanner. At exactly ten, a gold Mercedes pulled up and out stepped an elegant older woman. She wore her white hair tied back with a gold clip and extended a hand adorned with a rather large diamond toward Bailey.

"Mrs. Douglas?"

"You must be Bailey. My, aren't you a pretty girl. You favor your mother, I think."

She opened the door and flicked on a few lights, chatting as she went. "I'll put on a kettle of hot water for our tea. Sign in as a visitor, listing your name, phone number, and address." She pointed to an open ledger. "You can start with filing cabinet number four on the left. Use this little desk here." She patted the wooden surface as she flitted by on a whiff of powdery lavender.

An hour later, Bailey had found bits and pieces about Arthur by scanning the scant articles from 1964 through 1968. Evidently, he had often made headlines while in school and well beyond graduation. Inquiring social minds needed to know about their local prince, she guessed. She also found one about Eugene's engagement.

"Are you finding what you need?" The woman peered over Bailey's shoulder to read her notes. "Oh, my. Is this about your grandparents' horrid accident?" A wry, wrinkled smirk crossed the lady's face. "Your mother won't discuss it, I gather."

Bailey blinked. Something about the expression on Mrs. Douglas' face made her arms prickle. Bailey set her pen down and pushed her spine into the back of the office chair. "Actually, Mrs. Douglas. I am wishing to learn more about Aunt Edwina. And her relationship with your brother, Arthur, that produced a son."

Mrs. Douglas scoffed. "Nonsense. Whoever told you that is mistaken."

"No, ma'am. I have proof. Pictures. Edwina was pregnant the summer of 1966, after her annulment to your brother. And she did give birth to a son the next February. Edwin *Arthur* Holston. I have a copy of the birth certificate if you'd like to see it." She rested her hand on top of her binder.

The newspaper proprietor stepped back. "I think you should leave now, Bailey."

Bailey glanced at the clock. 11:05.

"Now." Mrs. Douglas pointed to the door.

Bailey gathered her things and exited without a word.

She got in her car and slammed the door shut. Nasty old bat.

153

Contrition flooded her heart. *Sorry, Lord. I guess she had a right to react to the dropped bomb. After all, I did when Chase told me. I'll write her an apology letter and mail it. I doubt she has an email.*

She ran a few errands to cool down, then stopped to get a macchiato latte. A little after two in the afternoon, she walked to her apartment door. Eyebrows raised, she halted. A folded piece of paper lay crammed in the knocker. She unfolded it, thinking maybe Jessica or Shannon had left it. But they'd have texted her. Who then?

Her eyes scanned the handwritten note. She whispered it out loud. "Stop your research now. If you don't, more will happen."

More? What does that mean?

She stuffed it in her shoulder bag and unlocked her door.

As it swung open, Bailey dropped her purse and screamed.

Her living room was in shambles and Bower lay lifeless on her carpet.

Chapter 17

Bailey couldn't stop shaking.

Chase wrapped his arm around her shoulder. Shannon sat on the other side, rubbing Bailey's hand. Jessica crouched down near her, ready to lend support.

"You didn't touch anything except to get a towel to wrap around your cat?"

"No. I dashed him to the vet's office down the street. He's all I thought about." She grimaced. "I think I left my door unlocked."

"Girl, you left it open. When I peered in I almost had heart failure until I saw you coming up the stairs."

A crime scene team scurried through her small apartment, taking fingerprints and photos.

Chase gave Bailey a soft smile. "How long have you had him?"

She gave him a blank stare. Slowly the words registered. "Um, five years. He was a stray who hung around the complex when I moved in. Alone, scared and scrawny, the little guy stole my heart." She whimpered. "Why would someone want to hurt him?"

She buried her face in her hands as shoulder-shaking sobs finally erupted. Chase gathered her to his chest and she accepted his warm strength without hesitation. "The vet said there is a good chance he will make it, right? The blow knocked him out, but the head trauma may not be severe."

"Can they be charged with attempted murder?" Jessica's question blurted out with anger.

"No. But breaking and entering, vandalism, and cruelty to an animal come to mind. Whoever did this will get more than a hand slap, I don't care who they are or what their family crest says."

"I shouldn't have touched that note." Bailey stuttered. "S-sorry."

Jessica pulled some tissues from the box and handed them to her.

"It's okay, Bailey." Chase pulled back and held her face in his hands. "We have your fingerprints from your driver's license for elimination purposes, so if there are any others, we can decipher them."

She pulled the last tissue from the box and blew her nose.

"I'll get some more off her dressing table." Shannon lifted herself from the couch and wound her way down the hall.

Chase let go of Bailey. "Wait. Shannon, no. Don't touch anything."

She shuffled back in, her head down. "Sorry. Forgot."

"Why don't you two take Bailey over to your apartment? Let us finish up here."

Bailey glanced at the carpet where she'd found her pet and shivered again. A police evidence number marked the spot now.

Chase gently turned her face to him. "Who's your vet?"

"Dr. Anderson at the animal clinic two blocks away. Why?"

"We may need his statement."

Bailey nodded and let herself be led out the front door by her friends.

Numbness. It's all she felt. Bailey sat on Shannon's couch and gazed with pleading eyes at her friends. "Why?"

Shannon set a glass of water for her down on the beveled glass coffee table. "What did you do today?"

"I went to the neighborhood newspaper office and skimmed through their archives for articles on Arthur and Edwina." She groaned. "And the snooty, hoity-toity editor is his sister. I may have mentioned the baby…"

"You mean you rubbed it in her face."

"I know, I know. She got on my nerves. But how could

that have anything to do with this?"

"Dunno." Shannon raised one shoulder to her ear.

Bailey snapped her fingers. "Oh. I had to sign their guestbook, and list my phone number and address."

Jessica scooted to the cushion next to her. "How long ago did you leave?"

She glanced at her phone. 3:22 p.m. "A little before lunch. Then I ran a few errands."

"The woman moved fast." Shannon hiked herself onto one of the bar stools and spun it toward her friends in the living room.

"You don't think she did this?"

"No, Bailey, but she called someone, perhaps Arthur. I bet he then called the 'someone' who did this."

Jessica stood from the sofa. "You need to let Chase know. Want me to go get him?"

Shannon waved her hand to stop Jessica from leaving. "Girl, when you got back from the vet, why did you call him instead of 9-1-1?"

Bailey hugged one of the leopard-patterned throw pillows. "I don't know, Shan. I had his home number he'd written on the back of his card and his name popped into my head." She thunked her head on the back of the sofa. "I hope he didn't get the wrong impression."

A knock at the door made all three girls jump.

Shannon squinted through the peephole, gave them a reassuring smile, and opened it. "Come on in, Chase."

He entered, hands folded in front and head bent. "May

I speak to Bailey?"

"I'm right here."

He raised his gaze. "Hi. Um, the vet gave us his statement. Bower is showing signs of a concussion due to a blow to the head. Most likely a boot."

"The burglar stomped on him?" Shannon clenched her fists as her eyes narrowed. "Seriously?"

"Or kicked him in the head." Chase rubbed the worry lines across his forehead.

"Ooohhh." Bailey hugged the cushion closer. "Poor Bower."

Jessica gathered Bailey to her chest and rocked her. Nestled against her friend, she kept her eyes on Chase. Maybe for confirmation, it had really all happened.

He stood in the doorway, his weight shifting from foot to foot as if he didn't know what to do. After a minute, he coughed into his fist. "I guess I better leave."

Shannon grabbed his elbow. "No, don't. Bailey has something she needs to tell you. We think we know who orchestrated this thing."

His expression changed. He morphed back into a police investigator like Clark Kent changing into Superman—without the need of a phone booth. "Let me get my tape recorder app up and running." He punched the screen on his phone.

Bailey took a large gulp of water. "I'm ready."

"Sure?" He grabbed a chair from Shannon's dining room set and pulled it to the couch. Shannon and Jessica perched on either side of Bailey on the sofa like bookends, as if ready to hold her up if she started to topple.

"Yeah. It all started this morning…"

Chase listened and didn't respond except a few times to clarify what Arthur's sister had said.

Twenty minutes later, Bailey took a gulp of water. "You're very good at this. You let me talk and helped me put it all together."

He clicked off the app and pocketed his phone. As he pulled back his jacket, his badge, clipped to his belt, came into view. "It's my job."

"Well, you do it very well. And thanks for the update on Bower."

He gave her a soft nod. "Dr. Anderson said he's keeping him overnight for observation. He will call you in the morning with an update."

"Thanks."

"The evidence team is finished with your place. I've asked the crime scene cleaning squad to help put your things back in order."

Her lips began to quiver again as her mind returned to the toppled room. Would she ever feel safe walking in her door again?

Chase reached to touch her arm. "I am very sorry. We will try everything we can to find out who did this."

"And who paid them to do it." Shannon cocked an eyebrow. "Though it seems obvious."

"We can't jump to conclusions." Chase shot her a stern

expression and then sent it to Jessica and Bailey. He stood and towered over them. "Ladies, do not try to handle this on your own, and do not tell anyone of your suspicions, got it? Let us do our job."

"I'm not going to stop looking for my aunt and nephew." Bailey gazed at his blurred image through dampened eyelashes. "Or stop trying to discover who killed my grandparents."

"I'm afraid either of those may be the reason for this break in." Chase stared into Bailey's face. "Be careful. Please."

"Okay. I will. But I will continue my research."

"I figured as much, though I strongly advise against it." His jaw twitched. "In fact, I want—no, I insist you three share any information you find with me and how you discovered it."

The three women glanced at each other.

Chase crouched to their eye level as they sat on the couch. "There is one thing you need to know. Whoever did this wore gloves. They also stole your laptop. By now they probably know where you have been in cyberspace. They may try to monitor you."

Her heart flipped into her abdomen. "You're kidding?"

"'Fraid not. I suggest you only use library computers to continue your search. That goes for all of you." He pointed to each lady. "Your friendships are as thick as hairs on a rabbit and everyone around here knows it. So be aware

161

of who is around you at all times. Bolt your doors, even when you are home. Got it?"

Bailey eyed her friends and mouthed "sorry" to them.

Chase turned to leave.

Shannon rose off the couch and followed him to the door.

He dug out his wallet. "Here's my card. It has my cell phone number on the back. Just in case."

"Gotcha."

He pointed his finger back to the sofa. "One more thing, Bailey. I hinted at it before, but now I mean it. Do not jog alone."

"Right." The memory of how frightened she'd been before she realized her track companion had been a dog flooded back. "I won't."

"Good." His voice softened as his hand turned the doorknob. "You should call your mom. You know she'll find out."

Bailey tossed the cushion to her side. "She'll want me to come stay with them."

"May not be a bad idea." He grinned and opened the door to leave. "Bye."

As soon as he closed the door, Shannon flipped the bolt.

They heard his voice bellow from the other side as he tapped the door. "Good girl. Keep it bolted. All of you."

Shannon clicked her heels and saluted.

For the first time that day, Bailey laughed.

Chapter 18

Shannon drove Bailey to her parent's house.

In a rare show of motherly affection, her mom squeezed Bailey's hand as her friends relayed what had happened. After hearing them out, her father spoke up. "I think under the circumstances your apartment manager should release you from your lease."

"Dad, I like my place." She turned to him and flashed him a brave smile. "And Shannon lives right down the way. I'll be fine."

Her mother nodded. "Of course, you will. The crime scene cleaners should be finished by now, but your carpet has to dry for at least twenty-four hours, I'm sure. Then we can go in and redecorate. We'll head for the home décor store first thing on Monday. You are taking a day or more off from work, I assume."

"Yes. I already called my boss." Bailey nodded. "But

Mom, it really isn't necessary."

"Of course, it is, dear. A fresh look will do wonders. Erase all those horrid memories of the crime scene."

Bailey surrendered. Her mother did make sense. And it was her way of helping out. "You do have a point, Mom. Thank you. It'll be fun. I haven't redecorated since I moved there after college."

"With most of the stuff from your dorm room." Her mother smirked. "You need a more grown-up environment anyway. Soft grays perhaps. And rose tones."

Bailey cocked her head. "Maybe something like purple, yellow and gray."

Her mom opened her mouth to speak but stopped. "Whatever makes you happy, dear." She rose. "I'll go make us some tea."

Shannon leaned in and whispered in Bailey's ear. "Go totally Goth. Black, blood red…"

Bailey swatted at her and chuckled.

Her mother attended to Bailey's every whim the rest of the evening, and Bailey suspected she wanted to tuck her into the guest room bed and read her a story. Luckily, her mother refrained, told her goodnight at the top of the stairs, and retired to her own room.

For some reason, Bailey's mom also refrained from mentioning the sudden camaraderie between her and Chase Montgomery after he had dropped by that Sunday afternoon to ask Bailey more questions. For that, Bailey almost hugged her. Still, she wondered why her mother acted so, well, un-Mrs.-Matteson-like.

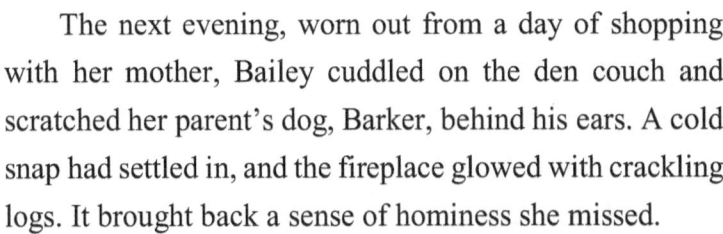

The next evening, worn out from a day of shopping with her mother, Bailey cuddled on the den couch and scratched her parent's dog, Barker, behind his ears. A cold snap had settled in, and the fireplace glowed with crackling logs. It brought back a sense of hominess she missed.

Her father snapped his paper. "I don't understand your insistence on pursuing this genealogy thing. Especially your mother's side of the family."

"But I know more about your relatives. We have gone to your family reunions at least six times during my life. I adore Aunt Susan."

He peered over his glasses. "And she adores you."

"Mom and her siblings are not even communicating, and yet all of us kids want to meet each other. That speaks volumes to me."

"Fine, but leave this Edwina and her son out of it. You're only kicking a fire ant mound."

Bailey stared into the flames. Her dad made sense, too. When did her parents become so wise?

Even so, her curiosity wouldn't be quenched. She couldn't shake the inkling that Edwina and her son had been wronged somehow, and it was up to her, Bailey, to help right it. Don Quixote had his windmills to battle. She had a family tree with broken limbs to re-graft.

Besides, her anger over her home being vandalized and someone hurting her pet had piqued more than her curiosity. The incident didn't frighten her, as she suspected whoever was behind it thought it would. It made her want to fight even harder. Someone had become fearful of what she'd find out. That meant they had secrets to hide. Secrets that had hurt her, and her family. If only she possessed a superhero power belt...

"Dad, I'm going to the mall. I need to buy a new laptop."

He reached in his back pocket for his wallet.

"Oh, don't bother, Dad. The insurance company said to send them the receipts and they'd reimburse me."

"Only if you buy a similar one in price and features, remember that."

"Right. I will."

Surely if she had a new laptop and set up new passwords, whoever had her old one couldn't locate her. Unless they hacked into her cloud. Not possible, right? Anyway, it only held data. Convinced Chase had been overprotective with his comment about only using library computers, she headed out. No way was she holing up in a musty cubicle unless absolutely necessary.

A co-worker's spouse worked in the electronic section of a megastore, and she trusted him to steer her right. Within a half hour, she walked out with her new computer, the kind that could also detach from the keyboard and become a tablet. An upgrade, for sure, but on sale for half price. A silver lining.

He'd showed her how to set up her new email, retrieve her old messages, and access her cloud. It took her about an hour and a half to set it all up. Once done, she noticed that Chase had sent her the scanned file of the annulment papers from 1966. She opened the document and scrolled to the last page. Sure enough. Two signatures and that of the notary. Edwina had agreed to end her marriage with Arthur.

How sad. Bailey sat back on the guest bed, her heart bleeding for a relative she didn't even know she had a month ago. As she stared at the signatures, her resolve strengthened. She wanted to meet her aunt, hear her side of the story, and then convince her to come to the reunion in May.

Who had Edwina known in El Paso? Perhaps she lived there before and had returned. She had to have made a living for her and her young son. She did a past address search. But the site she'd paid $49.99 to join only went back to 1980.

Bailey puffed through her cheeks. "I should've known."

She pulled up the census for 1960, hoping it would list her mother's relatives and their addresses at the time, thinking one of them may have lived there. But she learned, because of the 72 Rule passed in 1978, very little info gathered by the Census Bureau can be made public until seventy-two years from the date of the survey. Great, she'd have to wait until 2032.

Next, she tried driver license records through a website search. But it led her on a merry-go-round, and then wanted her credit card info to continue. No thanks.

Her efforts proved fruitless. Long shot anyway. Perhaps Edwina simply hopped a bus with her child and stopped when she ran out of money. She settled in El Paso and camped out at homeless shelters or YMCA's until she got a job.

She phoned Shannon to bounce her thoughts off her.

"I hate to say it, girl. But El Paso is on a major highway that goes all across the U.S. She could have gotten more money and headed out again."

"She could be anywhere by now."

Shannon's voice quieted. "Bailey, she may not be alive. If her life spiraled downhill…"

"We don't know that. She may have gotten her high school equivalency diploma, gone to college, met a nice guy and gotten married. Maybe have a career. She could be an executive to a major corporation for all we know."

"Uh, huh."

Bailey pouted. "Well, it could happen."

"Look, tell you what. I'll research her son, now that we know his name and birthdate, and you keep seeking info on her."

"Really, Shannon? You don't mind doing it?"

"Not at all. The hubs isn't back until next Tuesday. Better than most anything on TV."

Bailey chuckled. "I have the best friends ever."

Something told her to review the printouts she had. She sat at her dinette munching on some carrot sticks and hummus, pretending they were potato chips and onion dip. That's what she really craved.

She didn't see anything new so she laid them out side by side. Edwina's annulment papers, the goodbye letter, the photos, and her son's birth certificate. She'd searched online for the marriage certificate, but had not found the actual document, only the entry on the chapel ledger.

"What am I supposed to be seeing?" She grasped her chin in her hands and peered at each piece of evidence, just as they do in the crime shows. She rubbed her eyes and stared again. "Wait a minute!"

She sucked in a breath of air and dialed Shannon. She answered on the second ring. "Hey, girlfriend. What's up, now?"

"Shannon, you won't believe this."

"Try me."

"Edwina's signature on the annulment papers doesn't match the signature on her letter. Not even close."

"Are you saying…?"

"Yep. Edwina may not have consented to ending her marriage with Arthur Archer. Someone else signed those papers for her. But who?"

"Worse than that, girl. It may mean she is still married."

Chapter 19

Bailey hated to do it, but she called her father's attorney. She asked for an hour consultation and gawked that it would cost her $350 dollars.

"Um, thanks. I'll get back to you."

She surfed instead and found that teens sixteen or older can marry, but if one or both of the people are under eighteen, and do not have parental consent, the marriage can be annulled by one of the parents. Obviously, Edwina and Arthur's marriage didn't have parental blessings. Since Arthur had been seventeen or eighteen at the time, an attorney, representing Angus Archer, could file it without his or Edwina's permission since they were underage.

So why forge her signature? Beyond that, who forged it?

Since Arthur's parents had whisked him off to Europe, they no doubt left the attorney to clear up the matter. But surely an attorney wouldn't have broken the law like that when it wasn't necessary at all. It made no sense.

She researched the attorney only to find out he had passed away from a heart attack ten years ago. Perhaps this piece of the puzzle would never be found. Not that it mattered anyway.

Then she read something else. Children produced by the annulled marriage are still legitimate and considered heirs. Wow. That meant Edwin Arthur had to be Arthur Archer's first-born male heir... as far as she knew. It also meant he'd owe Edwina child support. Did he ever give it to her? Doubtful.

This can of worms kept producing more and more issues, each wiggling to the surface to slither out. Bailey felt a headache tapping at her temples. There remained only one course of action. Find either Edwina or Edwin. Get their side of the story.

Shannon texted her. *Found him. Call me for his last known address.*

Talk about timing. She winked at the ceiling and mouthed a thank you before snatching her phone. When Shannon answered, she blurted out without even saying hi. "Really? You found him? How?"

"Whoa. Slow down. I found his social media page. It said, 'born in Beaumont, graduate of...' get this... 'El Paso High School.'"

"Seriously?"

"And, he still lives in El Paso."

Shannon, are you sure it's him?"

"I mean how many fifty-year-old Edwin Holstons could there be who were born in Beaumont?"

Bailey's heart pumped a bit faster. "You have his address?"

"Easy. Phonebook white pages online revealed it. It's 1907 Calle Verde. Road trip?"

"Yes. This weekend. But won't your hubs be back in town?"

"No, Jayden leaves Friday evening. Has a long haul to San Diego, up to Seattle, and then back to Texas. He'll be gone at least a week."

"Sorry, he won't be here very long before he has to head out again."

"I know." Her tone drooped. It meant he'd miss their anniversary. "Hey, but that's not all. I scanned Edwin's social media friends. Your Aunt Edwina is one of them."

"Shannon! Oh, my gosh. Why didn't I think of that? I'm looking her up right now." Tears fuzzed her screen. She wiped her eyes. "I gotta go. Thanks, Shan."

"You're welcome. I'll call Jess to see if she wants to come to El Paso, too."

"Sounds good. Bye."

Bailey sat cross-legged on the bed and stared at the screen displaying the social media page of her newly-found cousin. He definitely bore a resemblance to her mother's side of the family, except that he had lighter hair like Edwina. She recalled something from biology genetics that the boy babies often resembled their mothers while little girls looked like daddy.

His photo folder revealed two digital pictures of his wife and several of their two children. A boy and a girl, appearing to be in their twenties, smiled back at Bailey over the web. One had on a university graduation cap and gown.

She pressed her finger to the laptop's glass and clicked on the name Edwina under the friends tab. Her page appeared, with a banner photo of a mountain. A thistle for an avatar. Rats. No photos of her.

Her mouse scrolled through the scanty posts, mostly containing a few cute memes she'd shared, and quotes. No family pictures. Not of Edwin or his kids. Odd.

She flipped back to Edwin's page and typed in a friend request with a private message. *I think our mothers are sisters. Mine is Emily Sue Holston Matteson. I'm doing a genealogy and would like to meet you and your family. I live in San Antonio but could drive to El Paso.*

Her hand slid the mouse to the send button. She hovered over it, closed her eyes, and pressed her finger. Click.

Now she'd see.

When Bailey got back to the guest room from dinner, her phone blinked that she had a message. Already? Her thumb shook a bit as she swiped the app open.

I'll meet if you like. But I don't care to know about my past. Mother and I are not on the greatest terms. Haven't been for years. I'll explain when I see you. Ed.

Bailey typed back a thank you and that she'd see him

Saturday evening. She clasped her hands to her mouth to stifle a happy squeal. El Paso here she came.

But for now, she would lay low and put it out of her head, if she could. Otherwise, the eggshells she'd have to walk upon here at her parents' home might crack into tiny, un-glueable pieces.

She and Bower, who'd bounced back to his old self, would return to her own place by Thursday, away from the motherly octopus tentacles that had been enclosing her so tightly after the break-in. Bailey decided to wait until then to continue her journey into the family genealogy.

No way was she telling her mom where she planned to travel this upcoming weekend. She would drive all night to make it back in time for Sunday dinner if necessary.

As Bailey arranged her new things Thursday evening, Jessica brought her some soup and salad. "I came to help out. I want to see everything you and your mom bought."

"Great you can help me make my bed."

She and Jessica smoothed her new lavender quilted bedspread over her bed. "How are you doing? Is it good to be back here?"

"I guess. Everything has been such a swirl. Did I tell you Shannon found Edwin in El Paso?"

"Seriously?" Jessica plopped deep purple and sky-blue throw pillows at the head of the bed.

"I've already communicated with him and he has invited me to come visit. Shannon insists on going with me."

"Well, she is taking what Chase said seriously, I guess."

Bailey detected flatness in her response. Of course. She hadn't even asked Jessica to join them. "Wanna go with us to meet him?"

"Sure." Jessica did a swivel of her hips and arms. "Road trip."

Bailey laughed as she added a round, purple and blue flowered accent pillow in the center nanoseconds before Bower hopped up, made three turns, and settled into it

"Guess we have his royal highness' approval." Jessica reached to stroke his ears. "I'm so glad he is okay. Has Chase made any progress on finding out who broke in?"

"He hasn't said one way or the other."

Jessica let out a long sigh.

Bailey put her hands to her hips and gazed around her bedroom. "I have to admit it. Mom was right. It does make a difference. She's been really great." A guilty twang thumped her heart like a sour note on a guitar. "Now I feel kinda bad about wanting to get out of that guest room so fast."

"You're an adult. You need your privacy." Jessica plopped on the bed. "Bet this set her back a few bucks, though."

Bailey leaned against the door. "Yeah. And she never

blinked an eye. Of course, the sofa *was* half-price on clearance. And I bought all of this stuff out of the insurance settlement." She waved her hand over the bedding.

"Keep justifying." Jessica hoisted herself on her elbows.

"I am doing that, aren't I?" Had she been justifying about her upcoming excursion as well or her motives for finding Edwin and his mother? She pushed that thought aside.

"Confession is good for the soul, as Mrs. Perkins says."

Bailey blinked. Did her friend read her mind?

"Well, I better get going. I have one more article to edit before tomorrow." Jessica stretched her arms behind her head. "What time Saturday?"

"Eight. It's a nine-hour drive, so with rest stops, I figure we'll get there about six-thirty or seven in the evening."

"He better offer us food, then. And I'm not sleeping on a cot in a motel room. Just saying…" Jessica winked and waved goodbye. "See you."

"Bye. And thanks for helping." Bailey chuckled as she waved.

Her friends blessed her and filled her life. And despite getting on each other nerves occasionally, she and her mom had a decent relationship. She sat and rubbed her hand down Bower's back, pondering what could have happened to make Edwin and his mother stop talking to each other?

It seemed Aunt Edwina had alienated everyone in her life. How sad.

Bailey wondered why.

Saturday morning, the sun blared in a clear, azure winter sky. The girls loaded up and headed out They took turns listening to each other's iPod faves and giggled when all three shared several selections on their lists. They pulled into Edwin's driveway at 6:22.

Bailey turned off the car and stared at the modern Spanish-styled, two-story house. Cacti, aloe vera, and maiden grass dotted the gravel-covered yard. Water-saving zero-scape made sense in this climate, but its prickly appearance didn't scream "welcome" to her.

"Bailey, are you all right?" Shannon touched her arm.

She pocketed her keys. "Yeah. Kinda nervous."

Jessica reached from the back seat and rubbed her shoulder. "Of course, you are. That's why we came with you. Moral support."

She half-turned and patted her friend's hand. "Thanks. Let's do this."

"Wait, girlfriend." Shannon arched an eyebrow. "First, we pray."

They did.

As they exited the car, the front door swung open and a balding, middle-aged man emerged. Slender and tall, his stride met theirs in only a few steps.

"Am I parked okay in your driveway? I saw no one else parking at curbs so I thought perhaps your homeowner's association frowned on it, but I can move my car..." Bailey realized she talked like a rapid-fire semi-automatic rifle.

"You're fine." His baritone voice carried no emotion.

She clamped her lips, swallowed, and extended her hand. "Hi, I'm Bailey. These are my friends, Jessica and Shannon."

His face held the tiniest smile. "Edwin Holston. Nice to meet ya, cuz." He shook hers and her friends' hands and then motioned them to head inside. "Maria is at evening mass. She'll be here in a little bit. So will my kids, Angelina and Joaquin. Angelina is a freshman at the University of Texas here in El Paso, and Joaquin graduated from trade school last year. He works in IT for a staffing and outsourcing company. Both still live with us."

He led them toward the house. As they entered the foyer, he motioned them in. "I figured y'all might be hungry so I ordered pizza. One large pepperoni, one supreme, and one vegetables-only. And two types of wings. Honey mustard and barbeque. Is that all right?"

The three women glanced back and forth to each other then nodded in unison. "Yes. Sure. Thanks."

Bailey leaned toward her friends. "I'll just eat salad the rest of the week."

They both nodded.

Edwin showed them into a sunken, Spanish-tiled living room with an adobe fireplace hugging one corner. Leather couches angled near it, and a woven rug added warmth. "Have a seat and I'll get you something to drink. Iced tea? Water? Soda? We have cola, root beer, and diet ginger ale."

They gave him their preferences. After he left the room, Jessica and Shannon sat down, but Bailey strolled, eyeing the snapshots of his family's milestones on the mantle. She picked up one of him, his wife and their kids, all with wide grins.

"You will meet them in a bit."

Edwin's voice behind her made her jolt. She set the photo frame down. "I'm sorry. I didn't mean to snoop."

"Sure, you did. That's why you've driven nine plus hours." He set down a tray of tumblers, and the ice cubes clinked against them. "So, tell me why."

Her throat closed. However, when she gazed into his face, his expression held no malice. Bailey chose one of the iced waters and sat down. She took three gulps and held the glass in her lap. "It's the genealogy thing. Well, and the fact I know so little about my mother's side of the family. I've never met anyone except Uncle Elliot, and that's only been a few times."

Edwin lowered himself into a chair that flanked the fireplace. He shot a glance at Jessica and Shannon. "I gather I can speak frankly in front of your friends."

"Of course. They are my closest pals and have been

helping me with my research."

He pressed his lips together and turned his face to the picture window overlooking the street. After a long moment, he spoke again. "I haven't met any of them. Mother wouldn't talk about them at all. I didn't even know their names until a week ago. That doesn't mean I want to know them."

"Excuse me?"

Her cousin stood. "Before my wife and kids come home, I think I better show you this." He went to the bookcase, pulled back some books and produced an envelope. Walking toward Bailey, his expression soured. "I don't know what you are digging up, but I'm telling you right now. I do not, I repeat not, want anything to do with it."

He jutted the envelope toward her face. Bailey took it, opened it, and unfolded a picture of everyone at Emily Holston's birthday party. The names had been written in red ink over each person in the background behind her and Edwina. Edwina's tummy had been circled with YOU scrawled next to it.

"Where did you get this?"

"Someone laid it on my windshield. I found it yesterday morning as I left for work." He pointed at it. "Turn it over."

In large, red letters Bailey read, "Do not try to find your father or your family will suffer."

A shaky hand went to her mouth as she passed the

message to her friends.

Edwin peered down at her. "So, tell me, Bailey Matteson. What the heck is going on?"

Chapter 20

Bailey spent the next few minutes explaining about his mother and Arthur Archer, the forged signature, and the threatening note she'd received. And about Bower. Tears threatened as her mind once again flashed the image of her beloved pet lying still on the carpet. Thank the Lord he had survived.

She handed him back the message. Her mouth opened to say something, then closed again.

Edwin took it, folded it and placed it back behind the books. Then he stoked the fire.

"And yet you keep pursuing this? Why?"

"Justice." She firmed her chin. "For you and your mother. Edwin, you are an heir to a very wealthy and powerful family. By law, they owe you…"

"No!" He turned back toward her and moved his hands in fast swipes. "I want nothing to do with that man. Mother would not have married him if he hadn't conned her into

183

doing it."

"Wait, she didn't love him?" Shannon sat forward. "We all assumed…"

A scoff clucked on Edwin's tongue. "My mother wrote her whole sob story to me in a seven-page letter. I got to read it when I turned eighteen. I'd show it to you but my wife burned it after we got married. She said I needed to let go of the past and forgive my mother if we were to have a future. Said Jesus tells us to do it. So, for the past two and a half decades that is what I have been trying to do." He stood, legs spread in an at-ease stance, his arms folded. "I recall enough to tell you what she said, though."

"Do you mind doing that?" Bailey felt uncomfortable even asking him to bring it all up again.

"It's why you came, right?" He gazed out the window. "According to my mother, Arthur Archer slipped drugs into her purse when a cop pulled them over on the way to a party. She didn't want anything more to do with him, but he said if she eloped, he'd make sure she got off easy. So she did."

"Why?"

"He wanted to escape his daddy's claws. Live his own life as a free child of the Age of Aquarius, I guess." Edwin scoffed. "He figured if he married, his father would back off, according to my mother's side of the story. He'd basically flunked out of high school anyway. A party animal. His dad's money kept him out of jail."

Bailey's eyes spread so wide they ached. "I, um, I had

184

no idea—"

"Yeah? Well, now you do." He took a chair across from her. "Mother said she thought she loved him for some reason so she agreed. Young, stupid kids, right?"

Bailey glanced at her friends who both had blank expressions.

Without facing Bailey, he continued his story. "Mom never really wanted me. Well, I think at first, she may have. But being eighteen and saddled with a baby that needs your attention twenty-four seven? It proved too much for her. At eighteen myself when I read all of it, I began to understand why. I mean if my girlfriend back then…"

He set the poker down and rested his elbow on the mantle. "Once I had kids of my own, I really got it. They demand all of your time and energy. And I had a wife to help." He turned to her and shrugged.

Bailey smiled.

His face relaxed a little. "My wife took it upon herself to locate Mother after Angelina was born. I'd thought of contacting her and making amends, but we've been at odds way too long. Anyway, we paid for her to take the bus here from Amarillo. It didn't go well. She really didn't want anything to do with my children. She left the next day." He blinked. "Guess the maternal gene passed her by."

"So why didn't she let you be adopted?" Shannon blurted the question out then dashed her gaze to her hands. "Sorry. None of my business."

Edwin rubbed his eyebrow. "I have no idea. A

momentary pang? I recall the whirlwind of emotions that blew through my heart when I held my newborn son for the first time. Whatever possessed her didn't last, though. She gave me up when I was four. So frankly, I only had a vague memory of her. When I saw her again, she could have been a stranger."

"I'm so sorry." Bailey set her glass on the coffee table. She glanced over to see Jessica's eyes downcast. Being adopted so young, Bailey doubted Jessica ever knew her birth mother.

"It's not your fault. Not every child gets to have a loving home. Eventually, I did thanks to my foster parents. So, God shone His light on me, I guess." His tone held an old anger, though.

"Did she say where y'all lived?"

"Amarillo. That's as far as she got after emptying her aunt's pocketbook." He shrugged. "Yeah, she wrote me about that, too. And then went on about how there aren't too many ways for a single woman who never finished high school to make a decent living. She worked at night, it seems. It meant she mostly slept while I played in a playpen during the day. That is until I became big enough to scale it, I guess. That's one of my first memories. Climbing over and eating a whole box of sugary cereal then throwing up a lot."

Bailey gulped. She wanted to say she felt sorry, but that seemed silly. She hadn't even been born yet.

Edwin looked at his fingernails. "After that, Mother

said she borrowed a car and took me to San Antonio, but we didn't stay long. Perhaps a couple of months. After her parents died, her siblings shunned her. She didn't say why."

Bailey thought she knew, but she couldn't decide whether to say anything or not. It might only fuel his anger toward his mother if she told him.

He paced the floor in silence. Finally, he spoke again.

"When we got back to Amarillo, Mom found a day job. The landlady of the rent-weekly motel where we lived babysat me for a few years. Mrs. Carson. All I remember is she used to rock and hum to me." His mouth curved into a sad smile.

Bailey tilted her head and waited to see if he'd reveal more.

Shannon remained quiet, for once.

After a moment, Edwin sucked in a breath and began to speak again. "Then, one day when I was four, I think, Mother packed me up and we headed to Beaumont for some family thing. That's the first bus ride I remember. But she left the shindig crying. I'd never seen her cry before so I wailed along with her. She let me have peppermint ice cream to shut me up, I guess." He rubbed an eyebrow. "Funny what we recall, right?"

"Your Uncle Elliott's graduation in 1971. I have a picture of you and your mother there." Bailey showed him the copy of the newsprint. "Did you return to Amarillo?"

"No. We came here. Mrs. Carson's daughter had

landed a job in El Paso at a finer restaurant and persuaded them to take Mother on, according to the letter. But Mother got really depressed, slept a lot, and lost the job. She'd leave PB and Js on a plate for me to chew on all day while she lay in bed and stared at the wall. CPS found out and took me away from her."

A cold, hard stone dropped into Bailey's gut. She really didn't know what to say.

He shrugged. "Guess she never tried to get me back. Several years later, my foster parents learned she'd signed away her parental rights and moved back to Amarillo to be a motel maid for Mrs. Carson again. That's when they agreed to keep raising me until I graduated from high school."

"I had no idea about any of this."

He flicked a piece of lint off his sleeve as if to keep the memories from clinging to him. "Now you do."

"Edwin, did she ever tell you she blamed herself for her parents' death?"

He sat down across from her. His response barely audible. "No."

"It's not my business." Jessica piped up. "I'm adopted, you see, so I have another perspective. It seems she went through a really rough patch. Maybe she didn't try to get you back because she knew her life was in shambles. It might have been her way of loving you. That's what my adoptive parents told me about my mom."

The rims of his eyes reddened. "I never considered that

angle."

Bailey waited and let the idea sink into his heart. He perched in the chair, his hands clasped and his head tilted to the rug. She scooted forward in her seat. "I see you are friends online now."

"Maria, my wife, found her. I wouldn't say we are friends, though. But I know that's what they call it on the site." He swiped at his eyes. "Not family either."

Bailey rose, crouched down in front of him, and took his hand. "Well, I'm your family and I am glad to meet you. But I hope you understand my desire to meet her as well. Do you know how I can reach Edwina?"

"She doesn't do maid work now, of course. She's seventy. But she runs the fleabag motel in Amarillo where we lived. Mrs. Carlson left it to her in her will. I can't recall the name but Maria might." He rose and walked to the window. "A lot of truck drivers stop off in Amarillo since it's on a major east to west route. It's been lucrative enough for her, I imagine because she's never asked me for money. Even paid me back for the bus fare here that one time. Not that I'd give her any."

The finality of his tone chilled the room like a Blue Norther barreling down from Canada over the Texas plains.

Shannon raised her hand to her mouth and stared at Jessica.

Bailey closed her eyes to keep from weeping. It would only embarrass both her and Edwin.

189

The whir of the garage door sounded. Then car doors slammed.

Edwin sighed. "They're here. I don't want to discuss this further. Understand?"

Bailey bobbed her head. "But, there is one more thing."

His eyes dashed toward the kitchen and then back to her. "Yes?"

She swallowed again and decided to plunge ahead. "Mom and I are hosting a family reunion next May. The 50th anniversary of her parents' death. I already have positive interest from Edmond, both of his children, and Eugene's son, and I hope more will agree. We'd love for you and your family to join us."

She dug in her shoulder bag and pulled out the flier.

He took it from her and scanned it. "The note said…"

"But surely they don't mean you can't have any contact with our side of the family. It simply warned you to stay away from the other side."

"Yoo-hoo. Ed?" Heel clicks sounded across the terrazzo tiles. A slightly plump Hispanic woman with a kind face entered.

Edwin handed the flier back to Bailey and went to hug his wife. "Maria, this is Bailey, my cousin. And on the couch are her two friends, Shannon and Jessica."

Maria's smile twinkled as she extended her hand. "*Mucho gusto.*"

Bailey, Shannon, and Jessica rose to greet her.

"I see my husband has seen to your thirst." She gave him a love pat across his stomach.

Bailey liked this sweet woman already. Her cousin had married well. "Yes, ma'am, I mean Maria. Thank you."

"Hey, Mom. Pizza's here. The delivery guy pulled up in the driveway before we closed the garage door."

Two college-aged kids with fawn eyes and dark wavy hair carried three large, flat boxes and two smaller Styrofoam ones. Joaquin addressed his father. "Dad, I signed for it."

"Okay. Put them on the table. Ladies?"

Bailey, Jessica, and Shannon helped Angelina open the boxes of pizza and wings as Maria set out plates and napkins. They spent an enjoyable hour or so chatting. Angelina relayed some antics they pulled in her dorm and Bailey told them about her childhood and her job now as a junior accountant for one of the largest fast food chains in Texas. "We are responsible for all eighteen restaurants in and around San Antonio and Austin."

"Wow. There is one here right on the edge of the campus." Angelina rubbed her hands on a paper napkin. "Next time I eat there, can I ask for a discount?"

"Sure, but I doubt it'll do any good." Bailey winked. They shared a hearty laugh.

Maria wiped her mouth and laid her napkin on the

table, a universal sign that the meal had concluded. Joaquin pulled out his mother's chair, while Edwin came around and pulled out Angelina's, Bailey's and her friends'. The grandfather clock in the hall chimed eight.

"Anyone for coffee? I can bring it in the living room."

Bailey shot a glance at her friends who both shook their heads. "No thanks, Maria. We're good. Look, it's been a very long day. Perhaps we should head out."

Edwin nodded. "I'm glad I met you."

She thought their visit had ended, but then her cousin spoke. "Bailey, show Maria that invitation."

Startled by his request, she pulled it out again. She gave it to Maria. "We hope—," she shifted her gaze to Edwin who gave her a small nod, "—that all of y'all will be able to attend. I know it's a long drive, but Mom and Dad have guest rooms and my complex has guest apartments for their residents' out-of-town guests to use. They are only fifty dollars a night and have a pull-out sofa along with a king-sized bed."

Maria grinned. "Oh, Ed. Do you think we could? I haven't been to the San Antonio area since—"

"—Our honeymoon." He pecked her rosy cheek. "I know. We'll talk about it."

Bailey's torso relaxed as she exhaled. Perhaps the trip had turned out well after all. "There is plenty of time. You let me know whenever you decide." She pointed to the bottom. "There is my email and telephone number."

Edwin extended his hand. "Thank you, Bailey. And

thanks for driving all the way out here to meet my family and me."

Bailey took it and felt his firm grip. "You're welcome. Thank you for inviting us into your home."

Shannon patted her belly. "And feeding us."

Jessica chimed in. "Yes, thanks so much."

As she held onto his hand Bailey gazed into his face. "You have a wonderful family. May God's peace and protection always dwell here."

His eyes registered her cryptic meaning. "Thank you."

Maria gave her a warm hug then waved as they drove away.

Jessica scooted forward and rested her elbows on the backs of the bucket seats. "So, who sent that threat?"

Bailey shrugged. "The same person who trashed my place and hurt Bower is my guess. That handwriting looked mighty familiar."

Jessica let out a harrumph. "But how did they get that photo?"

"Easy, Jess. They had Bailey's laptop." She slapped her head. "Oh, we should have taken that photo they sent Edwin. It may have prints."

"Doubt it." Bailey turned right to get on the highway. "The police didn't find any besides mine and y'all's in my apartment. And the maintenance man's from checking the air filters." She flicked on her blinker and accelerated to merge into the fast-moving traffic. "They wouldn't leave any on a photocopy of a picture. One thing for sure. We are

193

not dealing with an amateur."

"But why send it to Edwin? How did they even know his address or that we were coming?" Jessica's voice sounded in Bailey's right ear.

Bailey stared at Shannon next to her, and then at Jessica in the rearview mirror. She felt her cheeks and scalp chill. She exited the highway, pulled into a gas station, and turned off the engine. Her hands began to quiver on the steering wheel.

"What's wrong, Bailey?" Shannon reached across the console.

"Someone has either bugged my apartment or hacked into my text messages." She whimpered as she turned to face her friends. "How else would they have known?"

Chapter 21

Her phone beeped, and Bailey jumped. She pulled up the message. *Here is her last known address. 2816 Western Ave. Amarillo, TX. Good luck. Ed.*

"What is it?" Shannon craned her neck as she drove, giving Bailey a break until her nerves returned to normal.

Bailey angled her phone so Shannon could view the screen and the road at the same time. "Ed texted me his mother's address."

"Surely you aren't planning to go see her?" Jessica's voice raised a pitch higher.

"Maybe." Bailey lifted her chin to view her in the rearview mirror. "If I talk myself into it."

"You can't. She and Edwin are estranged. You have built a bridge with him and his family, don't burn it."

Bailey spun around. "I know, but he volunteered it, so that's like giving me permission, right? Besides, I still want to hear her side of the story."

"According to Edwin, she wrote him her side of the story. She never wanted him and practically abandoned him." Shannon scoffed.

"Because she had to work nights to make the rent? And then went through a depression over losing her parents? I mean, who knows what any of us would have done in the same situation. And I don't believe all the stuff about Archer. I think she truly loved him, or why would she come back when she neared twenty-one?"

Shannon eyed her. "M-o-n-e-y. And lots of it. Edwin was his heir. She wanted a portion of the Archer financial pie."

"Maybe. Edwina is the only one who can tell us."

Shannon groaned. "You cannot be serious about going to see her, girl."

"You don't have to come." She turned to Jessica in the back seat. "Neither do you, Jessica."

"Then who will go with you? That's a long way from San Antonio, Bailey." Jessica's brow furrowed.

"I don't know. Maybe my mother?"

Shannon broke out laughing. "Are you for real?"

Bailey felt her breath steam. Her friends were right. She had no business trying to meet an aunt who had broken off all ties, not only with her siblings but with her own son. So why did Bailey feel this tug on her heart? Selfishness on her part or something else? She sent up a quick prayer for wisdom then sunk down into the seat. "Let me know when we need to stop for gas. I'll take over the wheel again."

"You've done most of the driving. You need to get a good night's sleep. Jess and I will take turns."

Bailey burrowed her backbone into the bucket seat. "Thanks, Shannon. You two are great to come along on this trip. I'm sorry if all I've thought about is myself."

"Not a big deal. You'd do it for either of us." Shannon's voice carried on the swish of a car they passed. "Look. When the hubs gets in I'll ask him if he knows anything about this motel or its proprietor. Long-haulers talk. It's a pretty tight-knit community."

"Really? Thanks." Bailey sat up and reached for her phone. "At least we can look it up and find out the name." She tapped her thumbs. "Here. Shady Acres Motel."

Jessica jeered. "Appropriate name, don't you think? I mean her life seems to have been that way."

Bailey shot her a narrow-eyed glare.

"Sorry." Jessica shrugged and sat back. "Who knows what my real mom went through? We don't get to pick our parents."

"Yes, but your mom and dad picked you when they adopted you." Bailey clicked the keys on her qwerty board.

"What are you doing?" Shannon eyed her and then the road.

"Emailing her. It's on the website."

"No, don't." Shannon took one hand off the steering wheel and stretched for the phone, but Bailey twisted away.

"Already done."

"Heavens, Bailey. You're either really stupid or really brave."

Bailey huffed through her cheeks. "I think a bit of both."

As they traveled down the highway, Bailey stared out the side window and pondered their visit with Edwin. She could still feel his residual anger over the mother who gave him up. She didn't know how to explain this urge inside of her to locate Edwina. It felt as if a magnet somehow pulled them together, closer and closer, and she felt powerless to break free.

For a long while, Shannon didn't respond. Then she tapped the steering wheel. "Well, then we need to pray about it. If it is from God, He'll confirm it. If it is from the devil, we need to dispel that from your heart right now." She pulled onto the shoulder and put the car into park.

Jessica scooted forward and the three of them bowed their heads.

"Absolutely not." Her mother slammed the kitchen drawer closed.

"But Edwina responded to my email. I want to meet her."

"Bailey Jean, I cannot believe you would even fathom such an idea. And had I known you'd flitted off to El Paso..." she twirled the mixing spoon in the air.

Bailey wanted to kick herself. She shouldn't have brought it up during a holiday when the family was happily together. She bit her tongue and chopped the celery for the stuffing. Her mother always made it a day early and then crammed it inside the turkey so at four in the morning Thanksgiving Day, when she put the bird in the oven while half-asleep, it would go quicker. Her reasoning? "That way I can go back to bed instead of fussing in the kitchen like three-quarters of the women in the US." Some years, Bailey's dad, Chester Matteson, let her sleep and slid the bird in for her. Now that showed selfless love. She needed to display more of it in her life. Blessed are the peacemakers and the pure in heart. She recalled that from her study of Matthew.

Her mom had an innate wisdom for hosting as far as Bailey saw, especially when it came to Thanksgiving dinner. Well, to be truthful, her mom had many skills, including womanly intuition. Bailey couldn't blame her for not wanting her daughter to dash off to Northwest Texas to meet a woman who'd had no contact with her relatives for half a century.

She didn't broach the subject again for three weeks. Then one evening, the theme song from Jaws played on her phone. Bailey took a deep breath and answered. "Hi. What's up, Mom?"

199

"Okay. We'll go. But we wait until the weather thaws. It snows up there."

Bailey shut her eyes and pumped her fist. "Thanks, Mom."

"Hmph. I don't think we should tell your father. Let's tell him we're going shopping in Dallas for your birthday."

"My birthday *is* in March, but that would be lying."

"Yes, dear. Sometimes in marriage, it's necessary. But to make you feel better, we could make a detour to the Big D on the way back. That would add at least a day to our travels, though."

"I'll think about it. Talk later, Mom. Bye." She sat back on her gray sofa and pulled one of the purple pillows to her chest. What her mom said irked her. She always assumed honesty and trust anchored a marriage. At least she hoped one day hers would be... if she ever decided to fall in love again.

Her cell phone beeped to tell her she had a text. She pulled it up.

You don't listen well, do you? Stop or someone you know will have an accident.

Bailey gasped and dropped the phone. She ran out of her apartment and banged on Shannon's door.

When Shannon answered, Bailey sputtered as she told Shannon about the text.

"I'm calling 9-1-1."

Bailey grabbed her shoulders. "No."

"Why?"

"It's not an emergency, really. I don't want sirens and..."

Shannon released Bailey's hands. "Okay. Then let me call Chase. I still have his card."

Bailey didn't argue.

Chase arrived within fifteen minutes to Shannon's apartment. By that time, Shannon had retrieved Bailey's phone and locked the door to Bailey's unit.

He read the message and got out his cell. "Hey, Bob. Run this number for me. See what pops up." He called off the phone number of the sender.

A few minutes later, he got the text. "Burner phone. Of course."

"Can you trace that? I mean, to where someone purchased it?"

"Bob's already on it, Shannon. It's protocol. But it may take a while. And if they paid cash for it, well..." He shrugged.

"Right. And they would." Bailey slouched into the couch cushions.

"Most likely. You aren't dealing with dummies here, Bailey." He leaned in and tapped her forehead. "Someone has hacked into your phone calls, emails, and texts. You better tell me what you've been up to." He stepped back and sat in a side chair across from her.

She told him about El Paso, Edwin's side of the story, and the threatening photo. When she got to the part about her mother agreeing to head for Amarillo in March he

201

bolted to his feet. "Are you nuts, woman?"

"That's what I told her." Shannon waggled her head. "But she won't listen."

Bailey sucked in her breath. She shifted her attention to the man blowing steam puffs through his nose. "It isn't that big of a deal, Chase. We will meet her for lunch someplace public and well lit. In the middle of the day. Mom and I will be fine."

He jammed his finger to her phone screen. "You sure about that?"

Tears threatened, but she blinked them away. Every time they met, she teetered on the verge of distress. He must think her to be the weakest person he'd ever known. "I'm sorry we called you. You don't have to waste your time anymore. And tell your buddy, Bob, that too."

She rose, stomped to the front door, and opened it. Then she turned her head back and motioned for him to exit.

He didn't move. He remained seated, his eyes still fixed on Bailey, as he addressed Shannon. "This is your apartment. Do you want me to leave?"

Shannon sighed and rose from the couch. "No." Her heels clanked across the floor. She reached past Bailey and pushed on the door, releasing it to close. "I'd like you to stay and talk some sense into her."

"I'm not five years old." Bailey stomped her foot.

Chase pressed his hands to his knees. "You're acting like one."

If he'd been within arm's reach she'd have slapped him. Why did he stir up so many emotions in her?

His gaze bore into Bailey. "Shannon. Get three glasses of water, please. I think we all need to cool off."

Bailey rolled her eyes. She sauntered over and flopped on Shannon's sofa again, refusing to let her gaze meet his. But in her peripheral vision, she noticed him rub the corner of his eyebrow as he stifled a smirk.

Ooohh. The man could be irritating.

Shannon set two of the drinks on the coffee table within their grasp. She sipped her own while she remained standing next to the door as if guarding the exit.

Chase took a long guzzle then set his glass down. "Bailey. I am not adhering to your wishes for two reasons. First, you have been threatened twice. That is criminal *intent*. This message could lead us to discover who broke into your place and almost killed your cat. A criminal *offense*. Both warrant a police investigation. And I'd like Edwin to send me a photocopy, front and back, of the message he received on his windshield." He raised his hand in front of him. "It's a long shot, but sometimes we get lucky."

Bailey popped her neck to relieve the tension. He did have a point. "And the second reason?"

Chase glanced at Shannon ever so briefly then focused again on Bailey. His voice lowered. "Is a personal one. I can't go into detail right now."

What? She blinked.

He took another few sips of water before he walked to the door. He halted with his hand on the knob. "Look. Even if you aren't acting that way at the moment, you are a grown woman. So is your mother. If you two want to traipse off to Amarillo, I can't stop you."

"No, you can't."

"However, I can ask to come along."

Her mouth opened. "Um…"

Shannon sat down next to her. "It's not a half-bad idea."

Bailey gazed into Shannon's chocolate eyes. She then lifted her own to Chase. "I'll run it by Mom."

"Good. Thank you." He jerked the door open. "Look at it this way. If you have a flat, I can be the one to get grungy changing the tire."

The twinkle in his eyes nabbed her. Despite her best efforts, a grin began to sneak onto her face.

As soon as he noticed it, his smile increased as well.

Within a few seconds, they were all laughing.

After he left, Shannon shook her head. "Bailey, he's a great guy."

Bailey stared at the closed door and puffed out her cheeks. "Yeah, he is. He always knows how to cheer me up. He really gets me."

Chapter 22

Their rendition of the choruses from Handel's Messiah brought smiles, even from their senior pastor. At the Hallelujah chorus, he stood and encouraged everyone in the congregation to uphold the long-held tradition. The Christmas spirit began to envelop Bailey as she hummed what they'd sung. Yet her heart remained heavy. If she'd never researched her family, she'd never had known such gut-wrenching sadness existed in it. If the truth set one free, as the Bible said, she wanted to know how. Right now, she felt shackled by it.

"Great performance, right?" Jessica shook out her choir robe with a wide grin and placed it on a hanger.

Bailey made every effort to return the smile. "Yeah. I think everyone liked it."

Shannon edged in. "Let's go get some hot chocolate. They are serving it in the fellowship hall."

Bailey spotted Mr. Hanson and Mr. Garcia in her peripheral vision. Time to share the Christmas spirit. Part of her new resolve to be kinder to everyone and think less of herself. She turned to them. "Mr. Hanson? Mr. Garcia? Will you join us?"

The expression on Mr. Hanson's face made her step back. He shook his head and walked away. Mr. Garcia harrumphed and followed.

Shannon whispered in the close range of their ears. "That's kinda weird."

Jessica picked up her purse. "They're weird. More than most older folks."

"Jessica." Bailey gave her a motherly glare.

"I know. I know. Peace and goodwill. We should try to get along with everyone, I recall that from Bible study. It's just hard sometimes." She raised her hands in the air and headed out of the choir room.

Shannon shook her head. "So, have you heard from Chase?"

Bailey closed her locker door. "Last week. He said they traced the burner phone to a convenience store two blocks from where we live. Purchased November 23rd in the evening and the cash register records show guy paid cash."

"Did Chase review the surveillance camera?"

"Broken."

"Of course." Shannon scoffed. "The dude probably knew it. That's why he bought it there."

Bailey sighed. "With so many people coming in and out, the clerk couldn't give a description. He thought the guy might have been an older man. Not a teenager or anything."

"Like Arthur Archer?"

"I think the clerk would know him, don't you? I mean his car dealership commercials are on every fifteen minutes, it seems."

Shannon snickered. "True. And with A.A. running for comptroller, his daddy seems to get them both in front of the camera a lot lately."

"You're not kidding." Every time Bailey saw his face on the TV she shuddered. "I've stopped watching the local news."

"Not a bad thing necessarily." Shannon sniggered. The two of them traipsed down the corridor toward the hum of conversations in the fellowship hall.

Shannon spoke again. "Who bought the burner phone, do you think?"

"Chase won't speculate, but I'm guessing one of Arthur Archer's thugs. You know, the type who repossess cars when the new owner doesn't make their monthly payments?" She pictured a man with the physique of a wrestler and a cauliflower nose. Yuck.

That night she dreamed a thug like that chased her around her complex with a tire iron, waving the photo from Elliott's graduation. Her heartbeats became his footsteps slapping the pavement.

Bailey actually got an email with an animated Christmas card link from Eugene and his new wife Clara. Edwin and family sent her a postcard with their photo—all in Santa hats and shorts around the aloe vera plant in their graveled front yard. Edmond emailed her a card with a palm tree lit up with Christmas lights. It read, "Merry Christmas from the Hide-away-Huts, Leon, Nicaragua."

She sent e-cards to all of them, including the youngest of Edmond's sons, Michael, who she secretly thought might make Jessica's heart rate increase. But he lived in Chicago. Still, she wondered how to finagle her best friends to be included in the guest list.

She showed the correspondences to her mom at Sunday dinner.

The expression on her mother's face varied as she gazed at each. What emotions must be swirling inside her? Bailey didn't begin to know. After she'd viewed the e-cards on Bailey's phone, she took off her readers and wiped the smudges with the hem of her skirt. "Well, your Uncle Elliott has agreed to come for Christmas Dinner. How about that?"

Bailey's mouth flew open.

Her mother repositioned her specs and peered into her daughter's face with that motherly scowl that always made Bailey's skin tingle. "Please do not monopolize him playing twenty questions."

"Yes, ma'am. I won't." But she knew she would. She hadn't seen him in years, and back then she had been too self-aware to pay him much attention. She'd encountered one other person with his developmental condition, a janitor at one of the restaurants she audited.

When she returned home, Shannon dashed out of her apartment. "Bailey, come here."

"Let me set my things down and change out of these Sunday clothes. These heels are killing my feet."

"No. Now." She motioned rapidly with her hand. Her face held a seriousness Bailey rarely witnessed. Sort of like a vice principal she once had.

"Sure, Shan. What's up?"

Shannon practically pulled her inside. She closed the door and locked it. Then she snatched a piece of paper off the table. "This."

Bailey took the note-lined sheet from her. She read out loud the hand-written words. "Your friend won't listen. You better tell her to stop snooping or I'll get you both." She gasped. "Shannon? Where did you find this?"

A male voice sounded behind her. "Someone slid it into her mailbox slot."

Bailey almost jumped out of her shoes.

Chase rose from the sofa. "We've already dusted it for prints. None. Give me your key and I'll check your mail."

She bit her lower lip as she held out her keychain. "It's the small gold one."

His hand felt warm as he took it from her. She imagined hers resembled ice.

"I'll be right back."

Bailey shuddered as she edged into one of the side chairs in Shannon's living room. "It's the same handwriting as the others. He doesn't even hide that fact. Who is this guy?"

Shannon rubbed the goosebumps from her own arms. "I wish I knew, Bailey. I wish I knew."

A tap on the door jolted them both. Shannon peered through the peephole and sighed. She jerked the knob and let Chase inside. He handed Bailey two grocery store fliers, an advertisement to apply for a credit card, and her utility bill. "No nasty note."

Bailey exhaled. "Good."

He sat down on the couch and propped his foot on his knee. "Have you been doing more online research?"

"Well, yes. But on my new laptop. So...?"

He thumped his head against the wall behind him and stared at the ceiling. "Why didn't you follow instructions?"

"Excuse me?"

Chase rose and paced. "You are the most stubborn woman I've ever met."

Bailey's nostrils flared. She felt anger bubbling up her throat. Why did he push her buttons? She wadded up the note and threw it at him. "I'm sorry I ever called you the first time."

He caught it with one hand. "Do you want me to ask for someone else to be assigned to your case? I'd be happy to do so."

You arrogant... ugh. She jutted her chin and rose to

respond.

"Whoa." Shannon straddled between them, arms spread. "Take it down a few notches, y'all." Her hand met Chase's chest. It moved up and down with his quick breaths.

"Whatever." Bailey broke eye contact and walked to the window.

"Chase, I don't know about her, but I want you to find out who stuffed this in my mail slot. When my man hears about this he is not gonna be happy."

Bailey flipped her hair off her shoulder and turned around. "I'm sorry. I honestly thought there would be no difference between searching on a new laptop and doing it at the library."

She watched as the veins on Chase's forehead receded. "Perhaps I'm too close to this case. I've acted unprofessionally." He un-wadded the piece of paper. "I'll take this with me if you don't mind, Shannon. I'm not sure what we can do, but you never know. I had one case where the perp left a stray eyelash stuck to a ransom note's crease."

"Wow. Cool."

He snickered. "Don't get your hopes up." He swiveled his head to Bailey. "And please, no more surfing for long lost family or drunk drivers from 1968 until after the holidays, okay? I want us all to have a merry Christmas."

"Fine with me." Shannon shot a glance at Bailey, another one that reminded her of her middle school vice principal—or Cinderella's wicked stepmother in the movies. She couldn't decide which.

"Yes, yes. Fine." Bailey lowered her eyes and rubbed the toe of her boot against the carpet. "But I haven't pursued the drunk driver. Not really, other than a few more online…" She looked up, her hand to her mouth. "Oh."

"That's what I figured. I'll ask the San Marcos police archives to dig up the file. It seems it may now pertain to this current case."

"So, you see this as a good thing?" She scrunched her nose.

His footsteps edged toward her. "Perhaps. Friends again?"

She wagged her head. "Yes. Of course, we are."

He kissed her cheek. His voice became a low whisper. "At least I got to wish you a Merry Christmas, even if it is a few days early."

The place where his lips touched warmed her skin and spread down her like syrup over a stack of pancakes. She sputtered for a response. "Um, yeah… you, too."

He gave her his famous Chase wink and left.

"I'm not saying another thing." Shannon shuffled into the kitchen.

Bailey blew out the breath she'd been holding. Good, because she didn't have any desire to hear it. Her mind already swirled with enough confusing emotions.

Chapter 23

Christmas Eve services lasted past midnight and they always fixed a big breakfast afterward so Bailey spent the night at her parents' house. Egg, sausage, and cheddar casserole, cranberry muffins, along with hot oatmeal with raisins, apple chunks, and pecan pieces smothered in butter and brown sugar... same menu every year. Tradition.

Her mother still liked to do the stocking thing on Christmas morning so they were up by eight. Then she and Bailey spent the next four hours in the kitchen preparing the family meal, mostly in silence as they maneuvered around each other in a well-orchestrated culinary dance. She often wished she'd been born a boy so she could lean back and watch football like her dad.

Elliott arrived a little after one that afternoon. He brought a pecan pie from a renowned bakery in Houston as his contribution to the table. Bailey felt her hips growing by the second.

213

After the table had been cleared, Elliot motioned to Bailey. "Tell me about the party in May. W-why?"

She took his elbow. At first, he jerked, but then he relaxed.

"Sorry. I didn't mean to startle you. Let's talk in Dad's office." She motioned down the hall and he followed her.

"Uncle Elliot, what do you recall about Edwina and the baby?"

His face lost all color. He waggled his head back and forth. "We don't talk about that. No. No. We don't. Ever." His eyes darted to the partially closed door.

She wedged between it and him to catch his gaze. "It's okay. Tell me about Edmond and Eugene then. Wouldn't you like to see them again?"

His face became blank. "They used to tease me."

"I know. But they were stupid boys. They are grown-ups now. So are you."

His lip turned out. "Will they like me this time?"

She gently laid her hand on his arm. He didn't flinch this time. "I'm sure of it. And I'll be there, and Mom. It'll be fine. You can stay upstairs in the guest room between mine and Travis' rooms, too."

He stood still for a moment. Then he nodded. "Okay."

"Wonderful." She rose on her tiptoes and kissed his cheek.

He blushed, rubbed the spot with his hand, and shuffled out of the room.

When Bailey emerged, her mother flashed a stern glare

in her direction.

"Nothing, Mom. I promise. He worried that Edmond and Eugene would tease him at the family reunion like they used to growing up. I promised him it would be fine and he could stay in the guest room next to Travis."

"He's coming?"

"Yes. I talked him into it."

Her mother's face softened like icing on a warm cupcake. She drew Bailey into a rare hug. "Thank you, dear. That is the best Christmas present ever."

Her phone rang two days later. She looked at the screen and saw Chase's name. "Hi. What's up?"

"I got the file from San Marcos, Bailey. However, I am afraid it's of little help."

Bailey tucked her cell phone between her shoulder and her ear as she chopped pecans for the chocolate brownie batter. "Oh."

"I had to pull strings to get it. Someone back in 1968 did the same to keep it hidden."

She laid the knife down. "Meaning?"

"I may be reading between the lines, literally. Going over the transcript of that clerk's testimony, I think someone got to him. Maybe paid him off."

Exactly what she figured. "What gives you that impression?"

She heard Chase's chair hinges squeak and pictured him leaning back, the file in his lap. "Well, beer bottles littered the back seat. Some of them had lipstick, so I'm guessing he had a date at one point. Maybe the clerk didn't want to be fired for selling it to a minor? Only an assumption. San Marcos had a reputation of being a party college town back then."

"And Austin, with thousands attending its universities, isn't too far up the road either."

"True. Needle in a haystack."

"You're telling me there is no way to find out the identity of the driver."

"Well, it sounds to me like a university student whose daddy had money or power. Maybe local clout?"

She wiped her hands, sat down, and switched the phone to the other ear. "Money talks and the son walks."

"It happens. Especially in smaller towns, as you know. We both were raised in one."

"How well I know."

He cleared his throat. "Anyway, per the police report, someone bought your family a new car to replace the totaled one but kept it anonymous. Paid cash."

"Can we trace the money?"

"No, not really." He tilted his head and shrugged.

"Because it happened so long ago?"

"Even if it had occurred last week, we'd need to identify the sender to check bank statements. Besides, they probably wouldn't have kept records more than seven to ten years. That's all the IRS requires. But there's more. Your uncle Edmond, as the executor, signed off to end the investigation."

"They paid *him* off?"

"Inconclusive. Maybe he realized the police were at a dead end and thought it better not to pursue it. I imagine everyone's emotions were pretty raw."

"So, that's it?"

"Yeah."

She felt like a balloon accidentally released as someone blew air into it. "I appreciate all your work. Truly. And I am sorry I got so upset with you."

He chuckled. "Which time?"

She had no response.

After a few seconds, his voice came back through. "I haven't exactly been my best either. Clean slate?"

"Works for me."

"Good. Got plans for New Year's Eve?"

Was he asking her out? She stuttered a bit. "Um, yes, I do."

She planned to spend the evening with Jessica watching romantic comedies and eating decadently before resuming her diet on January first. Thus, the brownies.

He hesitated for only for a millisecond. "I'm glad. I didn't want you brooding."

"I don't brood."

Chase laughed. "Then tuck your lower lip back in, Bailey. I can picture your expression."

Of all the nerve… she did as he'd said, though.

"I have plans, too. Afraid I am on duty. It'll be a busy night."

"Sorry about that." Actually, she wasn't.

His tone remained cheery. "You've said you're sorry enough for one year, Bailey Matteson. I don't mind actually. It's an overrated holiday as far as I'm concerned. Each day is new in Christ, right?"

"Right."

"Happy New Year, anyway. If anything else pops up, I'll let you know."

Bailey lifted the phone from her face and stared at it as the call ended.

What was that all about? One minute, professional, the next, not. Jekyll and Hyde. Maybe she acted that way with him. She had to admit, she felt an attraction to him. From the same background as her family so he had her pegged, most of the time. And he had faith. And he could be nice… well, some of the time.

She shuddered. Whatever. Not worth her time thinking about it.

She set the phone down and scraped the nuts into the chocolaty batter.

"Yum. The cream cheese and caramel swirl in the center is delicious."

"New recipe on the web. Thought I'd try it." Bailey took one from the plate.

"You should do it." Jessica shoved the fourth brownie into her mouth.

"Do what, Jess?"

"Contact Edwina again."

"Well, not tonight. It's New Year's Eve."

"So?"

Bailey gave her a "well, duh" expression. Sometimes she could have blonde moments. "Edwina runs a motel. I'm sure she is very busy."

Jessica sputtered, lifting her hand to her mouth. "Are you saying it's that kind of a motel?"

"We don't know that. Not all truckers stay in those places. I bet Shannon's hubby wouldn't."

"True. We shouldn't judge."

"No, we shouldn't." Bailey chuckled and rose to get the door at the sound of a knock. "Bet that is our pizza."

When she opened it, a hooded man rushed her and pinned her to the wall with the pizza delivery box.

"Hey, what are you doing.?" Bailey began to push back. He pressed into her, the box firmly against her breastplate. The leather on his black gloves strained under his knuckles, making a crinkly, groaning sound.

He spun to point at Jessica who had jolted to her feet. "And don't you dare reach for that phone."

Jessica bobbed her head and took two steps away from the coffee table.

219

He motioned to her as his other gloved hand held the box flat against Bailey's throat. "You, get over here, too and be quiet." He swung his leg behind him and slammed the door shut.

Jessica shuffled over, her eyes darting between Bailey and the masked man.

Bailey tried to breathe through her nose. Her chest ached from the pressure as he leaned into her. Through the knitted ski mask, all she could see were two sinister eyes and full lips, but she could smell garlic on his breath. It almost made her eyes water, or were those tears threatening?

He jerked Jessica by the elbow and slammed her to the wall with Bailey. "Ladies. I'm not here to harm you. Only to give you a message. Stop playing games. I know you sweet talked that cop boyfriend of yours into digging up the past."

Bailey opened her mouth to object, but thought better of it. The man resembled a linebacker on Sunday afternoon football. And she felt like the practice battering ram at the moment.

He tossed the pizza box on the carpet like a giant, square Frisbee then grabbed them both by the sleeve, shoving them toward the couch. "Sit down."

Bailey raised her hands. "Okay. Calm down. We'll sit."

Bailey glanced at Jessica and motioned her to obey him.

Jessica gazed back at her, her blue eyes widened.

The man rushed them throwing her side armchair to the ground.

They edged onto the cushions and grabbed hands.

He glared down at them from what had to be a six-foot-three or more height. "What happened in 1968 doesn't affect you. Got it?"

Bailey swallowed hard, which made her chest ache more. "Got it."

But it did affect her, and her family.

He grunted, his angry, dark eyes boring deeper into her.

Her cell phone blared out the Jaws tune.

Bailey jolted. "That's my mother. If I don't answer..."

He yanked his head toward the phone vibrating on the table.

Taking that as a go ahead, Bailey reached for it. She punched the answer button while trying to control the shakiness of her voice. "Hi, Mom. Happy New Year."

"This isn't your mother." A gruff male voice sounded through the speaker. "And if you want to wish her anything, you'd better do as my friend says." Click.

Bailey let out a gasp.

Their captor rocked back and forth on his feet. "Now do you understand?"

Jessica turned to Bailey with a question on her lips.

Bailey shot her a not-now-glance and returned her attention to the man threatening them, and possibly her mother. She felt her heart thumping in her throat. "Where's my mom?"

"Safe enough. For now. Easy to lift her phone. She never shuts her bag when she's shopping. But you better do as my boss says. This is your final warning."

The hippopotamus-sized weight sitting on Bailey's chest lifted a bit. She took a breath. "What does he want?"

He jammed his gloved finger near her nose "Plan your little family reunion. Go see your aunt in Amarillo. But ask no questions about Arthur Archer, or May 10, 1968. Ever. Again. Or else…"

The man reached inside his black leather jacket.

Jessica squeezed her hand as Bailey stiffened.

Please tell me he isn't pulling out a gun.

Chapter 24

"Give your aunt this. He never wanted it." He took a black object from the inner lining of his jacket and tossed it. The pocket-sized photo album landed with a thunk on the table. "Mind what I say." Backing to the door with his finger still aimed at them, he turned the knob, barely glancing down, and left.

They both sucked in air and let it out in a long breath.

Jessica looped her arm through Bailey's and pressed her head into Bailey's shoulder. "Oh, my word. Did that just happen?"

Bailey heard her friend's voice quiver. She ran a hand down her long, blond hair. "It's over. He's gone."

She stared at the little album almost afraid to pick it up. Then something inside of Bailey steeled her nerve. First Bower, then Shannon, Jessica, and now her mother? This had to stop. Instead, she reached for her phone and dialed the number she now knew by heart.

It rang twice then someone picked up. "Hello?"

"Chase? Thank the Lord you answered. I've been threatened again."

"Where?"

"In my apartment. A man with a black ski mask."

"Are you all right?"

She ran a jittery hand through her hair. "Physically, yes."

His footsteps clunked, and then his office door opened and closed again.

"I'm on my way. Are you alone?"

"No, Jessica's here."

Jessica clutched a throw pillow, her eyes still wild.

"Has she been there the whole time? She witnessed it?" His footfall echoed as did his voice. He must be in the hall at the station.

"Yes. He threatened both of us. And they stole my mother's cell phone, too."

"Do you know why?"

"To prove they could get close to her I guess. He said they'd harm her if I kept pursuing what happened in 1968."

"Stay put. Do not move. Do not touch anything." His voice faded as she heard him say something to someone else. Then it became stronger again. "A unit is on its way, too."

When he clicked off, Bailey swiveled to her friend. "Chase is on his way. So is a patrol car."

"Good." Jessica's voice, unnaturally pitched high,

shook.

"He says to stay put and not to touch anything."

Her lips quaked as she bobbed her head.

Bailey tried her best to smile reassuringly. "It's going to be all right, Jess. Promise."

The idea that Chase headed to her rescue brought relief. Seriously, though. She had to quit treating him as her shining-armored knight. The man might get ideas.

"Let me get this straight. You opened the door to him?" The officer questioned Bailey and Jessica.

"Yes. We thought he was the pizza delivery guy."

He glanced over at the unopened box. "You mean that pizza?"

"Well, yeah. But…"

"So, it *was* the pizza deliverer."

"He did have the box, yes." Bailey rubbed her forehead. "However, most of them I've encountered don't wear black ski masks or shove you against the wall, pinning you to it with your order."

"Or threaten you." Jessica took two steps forward to make her point.

The policeman waved his pen back and forth between the two women. "Did he physically harm either of you?"

"No." The answer came in unison.

"Not exactly," Bailey added.

"Then exactly what did he do?" Chase edged through the open front door and around the interrogating patrolman.

Bailey almost rushed to hug him. Almost. Instead, she nodded a greeting with her head. "Thanks for coming."

Chase responded with the same gesture, their eyes briefly locking. Then he blinked and turned to the patrolman. "Officer..." he glanced at the badge. "Jamison. Why don't you take Ms. Warren out into the hall and have her relay her recount of the incident? I'll interview Ms. Matteson."

"Yes, sir." The officer motioned to Jessica. "This way, ma'am."

Chase and Bailey's eyes both followed them out. When the door had closed, Chase flipped his attention to Bailey. "Where shall we sit?"

She scanned the room as if she had never seen it before. The side armchair still remained toppled. The couch seemed a bit too informal. Besides if they sat there she might be tempted to fall into his chest and blubber like a three-year-old whose ice cream cone had been yanked out of her hand. She sucked in a breath. "Dining room?"

He opened his arm for her to lead then zipped around her to pull out one of the chairs for her. She whispered a thank you as she scooted closer to the table.

"Do you need a glass of water?"

"That would be nice. Shelf above the dishwasher."

He pulled out a tumbler. "Tap, okay?"

"I have a jug of filtered water in the fridge. Help

yourself."

Chase filled both glasses and brought them to the dinette set. Then he sat opposite her, took a sip, and got out his phone. "Do you mind if I record this?"

"Not at all." The cool liquid quenched the dryness in her throat.

"It's for official business, so I have to treat you as I would any witness." He winked at her, and once again she felt her cheeks warm. She figured he did it to calm her but his winks always had the opposite effect. She placed one hand over her pulse to reduce its racing.

He pulled up the app, and then using a professional tone, recorded the date, time, and the location. He clicked it off. "Ready?"

"Sure."

Chase tapped the on button. "Interviewing Bailey Matteson, age 30 residing at 1642 Magnolia Way, Apartment 4G. Tell me, Ms. Matteson," Chase knitted his brows in a serious expression. "In your own words, what happened this evening and why you believe you needed to call the police?"

Bailey obliged. When she reached the part about her mother's cell phone, the vein in his temple began to bulge.

"She's fine. No worries." She took a breath, appreciating his concern. "But they did steal her phone."

"I see. Did she file a report?"

"I'm not sure."

"I can check on it. Thank you for relaying what

happened from your point of view, Ms. Matteson." He peered down at the counter on the tape-recording application. "Now let's review a few details. You say he wore a black knit ski mask which covered all of his face except for his eyes and mouth, correct?"

"Yes."

"Do you recall the color of his eyes?"

"Um, brown, maybe. Dark."

"Describe his lips."

She scrunched her forehead. "Well, they were thick, I guess."

"No mustache or beard as far as you could tell?"

Bailey gestured no with her head, but when Chase tapped the phone, she leaned closer to it. "No, I don't think so. Honestly, I concentrated more on the pizza box shoved under my throat."

"What else did you notice about him? Stature? Build? Accent?"

"Taller than me and I'm five-six. His chin came up to here." She laid the side of her hand flat against the bridge of her nose.

Chase's eyes darted to the table again. "Can you explain the gesture you just gave, please?"

She rolled her eyes. "Sorry. Up to the middle of my nose. I'd guess six-three? And huge. Like a football player."

Chase winked again. She wished he'd stop that, it made her heart flutter. "You're doing well, Ms. Matteson.

Go on."

She hesitated to catch her breath.

"Take your time. Sometimes if you close your eyes you can visualize things better."

She squinted. "I'd describe him as hefty. Large shoulders, very strong. Oh, and his feet seemed very long. I noticed that when he stomped toward the sofa and upended my chair. He wore black jeans, a black leather jacket, gloves, and work boots. His accent mildly Hispanic. Articulate, though. He got his point across."

"Anything else? Something distinctive? Try viewing it in your mind as if you were watching it on TV. Remove your emotion if you can."

She closed her eyes again and let her mind replay the scene, then freeze-frame on his face. "Garlic. His breath smelled garlicky." Her eyelids flew open. "And he had a gold tooth. Right here." She pointed with her fingernail into her mouth.

"Note that the witness is pointing to her upper right bicuspid." Chase sat back. "Anything more?"

"I don't think... no. Yes, wait." She snapped her fingers. "He wore black leather gloves, like driving gloves, At least they smelled that way when he shoved his finger to my nose."

"Very well done."

Bailey opened her eyes.

Chase nodded and gave her the thumbs up gesture.

She looked down at her hands. The emotions rushed

back in like a tidal wave. She took a gulp of water to send them back down into her gut.

"Interview over at 10:42 p.m. December 31, 2017." He switched off his phone. "Nice job."

"Thanks." It came out in a shaky voice. She stood, arms wrapped around her, and paced to the couch and back again.

"What is it?"

She half-pivoted back toward him. "I'm antsy, I guess."

He rose to his feet. "Understandable." His hand reached to touch her forearm. "Would you be more comfortable on the couch?"

Her mouth flew open as she spun to face him full on. Did he just make a pass?

He back-stepped. "I only meant…" Chase ran his hand over the nape of his neck.

"I'll sit back down here, thank you." She returned to her seat at the table.

He followed suit.

Shuffles of feet made them shift their attention to the front door as Jessica and Officer Jamison reentered the apartment. Jessica focused briefly on Bailey.

Chase got out of his chair, bent to retrieve the pizza box, and placed it on the table. "Is this what you ordered?"

He opened it to reveal a large supreme with extra cheese.

Both girls nodded.

"How long ago?"

"I guess a little after nine-thirty?" Bailey shifted her gaze to Jessica for affirmation.

"Yeah." Jessica's head bobbed. "Because they said it would take about forty-five minutes."

"And the man arrived at…?"

"10:15." Bailey pointed to the clock on the wall. "I remember thinking, right on time. Even on New Year's Eve. That's why I opened the door without looking through the peephole."

"How did you plan to pay?"

"Cash."

Chase addressed the policeman. "Call the pizza parlor. Ask who they assigned to deliver it. Go interview him. Obviously, our assailant took it from him. I want to know if by force, by bribe, or how? Also, get a description from the delivery person of the man who took it."

"On it." He went to leave but halted at the doorframe. "You want my report in the morning, sir?"

"On my desk by 7 a.m. Yes. Thanks."

After Officer Jamison left, Chase motioned for Jessica to join him and Bailey at the table. "How did you order it?"

Bailey scrunched her eyebrows. "Online, with my phone. Why?"

"Obviously someone's been staking out your place and knew you were home. Either they hacked your phone and learned you ordered food to be delivered, or they got lucky and saw an opportunity."

Bailey swallowed to remain smooth and logical. She noticed Jessica had relaxed her shoulders a bit, too. "This had to be planned. They snatched Mom's phone. Whoever called in knew their goon would already be here."

"I agree. Well planned, in fact. The perp knew the law. We can't get him for breaking and entering since you opened the door for him."

"But—"

Chase held up a finger. "And he didn't physically harm you either. No assault."

"But the pizza box?"

"You have no markings. Basically, it would be his word against yours. My guess is once we track him down, he will say he was headed up there to deliver his message and took the pizza from the guy to save him the steps. Probably paid for your dinner and tipped him, too. He'll play it down and said he only meant to give you a warning then let you have your dinner."

Jessica slipped her hand into Bailey's. "He's right."

Bailey squeezed it. Then she let go and tossed her head to the ceiling. "Ugh. I hate this."

"You know how to make it stop, Bailey. Do as they say."

She narrowed her eyes on Chase. "That's your advice?"

"I'm asking you to let me take it from here. Someone snatched your mother's phone. That's theft. Do you have any idea of its value?"

"No, but she showed it to me. The one that came out a few weeks before Christmas. Dad bought it for her."

Chase whistled. "That set him back a bit. Very well. Grand theft. Still a misdemeanor since it's under fifteen-hundred dollars but it's worth pursuing."

Bailey crossed her arms over her chest. "And what about his threat?"

"Bailey. As I said, legally it's his word against yours. However, give me your phone a minute."

She handed it to him. He pulled up her history of calls and wrote the number down. "This is your mother's, right?"

She leaned closer to read his notepad. "Yes, it is."

He called it in and asked for a GPS trace. When he clicked off, he shrugged. "It'll be someplace very public. A popular bar, or outdoor event on New Year's Eve."

Bailey noticed the time on her phone. 11:25. Somehow, despite their recent history, having a policeman in her apartment a while longer sounded like a great idea tonight. "Want to stay and ring in the New Year?"

He opened the pizza, pulled out a wedge and chomped down. "Don't mind if I do."

"Hey, isn't that evidence?" Jessica pointed to the food.

Chase swallowed. "You said he wore gloves, right? And you did order it from the place on the box. If it's poisoned, I'll let you know."

Bailey shrugged and pulled a slice for herself. "And it's evidently paid for, too."

233

Chase raised his water glass and winked... again. Bailey cast her eyes down and concentrated on the pepperoni peeking out from under the cheese.

At 12:01 in the morning, Bailey, Jessica, and Chase exchanged New Year's handshakes. Bailey opened a can of black-eyed peas and nuked them. She brought the bowl to the table and handed out spoons.

"You're not superstitious, are you?" Chase bent to take a whiff.

"Of course not. It's tradition."

Jessica took a spoonful and blew on the steam rising from it. "Exactly." She shoveled it in her mouth, washed it down with the rest of her water, and shuddered. "Nasty tastin' things. No offense, Bailey. But I did it, so I'm out of here."

"You feel safe enough to leave?" Bailey set her spoon down.

"Yeah. Thanks, I do. Besides, I need my sleep and even though your couch is pretty it doesn't look as comfortable as my bed."

Bailey and Chase rose. They walked her to the door. Bailey hugged her and told her to drive safe. "Happy New Year. I know this is awful to say after all we've been through tonight but I'm glad you were here when it happened."

Jessica chuckled. "Me, too. I guess."

Chase stood by, his hands in his pants pockets. "Jess, let me walk you to your car."

"No argument."

He turned to Bailey and gave her forearm a tender rub. "Bolt your door. I'll call you if we find out anything."

She clicked both locks, and then leaned her back against the cool steel of the outer door, the place still tingly where he'd touched her. Not exactly the average way she spent New Year's Eve.

She cleaned up and then walked to her bedroom, curled up on the bed, and drew one of her throw pillows to her chin as her pet settled into the crux of her knees. But sleep wouldn't come, and she couldn't blame it on the pizza or the black-eyed peas.

Bailey rolled onto her back, disturbing Bower, who arched his back, yawned and jumped off the bed.

Her mind spun as scenes of the last few months zipped by. And in every other one it seemed, Chase appeared.

She pulled the covers over her eyes.

"Oh, for Pete's sake, it's because I keep ruffling someone's feathers and he is a policeman on the case."

And the fact she and her friends kept calling him.

And, he dashed to their rescue, every single time.

Chapter 25

"Honey, we need to talk." Her father's voice carried a worrisome tone.

"If this is about Mom's cell phone, I know all about it." Bailey tucked the phone to her chin as she crouched in front of the dryer, digging out clothes to be hung up.

"I know you know all about it. That's why we need to talk."

"Dad, let me put you on speaker. My hands are full at the moment."

"I said—" His voice increased by ten decibels. She'd forgotten she had the volume on high so she'd hear her alarm. Bailey slid the indicator back to the left. Better. "—Detective Montgomery wants to meet with us in an hour."

"Yes, Dad. He wants me there also."

"What is going on? Has this to do with your incessant

digging into your mother's past?"

Bailey shut the dryer door and pressed her backside against it. Where to begin? She described the events of the night before, keeping her tone even and unemotional as if she read the daily stock reports from a newspaper.

"Bailey, the Archer family is a powerful one. No one crosses their path unscathed. It's not worth it."

"But Edwin deserves his fair share. He is the true heir."

"Is that what he wants?"

She hesitated. No. But it didn't matter to her agenda, did it? Instead, she mounted her white steed and galloped head-on in the name of justice. Now she felt like an idiot. "I, um…"

His tone became harsher. "That's what I figured. You have a great deal to ponder, young lady, on your way over here." He disconnected the call.

The click echoed against her heart. She shut her eyes and drew in a deep breath. *Where has this gone wrong, Lord? I thought I was doing the right thing. Does justice have an expiration date? Are my motives selfish again?*

She let off an exasperated groan and headed into her bedroom to dress. Forget looking nice. Jeans and a sweater. Hair pulled back. Minimal makeup. It's a holiday, after all. No one spruces up on New Year's Day. As she wound the elastic band through her hair, she spoke to her reflection. "Mom will be mortified, but maybe it will send a message to Chase. Didn't dress to impress. Not interested."

She scrunched her lips to one side. The truth… right?

She thought it over as she applied a dash of mascara, chin tilted up. After she finished the second eye, she'd decided. Chase came with too much baggage—namely his job. Married to it. On call twenty-four seven. Worse than dating a physician. Besides, they had played together growing up. That made him almost a brother.

Bailey ran the tube of lip gloss over her mouth, nodded to the mirror, and headed down the hall. Let the day commence.

She pulled up while Chase got out of his car. They acknowledged each other silently and strolled to the portico. After he rang the doorbell, Chase glanced at her. "Get any sleep?"

"A little." She bore her gaze into the brass knocker. Be cool, professional. No vibes to send Mom chasing after wild geese. That thought brought forth a stifled giggle. Chase—wild goose. Her brain took off on a tangent.

"What?"

She continued to stare straight ahead. "Nothing. I hope you prayed today, Daniel of Babylon. We are about to enter the lion's den."

He didn't have time to respond. The front door creaked open and her father stood there dressed in a navy cashmere sweater with a white oxford collar protruding. A pipe might have completed the lord of the manner look, except he

239

didn't indulge.

Bailey leaned in and air-kissed his cheek. "Good morning, Dad."

Chase extended his hand. "Good morning, sir. Thank you for allowing me to pay you a call. I am aware it's probably not the most convenient time."

Chester Matteson pumped the man's hand. "Not at all. My wife is quite distraught over someone stealing her brand-new cell phone." He glimpsed beyond them, saw two cars parked at the curved drive, and relaxed his facial muscles.

Bailey gave him a stern glare. Did he honestly think they'd come together?

"My daughter knows I stress punctuality. I am glad to see you do as well." He gestured them inside.

Chase stepped back to allow Bailey to enter first. She gave him a quick thank you and preceded through the foyer to the formal living room, fully aware his eyes followed her. Her mother waited for them, perched on the edge of the couch with feet crossed and hands in her lap. On the coffee table sat a silver tray with bone china cups and bread plates, along with the sterling coffee urn, creamer and sugar. A three-tier tray of pastries perched off to the right along with linen napkins. Putting on the Ritz. Let's play high tea.

Bailey bent to kiss her, and then took a seat next to her. Chase extended his hand. "Good day, Mrs. Matteson. I hope you didn't go to all this trouble on my account."

Her mother's cheeks became rosier. "No trouble at all, detective. Have a seat."

He chose one of the winged chairs that flanked the fireplace. "Thank you."

"Coffee?" She scooted closer to the table and lifted the urn. "Bailey. Serve the gentlemen some breakfast breads."

"Delighted." Bailey took the tongs. Under her breath, she seethed.

Chase laughed inside at her having to play Miss Society. The twinkle in his eyes clearly showed it. Then he put up his hand.

"It's all right. They look delicious but I must decline. On duty, you know. Have to stay sharp. Coffee would be pleasant, though."

"Well, of course. We understand." Her mother smiled and handed him a cup.

Bailey tipped her head to him. Well played.

He barely nodded back, indicating he caught her silent message.

They had both been raised in blue-blood homes. Southern tradition, however antiquated, still reigned no matter how they tried to buck it.

"How is your mother, Chase?" Her mother peered over the rim of her cup as she took a sip.

His own cup halted halfway to his lips.

"I can call you Chase?"

He set it back on the saucer. "You may. She is well. Thank you, Mrs. Matteson. I'll give her your regards."

"Emily, this is not a social call." Bailey's father growled his displeasure from his favorite chair.

Chase set his cup down, signaling the end of the "high tea" and time to get down to business. "No, sir. Unfortunately, it is not. So, let me not detain you any longer than necessary. I know you are a busy man, even on a holiday."

Her father crossed his arms. "Well, I appreciate your consideration."

Bailey gave Chase mental applause.

Emily Matteson repositioned her woolen skirt over her knees. "Our daughter certainly decided to dress as such."

Oh, boy. Here we go. Bailey studied her hands to keep from seething.

"Your daughter is very lovely, Mrs. Matteson, even in casual attire."

Bailey's eyes shot daggers at him. *Don't encourage her.*

The twinkle in his eyes glistened brighter before he shifted his attention to his cell phone. "Nowadays we rely on these instead of little black notebooks. It has a recording application. May I?"

"But of course, man." Chester Matteson reached for half a bear claw. He placed a pastry on his plate and settled back into the winged chair opposite Chase.

Chase set his phone on the coffee table. "As you know, Bailey requested my involvement quite some time ago."

"Oh?" Her mother's ears perked as she glanced

between them.

Bailey narrowed her focus onto Chase's face. Now he'd done it.

He flashed an innocent "what?" at her before shifting his attention to her father. "There have been two other incidences prior to this one last night. You are aware of the one when her apartment was trashed. I believe she stayed with you for several days after that."

"And there have been others?" Her mother clutched her pearl necklace. Her face whitened as she turned to face Bailey.

Bailey half rose to object. "Chase—Detective Montgomery. Is this necessary?"

"Bailey. They need to be brought up to speed." His expression became stern as he punched up the tape-recording app and dictated the date and time into it.

She shrank back into the sofa cushions, like a child preparing for her parents to receive a failing report card.

To Chase's credit, he remained professional, commanded their attention, minimized their reactions, and segued into the current events.

"Now, Mrs. Matteson. When did you notice your phone had disappeared?"

"I guess about eight last night. We were at the Gillespie's home."

"Aw, their annual Christmas party. My parents attended it, too."

"Everyone does. I went to powder my nose and noticed

the phone no longer lay in my handbag. I figured I had left it in the car or on my dressing table, or perhaps on the table in the foyer. I do that occasionally."

"So, it didn't concern you?"

"No. Chester always carries his anyway, and I'm not quite used to all its bells and whistles yet so…" She blinked. "Not that I don't appreciate the gift, Chester. Quite extravagant of you. I know they are as rare as green diamonds this season."

Bailey's father nodded.

"So, when did you become concerned?" Chase bent to adjust his phone, subtly reminding her mother of the topic of the interview.

That's when Bailey noticed the raggedness around his face, even though he appeared freshly shaved. Had the man slept at all?

"Actually, I didn't. Until you phoned and told me it had been stolen. Had I realized it involved my daughter being threatened…" Her mother's voice quivered.

Chester Matteson spoke up. "Our insurance will cover the loss. I'd prefer we didn't pursue this any further." He redirected his attention to Bailey. "That includes you, young lady. Understand?"

Chase's eyes darted between father and daughter. "Sir, Bailey has been terrorized. Her apartment trashed. Her pet injured. And her friends have been stalked. As you know…"

Her father jolted from his chair. "I'm sure your

department has better things to do and far more heinous cases to solve."

Chase rubbed his hand down his chin. The two men exchanged glares.

Bailey knitted her brow. What message did they pass between them?

The detective broke the lock first and leaned toward his phone, still recording. "So, in regards to the stolen telephone. You are not pressing charges?"

"I filled out a report online simply for insurance purposes. I don't expect anything more since I and you both know who could do such a thing."

Chase narrowed his eyes and turned off the recorder. "Very well, sir. That is your prerogative. Thank you for your time." He rose and extended his hand.

Bailey's father shook it. "Good to see you again, Detective."

"You as well, sir." He turned to give her mother a slight bow. "Thank you for your hospitality and excellent coffee. I can see myself out." With a quick glance across the sofa, he bobbed his head. "Bailey."

They listened in silence as his footfall faded and the front door closed.

Bailey sat back. "Dad, that bordered on rude."

He pointed his finger toward her nose. "And you border on insubordination. I don't care how old you are or where you live, until you get married you are under my rules. I want this nonsense to stop."

He stomped out of the room.

Her mother sighed. "He is growling today. But he has no bite, dear. You know that."

"So, we are still—"

"Going on our shopping excursion in March? Absolutely. But I'd lay low until then." She patted Bailey's knee. "Now, tell me your impression of Chase Montgomery. He comes from a fine family, you know. Both times he has visited, he seemed intent on your attention."

The banana nut muffin in her stomach flipped.

Chapter 26

As she got to her car, her phone beeped inside her shoulder bag. A text from Chase. *Meet me at the diner on Walnut. I need a decent breakfast, and we need to talk.*

Yes, they did. She sent him back an okay emoji.

He waited at the curb, resting his hip on the hood of his car. He pushed off and opened her door for her. "Thank you for agreeing to meet me. I hope you didn't get too much of a tongue lashing after I left."

"Dad has banned me from any more research, laying down the law as if I were ten." She puffed between her lips. "Mom thinks you and I are an item."

He roared back and laughed.

She pressed her hands to her hips. "Is it that funny?"

He stopped in mid-chuckle but didn't respond.

Maybe she'd misread his signals. "Let's go in. I need some protein."

He opened the glass door for her. "Yes, ma'am. Will

you let me buy?"

She tossed her hair. "No. I'd hate for you to think we might be an item, too."

"Ouch."

They remained silent as they found a booth and ordered. Then Chase bore into her face. "Where do we go from here?"

"Excuse me?"

His crystal-clear eyes darted over her. Then they shifted to the waitress who brought their coffee mugs. A welcoming aroma rose from the steam. He addressed her. "Thank you, ma'am."

Bailey reached for the creamer.

He clasped his hand around his cup and focused again on Bailey. "As far as the investigation goes."

"I'm, um, not sure."

Chase took his time tasting his brew before setting it down. "If Arthur Archer is behind this, he will cover his tracks. His power reaches into all areas of the community, including being a golf partner of my chief." He leaned forward. "So, Miss Matteson. If you choose to pursue this, my you-know-what is on the line. You better be really sure."

"And you're not?"

"No. Frankly, I'm not. I cannot discuss why with you, however."

The expression on his face told her she better not try to wiggle it out of him. She decided to follow another trail.

"But someone forged Aunt Edwina's signature on the annulment papers. And Edwin is his heir. Arthur Archer needs to acknowledge that."

"Maybe he has, in his will. And as far as the forgery, it doesn't matter. They didn't need her permission since she was underage."

"Then why do it?"

Chase tapped his fingers on the diner's tabletop. "I haven't a clue. But it's not a matter for the police at this point."

"Because…?"

"Statute of limitations for one. Lack of provable criminal intent for another. This is more a matter for estate attorneys to haggle over." He downed the rest of the caffeine.

"Have you been to bed?"

He furrowed his brow. "Ma'am?" But laughter bounced in his eyes.

Her face warmed. Now she'd made the plunder. Turnabout, fair play and all, she couldn't be angry about his mind going there. "I simply wondered if your duties kept you up all night, and if it did, I hope not because of me."

"Yours is not my only case. New Year's Eve is one of our busiest nights of the year, as I explained."

"So, you didn't get any sleep?"

"I imagine a great many people in this country don't, which is why today is a national holiday."

"True." She detected from his tone he didn't want her to be concerned.

The waitress brought their food and laid it between them without having to ask who'd ordered what. Hers consisted of egg whites, scrambled in olive oil, with whole wheat toast—hold the butter—proving that she, like millions of Americans had begun a New Year's diet. His over-easy eggs, grits, biscuits, and sausage proved he chose not to participate in the tradition.

Chase took her hand, prayed over the meal, and then proceeded to shovel food into his mouth as if he hadn't eaten in days.

She let him.

He finished off his eggs and grits, and then wiped his mouth as he reached for a grape jelly packet. "To answer your earlier question, I'm off-duty as soon as I file this report. I plan to go home, close the drapes, and pass out for at least six hours. So no, Bailey Matteson, I won't lose any sleep over you."

His double entendre irked her. "Can we call a truce, for real this time?"

He glanced at her as he crammed the biscuit into his mouth. "Fine with me. We've known each other a long time. Used to play together."

"When you and Travis let me."

He wagged his head. "True. I know you are not interested in me in any capacity other than to help you shake your family tree. You've made that clear enough, several times." His face softened. "I respect that. You must have loved Jacob very much."

She stuffed a piece of toast in her mouth to avoid responding.

"Look, I'm sorry for the cat and mouse banter. I keep slipping into the old mold of teasing you like I did when we were kids."

"It got me riled. Still does."

"But you always did stand your ground, Bailey Matteson. Even when you wore pigtails." He wiped his mouth. "Still do. I admire that about you. You have gumption and plenty of it."

"Thank you." She really blushed now and hated that she did. "I'm guilty of bantering, too. I guess. You're right. Old habits."

He folded his napkin. "Tell you what. I will quietly investigate any connection between this latest incident and your apartment being broken into, your laptop being stolen, and your cat being hit in the head. Also, the threat Shannon and you and Jessica received. But, I want you to back off. I mean it. Let me do my job."

"But Edwin—"

"—has his own battle, if he chooses to pursue it. Do not fight that for him. You have no right."

She pressed her hands to her thighs. "True. Dad said so, as well."

His eyebrows disappeared under his side-swept bangs. "Mark the day. A woman actually admitted a guy is right."

251

Bailey snatched her napkin and swatted his hand. Some things never change.

The next few weeks slipped back into a routine. Work, choir, Bible study, home. She private messaged a few of the family members to update them on the reunion and to suggest hotel accommodations. All totaled, seventeen had confirmed they would be there. She, her brother, dad, and mom made twenty-one. Though she left several messages for Edwina and even had sent her a card with a recent family photo, she never heard back.

"Maybe we should cancel the trip." Bailey proposed the idea to her mother as they laid out Sunday dinner on the buffet table.

"I'll write to her. Elliott has mentioned he'd like to join us. He has some vacation time coming. He'd be so disappointed if we did."

"Good, then we'd have a male escort. I'll let Detective Montgomery know we don't need his services after all."

"Oh?" Her mother set down the platter.

"He only offered as a favor, Mom. Since you're friends with his mother."

"So, there is nothing—"

"—Absolutely not." Bailey turned away. Had she stated that a bit too empathically? Her mother's reaction, reflected in the dining room window indicated perhaps she had. Oh, bother.

"He's married to his job, Mom. He has no time for dating." She halted before going into the kitchen to get the seasoned new potatoes. "I wouldn't want to compete for his attention."

"You aren't getting any younger, Bailey. Next March you'll be thirty-one."

"I know, but that's my business."

"Everything we do is Mom's business, sis. Certainly, you've learned that by now."

Bailey and her mother gasped at the sound of a male voice. There in the doorway stood Travis.

As they rushed to hug him, Bailey lifted a silent prayer. Big brother to the rescue.

Over Sunday dinner he explained he would only be in town for a day because he had a corporate meeting in Dallas bright and early the next morning. "I drove down in a rental. Liza and girls came to the states with me but the jet lag coming from Tokyo has gotten the better of them. She stayed with her parents up there."

"That is understandable, I guess. But I'd love to see them." Her mother put on the brave face.

"We will all be back for the reunion in May and stay a full week. Promise." He leaned over and kissed her cheek. "Liza wants to help you with all the last-minute preparations."

Her dad plodded in the dining room, all smiles at the sound of his son's voice. The two shook hands and then drew into a male, back-slapping hug.

The four chatted over a leisurely meal. Bailey saw the weight of the world lift from her parents' shoulders. She chided herself for not realizing how much they missed the child who lived halfway around the world—nor how much their other one, who lived fifteen minutes away, had caused them grief.

If only she'd never studied the begats in the Book of Matthew. How dull and normal the last few months would have been. She drove away with a new resolve to concentrate on the family now, not in the past. A little late, considering the calendar showed the 28th of January, but she'd broken her diet twice now, so she decided to make a resolution she had a better chance of keeping, along with the Christmas season one of being less selfish in her motives.

She hadn't heard a peep from Chase, so most likely the case led nowhere and she'd never know who had been the person to cause her so much angst. Even if they did discover his identity, that didn't reveal who'd hired him. The goon may not have known. According to the shows on TV, they rarely do. An anonymous drop-off spot after secret phone texts deemed it better for both parties concerned. Then no one could testify against the others.

A little light on her dashboard caught her eye. Almost out of gas. With a grumbled sigh, Bailey turned into the nearest station. As she lifted the pump handle, she noticed a black Lexus pull up on the other side. Who should get out but Arthur Archer, Senior?

Bailey never believed in coincidences. She stepped over the concrete island that housed the gas pumps. "Excuse me. Mr. Archer?"

He frowned as he jammed the nozzle into his gas tank. "Yeah?"

She edged around him to meet his bent-over face. "I'm Bailey Matteson."

His face screwed up. "I know who you are. What do you want?"

"Your attention for as long as it takes your tank to fill."

His thumb flipped the lever on the pump handle that would automatically shut off the gasoline flow when it reached full capacity. He folded his arms. "You got it."

"How do you know who I am?"

He scoffed. "If you want to play games, I honestly do not have the time." He gazed at the numbers flipping on the monitor, counting the gallons.

"I'm going to see Edwina in March. May I give her a message?"

"I don't see why I would want to tell her anything after all these years."

"What about your son, Edwin?"

The nozzle handle clicked. "Time's up."

She pulled on his sleeve. "Wait. Are you telling me you aren't even curious—"

He swatted her hand away. "I fell stupidly in love with the girl. She talked me into eloping and then let me get her

255

pregnant. Dad guesses she wanted to land a big fish and live happily ever after on our fame and fortune. How did I know she wasn't on the pill?"

"You didn't want the child. Is that what you're saying?"

"Exactly. I hate to burst your bubble, sweet thing, but your aunt's brain rattled as loose as a rusty lawnmower bolt. Get my drift?"

"But you agreed to marry her?"

Arthur shrugged. "As I said, I fell stupidly in love."

"As she did with you?"

He screwed in the cap to his gas tank and ripped the receipt away. "I'm not sure about that. You'd have to ask your aunt. I'd be wary of her answer, though. She's conned everyone she ever met."

She stood on the curb, her mouth open, watching him peel out and drive away.

Bailey shook her head to let all he told her sink in. Could she believe him to tell her the truth? Or had time, power, and emotions clouded his view?

Chapter 27

Bailey dashed up the stairs, two at a time, and banged on Shannon's door.

Shannon opened it, her hair wrapped turban-style in a towel. "Bailey?"

"Can I come in?" Her voice shook.

"Sure, I have ten minutes until the rinse comes out. What's wrong?"

"Oh, my word, Shannon. Oh, my word."

Shannon grasped her by the shoulders. "Calm down. Come sit. Tell me what's going on."

Bailey did.

"Do you think Athur's telling the truth?"

Shannon played with the edging on the sofa's middle cushion. "I don't know. He may be trying to throw you off the scent."

"Of course." She slapped her forehead with the palm of her hand.

"On the other hand, he may be telling you the truth. He admitted he loved her."

"I doubt it. Evil flashed in his eyes."

She shrugged. "It does happen, girl. Some sense of protectiveness? Misguided love?"

Bailey slumped. "In the movies, yeah. From that snake, no."

"Maybe he's still bitter that the marriage didn't work out and his dad gave him the ultimatum, which he took."

"I guess." She tucked one leg under the other and turned to face Shannon. "Besides why did Edwina return to San Antonio?"

"Don't know. Maybe, in a way she loved him, too?" Shannon squeezed her hair into the towel. "Or she wanted to bribe him into giving her money."

"Or she got tired of trying to make it on her own." Bailey drummed her fingers on the arm of the sofa. After a moment she swallowed. "Mr. Archer is right about something. I have to ask Edwina. Only I'm not sure we are going to go see her. She won't respond now."

"There has to be a lot of hurt there."

"I know, Shannon." She pressed a throw pillow to her face. "Why do I have to play nurse and try to bandage up everyone's wounds?"

Shannon ruffled Bailey's hair. "Because you have a big heart, girlfriend."

"Yep."

"Of course, there is another way to prove paternity and

get the Archers to cough up what they owe."

Bailey appeared from behind the pillow. "Oh?"

"DNA. But we'd have to get a sample from Mr. Archer and from Edwin."

Bailey sat upright. "I have a letter from Edwin. If he licked the seal on the envelope…"

Shannon clapped. "Brilliant. Now, for Mr. Archer…"

They both spouted out the answer at the same time. "Hair."

"But it has to have a follicle or root, right, Shannon?"

"Hmmm. How in the world do we get that?"

The two flopped back on the couch and stared at the ceiling as if the answer would magically appear in the popcorn plaster.

"You two are insane." Jessica waved her hands away as they walked through the parking lot to Bible study.

Bailey scoffed. "It'll be easy. You two go knock on Arthur Archer's door."

"Why us?"

"Because he knows me, Jess. Tell him you're collecting for cancer research and ask him if he has ever considered having his DNA tested for markers."

Shannon bobbed her head. "We can make up the forms on my computer and my cousin works in a pathology lab, so I can ask him for some lab specimen bags."

"And he'll give them to you?"

"I'll tell him it's a birthday gag. Cousin Jay always loves pulling practical jokes."

"I don't know about this." Jessica quickened her pace. "Why would someone go door to door collecting DNA samples?"

Bailey gave her a whimpering puppy dog face. "Please?"

"And you're sure they can lift the DNA from the envelope Edwin sent you?"

"I researched it. It can be done. Not the preferred method, but…" She waggled her head back and forth.

"How much is this going to cost?"

"It's cheaper than you think, Jess."

She stopped in the hallway. "I don't think this is right. Isn't there something in the Bible about not fooling people?"

A wise, elderly voice sounded behind them. *"Therefore each of you must put off falsehood and speak truthfully to your neighbor, for we are all members of one body.* Ephesians 4:25."

"Oh, hello Mrs. Perkins." Bailey's shoulders lifted to her ears.

"Shall we go in, ladies?" She gave them the teacher look over her readers.

The three shared a wide-eyed expression. Silently, they followed their Bible study leader.

As they took their seats, Shannon whispered in

Bailey's ear. "We'll come up with something better."

"Right." Bailey wondered if breaking and entering to steal his hairbrush would be considered an eye for an eye. Probably not.

Then an idea hit her. Golf. The man played golf with Chase's boss, the chief of police. If she could find out their tee time and slip into the locker room... Oh, never mind. It'd get her kicked out of the country club. Oh, the society headlines would make her mother keel. Besides, it would be a long shot.

Her own pun rumbled a giggle into her throat. She swallowed it back down with a gulp of bottled water as everyone flipped open their Bibles to Matthew 17.

After Bible study, she walked out with her friends. She halted in the parking lot. "Jess, you're right. It is a stupid idea. And not like me to think of such a weird plan."

"So, you are giving it up?"

She thought for a moment. "No. But I don't want to involve you two anymore. No offense, but this is my family's battle. I'm tired of being shoved around and threatened." She jutted her chin. "It's time I fought back."

"Then what are you going to do, girlfriend?" Shannon shifted to her other foot.

"Walk boldly onto the battlefield with my little stone and see if I can fell a giant."

Chapter 28

Could she do it? Yes, she could. Chase said she always stood up when confronted. Well, she tired of being bullied by this supposedly invincible powerhouse. Her family's bloodlines could run circles around his.

Bailey tugged on her pencil skirt to make sure it fell below her knees. She wrapped her hair into a professional bun, donned some modest yet pricey earrings, and adjusted the buttons on her blouse. She pulled on her woolen business jacket and slipped into her most expensive heeled boots.

Ten minutes later, she pulled into the campaign headquarters of Arthur Archer, aka A.A. Jr. Only nine in the morning on a Saturday, but she'd take her chances the place would be buzzing, considering the primary election drew near. She counted to three and opened the door.

About ten workers sat at various tables licking envelopes, folding fliers, and hauling boxes. A young woman greeted her. "Hi, welcome to the campaign headquarters for the next State Comptroller, Arthur Archer, A.A. Junior." She flashed Bailey a large smile and held out a hand at the end of a stiff-elbowed arm. "A.A. stands for the double excellence he will deliver to the citizens of this state."

Wonder how much they paid an ad agency to come up with that one? "Thank you. Is the campaign manager in by any chance?"

She withdrew her hand with a puzzled expression. "Um, yeah. Why?"

"My name is Bailey Matteson. I'm on staff in accounting for Hamburger Haven and I'd like to talk to him about a contribution."

The girl's eyes lit. "Oh, wait here."

Bailey rocked forward onto her toes. *Not exactly a lie.* She did want to discuss a contribution, just from A.A. Jr., not Hamburger Haven.

A few minutes later a middle-aged man with a receding hairline approached as he rolled his sleeves down and buttoned the cuffs. He extended a warm, soft hand in a firm shake. "I'm Max Olson."

She took his hand and returned the grip. "Bailey Matteson. May I have a minute of your time?"

"Absolutely. This way to my office."

He motioned back toward the left to a space behind upholstered dividers. She took it as a cue to go first. When they reached the entrance, Mr. Olson shuffled around her and cleared a few boxes of stuffed envelopes from an office chair. Brushing it off with his hand, he pointed to it. "Please, have a seat. Sorry for the mess. It gets a bit hectic this time of year."

Bailey sat and innocently crossed her leg.

He moved a hand over his chin and smiled.

She noticed a gold band encircling his left ring finger. Is he sizing me up? Ew. Of all the nerve. Wimpy little man.

She uncrossed her legs and pulled her skirt over her knees. "I'm sure you are swamped. Hardly see the *wife and kids*, right?"

His eyes darted away as he eased into his chair behind the desk. "Yeah. But we'll get a break after A.A. Jr. wins the primaries."

"Ah. Good." Why did she stall? She steeled her nerves.

He moved a few papers over. "So, Miss Matteson, how can we help you?"

She scooted forward in her chair. "Actually, sir. I may have misled your worker. It is me who is soliciting your help. I need A.A. to make a contribution of one or two hair follicles."

"Excuse me?"

"For a paternity test."

His face lost all color.

"Oh, not for him, for his dad. Let me explain."

As she did, the man tented his fingers and swallowed a lot.

"This isn't a joke, is it?"

"No sir, I'm afraid not."

He reared back, and his chair hinges complained. "And if A.A. doesn't agree?"

"I go to the press."

"You have proof, you say."

"I do." She reached into her portfolio bag and pulled out the annulment copies along with the handwriting sample from Edwina.

He took them and studied them for a few minutes. "Well, they are very different."

"Yes. It doesn't matter because the annulment is still valid without both of them. But the press would love to twist this small deception into a tornado. And if it leaks out that Edwina Holston became pregnant by the well-known Arthur Archer with a son whom she named Edwin Arthur, a combination of hers and the father's names, who has never been acknowledged by the Archer clan, well…"

"I don't see how that would be a black mark on A.A. He wasn't even born then."

"There is a pattern of deceit from grandfather to father." She paused to let that fact sink in. "Mr. Olson, would it not make people wonder if it had spread down the family line? We all know A.A. is running on his father's coattails."

He cleared his throat. "What do you want me to do?"

"Talk to A.A. Get the sample. I'll come pick it up."

"And if he agrees, this stays under wrap?"

"Absolutely."

"Ms. Matteson. Why is this so important to you? The money?"

She rose and extended her hand. "No, Mr. Olson. Principle. If Arthur Senior is the father, he needs to do the right thing. I think A.A. can convince him of it better than I ever could." She handed him her business card. "You have one week. Good day."

Bailey walked with a purposeful stride out of the makeshift office, through the zigzag of tables and workers, and out the front door. She hurried to her car, clicked the fob and slid into the front seat. Only then did she exhale.

She texted Shannon. *I did it.*

The thumbs up emoji plinked onto her screen.

She started her car. "Now Mr. Archer. Let's see who has the upper hand in this game."

Three days passed. Nothing from the Archers. Did they not take her seriously?

Bailey grew antsy and tried to keep her mind on other things like the reunion, her job, and the choir rehearsals for Easter, which fell on April Fools this year. She thought of the verse from Paul's letter to the Romans, *"For although they knew God, they neither glorified him as God nor gave thanks to him, but their thinking became futile and their foolish hearts were darkened" (1:21)*. So, either you show up at church Easter Sunday or are foolish. She

267

stopped in mid-thought. Oops, she'd judged again. *Sorry, God.*

That Friday, as she stood in her closet and decided what to wear to work, her phone rang.

"Miss Matteson. Max Olson. We have the item you ordered. When can you come pick it up?"

A sense of victory filled her chest. Stand up for yourself and the bullies will back off. "I can be there at 12:15. Will you be open?"

"Yes, I don't take a lunch break. Not this close to the election."

Bailey barely ate her breakfast. The morning dragged slower than a waiting line of sloths at a zoo trough. She must have glanced at the clock on the lower right screen of her computer a hundred times before it finally flashed 11:58. She clicked on the sleep mode and left the office.

"In a hurry, Bailey?" Her supervisor poked his head out from behind his cubicle.

"An appointment, sir. Tills are balanced and the report is in your email as an attachment. See you after lunch."

She rushed to the elevator and tapped her foot, as the numbers, displayed above the double doors, counted down the floors. At last a ding sounded and the doors swished open. Several more people now crowded in with her, some chatting. She watched the declining dings until, at last, the letter L for lobby illuminated.

Bailey dashed for her car and started the engine. The headquarters would be a ten-minute drive in normal traffic.

If she beat the rush hour lunch crowds, she'd make it.

When she pulled into the parking space in front of the campaign building, she noticed there were no other cars around. Maybe the volunteers were out to lunch.

She got out and knocked on the glass entrance. Max Olson waved and walked toward the entrance. She heard the bolt unclick then stepped back for him to open the door.

"Sorry. Everyone has headed for lunch, and since we have cash on hand, well protocol."

"I understand."

He glanced around and scratched the back of his scalp.

Did he seem nervous? Her battle didn't lie with him, the messenger.

"The envelope is on my desk. Please follow me."

Something didn't feel right. A warning went off in her mind. "Why don't you go get it and I will wait here?"

He grabbed her arm. "Because those aren't my instructions."

"What?" She jerked away and reached to unbolt the door.

A strong hand pressed onto her shoulder.

Bailey gasped.

"Come with me, Bailey Matteson." A gruff voice commanded her as he placed his large gloved hand over her mouth. His other hand slammed across her shoulders and pinned her to him, pressing her arm to her side.

"Please come quietly, so I don't have to gag you. I'm to take you to pick up your order."

She struggled to get free until he unlocked a switchblade and waved it at her nose. "Be a good girl and I won't hurt you. My boss only wants to talk to you face to face. Got it?"

His grip tightened like a blood pressure cup on her arm. It made her fingers tingle. She moved her head up and down, noticing Max had conveniently disappeared.

The man half-dragged her to the back door where a black limousine waited, its engine running. Another thug, just as big, waited by the opened back passenger door.

Scream and run, or obey and go with them? Bailey's heart thumped as her eyes darted the empty alleyway. Run, obey, run, obey.

The first one hissed in her ear. "Get in, Ms. Matteson." He shoved her toward the other one. They blocked her escape.

She slid into the back seat, and the second man followed her. As he sat, the whole bench seat moved.

"I'll take that." He snatched her purse and tossed it to the driver. The odor of his breath made her eyes water. Why did all of these thugs have bad breath?

The first goon slid into the front passenger seat. "Let's go."

A whir sounded as a piece of glass rose between the back seat and the front. It and the tinted side windows grew darker. Soon, Bailey couldn't see a thing beyond them.

She closed her eyes and prayed.

Chapter 29

The man sitting next to her said nothing. Besides her own heartbeat in her ears, she only heard the rustle of his black leather jacket as he breathed in and out through his nose. That, and the constant whirr of the engine and thunk of the tires over the city streets.

Bailey scooted over as close to the door as she could then realized no handle rammed into her ribs. Of course not. Why would they allow her a means of escape?

She weighed her options.

She could scream bloody murder until the man sitting next to her either burst his eardrums or smacked her unconscious. Nope. Not the best idea.

No cell phone. No way to communicate, unless gorilla man next to her carried one. Maybe if she pretended to have hysteria and beat on his chest she could somehow slip her hand inside his leather jacket to find out. Well, maybe not a great plan either. He definitely could overpower her, even

271

if she did manage to nab it.

Wait. Sit quiet and do nothing. A small voice inside of her cautioned her. She'd discover what they planned to do with her soon enough. Instead, she played familiar hymns in her head. It almost drowned out the goon's raspy breaths. Maybe he had allergies.

Where were they? She couldn't detect the whoosh of traffic. The vehicle slowed and turned left. The pitch of the tires' humming changed and the road jostled her more. Definitely no longer on the highway.

She strained her ears for any sound that would give her a clue to where they were, but the goon's loud breathing stifled that effort. It finally dawned on her about ten minutes later. Her bodyguard had fallen asleep. Did she dare slip her hand under his leather jacket without making too much noise? She inched closer. Carefully reached out her hand...

He snorted and then resettled into slumberland.

Bailey bit her lip and tried again. Closer. Easy. Slowly. She squinted to adjust to the darkness. Since he wore all black, she couldn't detect a thing. With her luck, he probably had it in his back pocket.

Her hand shook. She brought it back to her chest and held it to steady it. She took three cleansing breaths before she tried again.

On the third inhale the car hit a bump. It lifted her out of her seat and flopped her half on top of the guy. He woke with a grunt and a growl. "What are you doing?"

"Um… sorry. Bump."

He lifted her off, scraping her head on the roof of the limo and slammed her rear into the upholstery. "Fasten your belt."

Bailey obeyed. She reached over, pulled the shoulder restraint diagonally across her torso, and clicked it.

He grunted again as he crossed his arms over his broad chest. Within a few seconds, his eyes closed again.

Onward Christian so-o-soldiers, marching as to war… she began to hum again in her mind. Halfway through the second verse, the car halted.

She waited as the engine died, the car doors in front opened and shut, and footsteps sounded closer to her. The man next to her yawned and stretched, his arm brushing her face. The smell of new leather assaulted her nose.

When her side opened, the afternoon light poured in, making her squint.

"Let's go."

She bobbed her head and un-clicked her belt nanoseconds before a hand cupped her arm and pulled her out. Otherwise, she may have donated part of her liver right then and there. She didn't recognize the hand's owner, but he appeared as large and bulky as the other two. Yep, had to be repo men.

They walked her down a wilderness path for about a mile. No one spoke, so Bailey decided she shouldn't break the ice. She glanced at the men in front of her then back to her car companion who brought up the rear. None of them held her purse. Great. No way to yank it from them, run like she raced in a sprint around the high school track and call for help.

Hill Country shrub mesquite, cedars, and a few oak trees lined either side of the path. Leaves and gravel crunched under their feet. Thank goodness she had worn sensible shoes to work today. And slacks. A slight dampness began to seep through her blouse under her arms even in the cool, late February temperatures.

Birds flittered above them in the tree limbs, disturbed by their footsteps. A squirrel wound around a trunk and chattered at them as he popped his tail. Did the furry guy issue a warning to her?

Surely, they wouldn't lead her into the wood to shoot her in the head and leave her body for the buzzards. No, no. She couldn't think that.

Her mind raced almost faster than her heart. Calm it down. The first goon said they wouldn't hurt her. Only take her to chat with their boss. Stop worrying. God is here.

But who is the boss? A.A., or Arthur, Senior? Well, she'd find that out soon enough.

She stumbled over a rut in the dirt road. One of the men jerked her arm and pushed her to keep walking.

Oh, why hadn't she listened to Chase and backed off? Because her stupid pride got in the way. Whenever confronted she became riled. She honestly thought she'd shown her strength and won the battle by not backing down.

A verse in Matthew six played in her head. "Don't be anxious. Don't be anxious." They'd talked about how fear is the opposite of faith in Mrs. Perkin's class. If she ever needed faith, she could use a huge dose of it now. *Put on the armor—the breastplate of truth and the sword of His word. God's right here with me.*

The trail curved to the right. They continued to follow it until a small, cedar-planked cabin came into view. A motorcycle leaned on its kickstand near the entrance. Not what she expected Arthur Archer to ride.

The man behind her gave her a shove in the kidneys. "Keep going."

Bailey hadn't realized she'd stopped.

The door to the cabin opened and a young man leaned against the jamb.

"You must be Bailey Matteson. Now, what's this about wanting a lock of my hair? Not as a memento, I gather."

"Not for my hope chest, I assure you, A.A."

He pressed his hand to his heart. "I'm crushed. Though I already have a rather sexy wife as it is." He scowled at her with a snicker before shifting his attention to his underlings. "Bring her inside."

The décor screamed hunting cabin. The underside of the cedar planks outside covered the walls. A rock fireplace dominated the room with a small Pullman kitchen off to the corner, housing a dormitory-sized refrigerator, a microwave, and a burner plate. Next to it, a two-chair

275

dinette hugged the wall. Two leather sofas draped with woven Mexican blankets flanked the fireplace and mounted deer antlers decorated the walls. In the other corner, a stuffed bobcat froze in a growling pose with one paw extended. At first glance, it made her jump.

A.A. laughed. "My dad bagged that when he turned sixteen. We named it Bob."

She glared into his face. "How original."

His smile disappeared, and his eyes narrowed. "Have a seat."

Bailey took stock of her surroundings as she obeyed. The bodyguards stood stationed like tin soldiers around the room, blocking the door and both windows. Two doors off to the right cracked open far enough for her to discern that they led to a bathroom and a bedroom.

"If you're thinking of escaping, I'd rethink it." A.A. lowered himself onto the sofa opposite of her and draped his hand across the top. "All I want to do is have nice chat."

She wanted to believe him, but her mind stayed on high alert. She breathed deeply to steady her heartbeat. Don't be anxious. "Okay." She sat back, hoping to convey confidence.

"What exactly do you hope to gain by obtaining a sample of my hair?"

"Paternity proof that your father had a son several years before you were born."

A.A. reared back and guffawed. The goons chimed in, probably out of loyalty. Bailey doubted they had a clue what this was all about.

After the din died down, A.A. wiped his eye. "Mac, get her some water. Me, too."

One of the men rocked forward on his feet and stomped over to the refrigerator. Its hinges squeaked when he opened it and pulled out two plastic bottles. He waddled back to the sofas with them.

Bailey reached out to retrieve hers. She twisted off the cap and wiped the rim with a corner of her blouse. "Thanks. Now can I be let in on the joke?"

A.A. chugged half the bottle then set it on the floor. "In a minute." He motioned for the other men to leave.

Why? What did he plan to do? Surely not shoot her or something. She took in his small frame and stature. Clean nails, expensive shirt, and trousers. Weak chin. She doubted he had the guts. The muscles in her shoulders eased, only a tad.

After his underlings shuffled outside and closed the door, he leaned forward, his hand on his knee. "I'm gonna let you in on a family secret, Ms. Matteson. But I need assurance it will stay that way. So here are your choices." He held up a finger. "You can promise to keep it, which as a Christian woman of integrity from good bloodlines I believe you will."

"Of course, I will." She straightened her backbone.

"Good decision. In that case, I see no need to discuss the other option, which is good." He scowled. "You don't do nature, do you? Kill and skin for your supper? Bet you've never baited a hook with a worm either, correct?"

"Have you?" She pressed her lips together and narrowed her eyes.

"This is my family's hunting cabin."

Well, true. She sucked in a breath. Back it down, Bailey.

He scooted forward a bit more and cupped one hand to his mouth. "Let's make a deal. You keep quiet and I will assure that you make it out of the woods."

"Deal. So, what's the big secret, A.A.?" She reached to take a gulp from her bottled drink, partly to appear nonchalant, but more to send the anxiousness lodged in her throat back down.

An evil twinkle gleamed in his eyes. He whispered the response. "I'm adopted."

Bailey sputtered her water.

He roared back in laughter again then shut it off as quickly as the humor had erupted. His face grew serious. He flipped open a knife blade.

Bailey jolted.

"Antsy, are we?" He smirked and proceeded to clean his fingernails. "And gullible."

Her blood boiled. Of all the nerve. Cocky little man with the big family name. She breathed heavily through her nostrils and counted to ten.

He pocketed the knife and slapped his knee with a vicious grin. "I'm kidding you." He rose and walked forward, towering over her.

Bailey remained stiff, refusing to let him get her goat this time.

He shrugged and sat next to her. "I'm not adopted. I came later after dad married the girl his father had handpicked."

"Not my Aunt Edwina."

"Hardly. My grandpa thought my daddy too young at eighteen. He wanted him to graduate, play football for UT, and make himself known to the senators and reps in Austin. Feather the political nest, so to speak."

"A teenage wife and baby wouldn't have been beneficial."

"No, it wouldn't have. It'd also show lack of moral restraint. Plus, let's just say your aunt wasn't exactly the type of gal grandpa would have chosen to bear his heir."

Bailey could see that. Though her grandparents had wealth, her mother Dupree's Louisiana family had been Catholic immigrants. The Holston clan, on the other hand, were true-blooded Texians who fought for the state's independence. Would that not have counted as clout?

"Did your dad love her?"

"Have you seen pictures of her? She could turn a head or two." His eyes scanned her like a package on the grocery belt. "You resemble her a bit."

Bailey let off a nervous snicker. "Is that a roundabout compliment?"

A.A. stood. "Take it however you wish." He glared down at her. "If you pursue this, Ms. Matteson, I will

279

spread your family through the mud. Say she got pregnant by another guy and tricked my dad. Your grandparents were behind the whole thing and tried to bribe our family out of money. Think of your mother's social standing. Think of your dad's business contacts and connections." He fluttered his hands like a bird escaping. "Bye-bye. It'll ruin him. And of course, they could always have an accident, like your grandparents did."

Bailey gasped.

He whistled through his teeth and his underlings appeared like obedient hounds. He motioned to the men. "Our little conversation with this lady is over, men. Let's go."

Bailey rose.

He pointed a finger at her and one of the gorilla-men pushed her shoulders down until her knees buckled and her behind landed back onto the couch.

"Not you, sweetheart." A.A. flashed a sinister smile and chugged the rest of his water. Then he spit in it. He crunched the plastic with one hand and tossed it into the corner. "There's your DNA sample, sweetie. But, remember what I said."

He pivoted to walk out of the cabin. Bailey twisted around. "Wait. You said…"

"You'll be fine."

"Where is my purse?"

"It'll be returned to you. Later." The goons followed him to the front door, the only exit as far as Bailey could surmise.

"Are you planning on leaving me here alone?" Her voice squeaked, and she hated it because it revealed her growing fear.

He stopped at the threshold. "Civilization is about five miles down the road. But it'll be dark by the time you try to reach it, so if I were you, I'd sleep here and head out in the morning. Bob's kin still lurk around here." His head pointed in the direction of the taxidermy statue. "Coyotes, too. And wild boar. Not to mention it's skunk mating season." He pinched his nose.

"Thanks." She glared a hole into his smirk face.

"There is a chicken salad sandwich, an apple turnover, and another bottle of water in the fridge, courtesy of the local convenience store you passed on the way here." He snapped his fingers. "That's right, you couldn't see it could you?" He let off a cackly laugh. "Nighty-night."

The door slammed, and she heard a bolt lock slip into place before she could rush to it. A few minutes later the motorcycle and car engines revved. Their tires crackled on the gravel, the sound growing fainter.

Bailey plopped back onto the couch with her hands intertwined between her knees. The soft late afternoon sunlight filtered through the shuttered windows. Winter darkness settled quickly in the woods.

Her stomach growled, reminding her she never had any lunch. Fighting back tears, she slapped her thighs and strolled to the little fridge. Inside, metal shelves greeted her with the sandwich and turnover the only items on them. In the doorway sat another bottle of water, just as he'd said.

Very well. Sandwich and the rest of her bottled water tonight. The apple turnover and the second bottle in the morning. Yummy.

Think positive. He didn't mean you harm. Only showing his teeth in a low growl. Five miles would be an easy trek. She went to the gym regularly and jogged. It would be like an hour on the treadmill.

Right.

She sat back down and prayed for peace, strength, and discernment. In fact, she had a really good talk with the Lord, one she had been needing. She asked forgiveness for her stubborn pride, which had blocked her reason and probably His Spirit. She recalled scripture and sought His guidance. Then sat in the stillness and listened for His response. It came in a loosening of her muscles and the soft sound of crickets outside lulling her.

A half-hour later, she opened her eyes and gasped. The room lay enveloped in total darkness. Instinctively, she reached to flick on a lamp. Nothing. She felt and found it had no bulb. *Oh, great. Bet he did that on purpose.*

Bailey felt the walls near the doors. Cold, dry. Two light switches produced no results either. The snake purposely left her in the dark… in February… in a hunting cabin. The drop in temperature caused a shiver to run through her body. Warmth, she needed to find warmth.

She went over to the fireplace and ran her hand across

the mantle. Her fingers hit cardboard and it rattled. She felt the rectangle. Matches. *Thank you, Lord.* She fumbled the box open and struck one. Nothing emerged except the faint smell of sulfur. No telling how old these were. She tried again and spark flicked. The end of the stick sizzled and lit. She lowered the match to the opening of the fireplace. There lay kindling, newspaper and four logs ready for use.

At least, A.A. provided a means of heat. She knelt and aimed the match to the paper. In a second, it caught, and a small flicker of a blue-yellow flame began to etch the edge of the newsprint in black then curl it. A bluish glow danced over the paper as it spread to the kindling. Bailey blew on it softly to encourage the fire to build. The edges turned red and crackled the wood as smoke licked the logs. She kept blowing steady, long breaths. Within a few minutes, a blaze of warmth and light filled the room.

Saying a prayer of thanks, she snatched one of the blankets from the couch, wrapped it around her shoulders and sat cross-legged on the hearth as she chomped down her meal.

Now, Lord, if it isn't asking too much, let the plumbing work.

Chapter 30

With food in her stomach, Bailey thought about her situation as she tried to keep calm and logical. She'd never returned to work. Her boss knew she wouldn't skip out without notifying him. Responsibility had made five stars on her last evaluation. What would he have done? Called her cell phone most likely. Of course, there would be no answer, Unless A.A. had someone answer and make up a story saying she got food poisoning or something.

She rolled her eyes. Let's hope not. So, her boss would get no answer. What then? Her parents were her next of kin contact in her employee file. He'd call them.

She slapped her forehead. Great. By now they'd be in a frantic state. Wait. Which would mean they would call Chase, right? They'd assume she'd been threatened again. Or they'd call Shannon and she'd call Chase.

A grin slid across her face. By morning, the smart

detective and his cavalry would ride over the hill and swoop down to rescue her. With that thought in her mind, she curled up on the couch and closed her eyes, lulled by the crackling wood in the fireplace.

Bailey awoke to birdsong. Not Chase hammering at the door. Oh, well. Even someone like him would need more time to figure out where she had been taken. She'd better head out and meet him halfway, then.

She unwound herself from the blankets and lowered her feet to the floor. Her back complained. Not the most comfortable couch in the world, but the fire crackled most of the night and kept her warm. Besides, she doubted the bed would have been less lumpy. The plumbing did work; however, there appeared to be no hot water heater. Men— they loved to rough it. She thanked God at least a sink and toilet existed inside the cabin. Slipping on her shoes, after shaking them for scorpions, Bailey grabbed her pastry and water and went to the door. She pulled. Wait, they locked it. How on earth did they expect her…?

She spun around the room. The windows on either side of the fireplace were shuttered from the outside. She darted into the bedroom. Boards covered its window, too, which left the tiny one over the toilet in the bathroom. She knelt on the commode lid and yanked. After a few tugs, the wood gave way, and it inched open. It took several more shoves to slide the pane up a few more inches.

Could she fit through? Did she have a choice? Bailey pressed the screen and it popped out, landing on the ground below. Satisfied she had an exit, she went back into the living room and ate a few bites of her turnover for fortitude. The rest she'd save for the hike. She wrapped it back in the cellophane and shoved it in her pocket.

Bailey yanked one of the blankets from the couch to wrap around her for warmth as she started on the five-mile trek. The early morning February chill would be a bit much for her outfit, though her pants were woolen. She justified it as not exactly stealing. When A.A. returned her purse, she'd return his bedcover.

She tossed the water bottle and wadded blanket through the opening, and then lifted one leg out the ledge. Half twisting her body, she eased herself through, clinging to the edge as she lifted her other leg out and then let go, dropping to the prairie floor.

Brushing off her pants, Bailey reached for the bottle of water, swung the blanket around her like a poncho, and began to briskly walk. Five miles. That should take her about an hour or so. Not bad. With renewed spirits, she traipsed down the path into the rising sun as its rays seeped through the trees.

As she walked, Bailey once again went over the events in her head, intent on remaining objective and logical. Fear only clouded her mind. Besides, she had escaped and had food and water. The sun dawned on a fine day. God walked with her. *Keep telling yourself that.*

She replayed last night in her mind. If A.A. told the truth, and she assumed he did, then they admitted Edwin is their heir. Did Edwina ever pressure them to make that claim? Edwina could tell her, but right now she refused to communicate.

Whatever had happened between them, Edwina obviously decided Arthur didn't make a good candidate for Father of the Year. Edwin didn't care to have a relationship with either of his parents. Perhaps Bailey should forget it and not pursue this anymore?

She stopped in the middle of the path.

No, now it had become personal. A.A. did kidnap her or have his thugs do it. That meant he could go to jail, right? Chase's speech echoed in her head. Criminal motive. Criminal intent. Well, now the Archers crossed the line into a criminal act. Her blood began to heat as she thought about how he'd treated her. Oh, she needed to bring him down.

Then a chill ran through her. His snide remark ricocheted through her mind like a marble clunking down a stairwell. An accident like her grandparents? She pulled the blanket tighter around her.

Did he mean the Archer family killed them to send Edwina a warning? Could it be true? Had Arthur been the university student the convenient clerk later recanted he'd served?

Of course, and they paid the guy off, didn't they? And Edwina knew it. That's why she ran away again!

Oh, my heavens.

Her hands shook. The gold-toothed thug's warning blared in her brain. Forget what happened in 1968. That had to be it.

The small pieces of baked apple clunked around in her gut like gym shoes in the dryer. She held her hand to her mouth, willing them to not lurch into her throat. She wobbled to a tree stump and sat, her breath shaky and shallow. Her eyes darted frantically around her, searching for the truth. And maybe the sound of policemen headed her way. That would be great timing, Lord.

No such luck. She calmed her spinning mind with a few deep breaths, took a swig of water and proceeded to walk again. Getting to civilization had to remain her priority right now. Stay focused. Don't panic.

After a few more steps her logical, accounting brain kicked in again. No, no. The Archers would never admit they had been involved in the deaths of her grandparents. A.A. simply tried to scare her into staying quiet.

But he had done something else. He'd made her promise, and Mattesons always kept their word. He knew that.... *a Christian woman of integrity from good bloodlines.*

She kicked a small rock out of the way. Arggh. A.A. Jr and his father trapped her with ethics, proving they had none.

If she pressed charges, they'd press down on her family. But what would she tell Chase when he found her?

289

Surely, he'd put it all together.

But not with her help. He'd told her to let him do his job then by golly she would. She whispered to herself under her breath. "Forget the Archer family. Concentrate on your own."

Which meant getting everyone to the reunion so they could mend fences. A part of her still wanted those Archers to squirm. Oh, how she'd love to topple their kingdom with one piece of viable evidence of their treachery. It would be like removing the right block in the Jenga game.

She halted again. She'd had it. And she'd left it in the cabin. The bottle. Oh, good gravy. How could she have not remembered to bring it?

Should she go back and retrieve it? Prove he'd been the one there in the cabin with her? No longer her word against his?

Wait a minute. She thought for a moment. Why would he be that stupid?

She shook her head. No, no, no. She'd not fall for another trap. Why else would he leave his spittle in a bottle?

Besides, if she went back, she'd have to break in. That would be illegal. She didn't know how much jail time she'd get for trespassing, but one thing for sure. She didn't want to find out. Talk about devastating her parent's reputation!

She took a long gulp from her water bottle and headed out once more. She walked, prayed, sang, and talked to critters as she tossed them pieces of apple turnover… and walked some more. At last, she saw wires looped from poles like garland and the dirt path end at asphalt. Down the road to the left, a bait shop sat with two gas pumps. It looked open. With a spring in her stride, Bailey sprinted toward the store.

The old man who ran the bait shop knew the cabin and the family.

"A.A. played a mean trick on me. He locked me in his cabin. I guess he got angry because, well, I wouldn't..." Bailey lowered her head. *Okay, Lord not exactly a lie. Only an innuendo...*

The clerk cleared his throat. "That boy should've been walloped a long time ago. The skunk always had a wild streak, though his pappy tried to hide it with good clothes and fancy cars. Heh, heh." He winked. "Hear he's running for office."

Bailey leaned on the counter. "Yes. Comptroller. If he wins."

He glanced her over. "Who do you want me to call? Your parents, the cops, or the press?"

She chuckled. "Actually, my boss has probably called my parents since I didn't show up for work. They have most likely called the police."

"Then you better call your mother."

"Actually, I think I'll call my best friend who lives in

my apartment complex. She'll be worried sick by now when she notices my car isn't in my parking spot. I'll tell her to call my folks."

He shoved the old-fashioned phone across the countertop. "Don't get good cell coverage out here. But Ma Bell still services us just fine."

Bailey lifted the receiver. "I'm afraid I don't have any money to pay for the call. He stole my purse."

The man swatted it away. "Never you mind about that. But don't talk too long."

"Right." She punched in the number to Shannon's phone. A wall clock, advertising a popular soda, read eight-fifteen.

"Hello?"

"Shannon, it's Bailey."

A squeal blasted into her ear. "Oh my gosh. Where are you? We've all been worried sick."

Bailey pointed to the receiver and mouthed *I told you so* to the clerk, who chuckled and wagged his head.

"Look I'll explain everything. Right now, please call Mom and Dad and tell them I'm stranded at a gas station and bait shop on…" She cupped her hand over the receiver. "What road is this?"

He motioned for her to hand him the phone. When she did, his Texas twang became even friendlier. "Hello. This is Bud Avery. I'm the proprietor of Bud's Bait and Beer out on FM 3351 fifteen miles south of Kendalia. Where are you?"

Bailey could hear Shannon's shrill, excited voice telling him she lived a few miles northwest of San Antonio.

"You're about forty minutes out. I'll keep your friend safe and warm until you or her parents get here. Write down this number in case y'all get lost."

He parroted off his phone number and hung up. "She's on her way. Now, how about a cup of coffee and a hot, fresh from the microwave sausage biscuit, on the house?"

Bailey could've hugged him.

At nine-thirty, Shannon's car pulled up and ran over the rubber wire, causing it to ding inside the bait shop. "That must be her."

Mr. Avery had spent the time keeping Bailey entertained with one tall tale after another as they sipped fresh coffee and listened to country music in the background on an old radio. Bailey rose off the stool from behind the counter and walked out into the winter sunshine.

Shannon bolted from the driver's side. Bailey waved and quickened her step to greet her. Then she halted. From the passenger side emerged Chase. He sauntered over to her. "Good morning. Have a fun evening?" His voice held a sarcastic tone but his eyes revealed concern.

"Not exactly." Her hand immediately flew to smooth her hair, and she hated herself for it.

"Want to tell me what happened?"

"Well, um…"

Shannon rushed toward her and pulled her into a bear hug. The aroma of her citrusy body-splash filled Bailey's nose.

She pulled back and stared into Bailey's face. "I've been frantic with worry. What on earth are you doing all the way out here?"

Bailey passed glances between the two of them. "Long story. I have no purse, no phone. Can I borrow five dollars to pay for the phone call, coffee, and this sweet gentleman's hospitality?" She twisted to point to the entry to the bait shop.

Mr. Avery tipped an imaginary hat to them with his fingers.

"I've got it." Chase reached into his back pocket and pulled out his wallet. He meandered over to the man, shook his hand, and presented the cash, which Mr. Avery refused.

Shannon still fussed. "Bailey, are you sure you're okay?"

Chase turned back toward them. "Yeah, do you need to go to the hospital or anything?"

"No, I'm fine really. They treated me quite well."

He strode to her side. "They?"

"A.A. Jr. and his, um, employees. They brought me out here."

"By force?" He scanned the area, his eyes shooting fire.

"Not quite. And not here, per se. About five miles that

way into the woods to a hunting cabin." She pointed up the road.

"For what purpose?" He squinted at her, and she didn't suspect it to be because of the bright sun. His jaw worked as he waited for her answer.

"Nothing heinous, Chase. I'll explain everything as we ride. But for now, I need to call my boss and—"

"I already spoke to him and told him you were called out of town on a family emergency." Shannon cocked her head. "That's wasn't a lie, exactly, right?"

Chase and Bailey both wagged their heads.

"Whatever." She pointed to the car doors. "Front seat or back?"

Bailey got in the back seat of the car. "This way I can stretch out."

The detective poked his head in. "You sure you're all right...?"

"I am. Truly. Only not as fresh as a daisy. The cabin had no hot water, so I couldn't wash up. You may wish to sit up front."

Chase held up a finger. "I'll be back in a minute. Shannon, coffee?"

"That'd be great, with a little creamer. And a pastry if they have it." She leaned into the car. "You?"

"I'm good. I've had some."

"Okay. If you're certain..."

She nodded and he backed away, walking to the store with his hands shoved into his pockets.

295

"You're not mad at me for asking him to tag along, are you?"

She smiled. "No, not at all. It's good to see you both."

He came out a few minutes later carrying two to-go cups and a small sack. He distributed the breakfast between him and Shannon. He also produced a small pack of waterless wipes. "For your hands and face, Bailey." He pointed to his own cheek. "You have a smudge."

"Thanks." She ripped open the seal.

He crawled in the back seat. "This way I can do the recording thing. You don't mind playing chauffeur, right, Shannon?"

"Nope."

Bailey scooted over to give him room and clicked her belt.

"This is from your new friend." He held up a postcard with a photo of a bobcat on it.

Bailey took it and laughed. "I'll keep it always." She shifted her focus between the two perplexed faces in the car. "Guess I better explain."

Shannon started the engine. "Yes, you better."

She spent the next thirty minutes relaying what had happened to her, or tried to, in between the assault of queries the two tossed her. When she finished, she stared at the floor mat.

Chase pivoted in his seat to face her. "Are you sure you don't want to press charges?"

"No. They didn't really force me. More like persuaded

me quite well, and though they left me stranded, they provided food, water, a fire…"

"Okay. You're call. If I can't persuade you otherwise." He crossed his arms and breathed through his nose as he clicked off the recorder app.

Bailey let out a nervous laugh. "You're really irritated, aren't you?"

"Yes, ma'am, I am." He shoved his finger into her face. "You got yourself into this mess. You disobeyed my orders."

"Orders?" Bailey felt her face heat… again. Oh, how this man could push her buttons. She jerked around as much as she could, restrained by the seat belt, and stared him down. "What gives you the right to order me to do anything?"

His nostrils flared, but he held his tongue.

Bailey's heart pounded, and not because of his deep blue eyes. "Why are you here anyway?"

"Strictly professional." His jaw twitched, again but his breathing eased.

Shannon craned to peer in the rearview mirror as she drove. "I called him. First, I noticed your car was missing. You didn't answer the ten messages I left on your cell, and then your parents phoned about six this morning in a panic."

"They'd already phoned me last night. So, I put out an all-points bulletin after convincing my chief your uncharacteristic disappearance may be of a sinister nature.

About five-thirty this morning, a patrol officer located your car parked in an alley in the warehouse district by the railroad tracks. Empty, of course. It's being dusted for prints."

"But of course, you won't find any." Bailey puffed a long breath. "I should have known A.A. wouldn't leave it sitting in front of his campaign headquarters. My keys were in my purse, so I guess he had one of his goons move it." A flash of iciness shot across her heart. "You don't think they trashed my place again? Bower?"

Chase lowered his chin to meet her gaze, the way a boss glares at a truant employee. "I already have an officer stationed there. Protocol."

His sudden formality irked her further. Why did he annoy her so much? What did she want? For him to draw her into his arms and tell her he'd been worried sick?

"But Mr. Avery told Shannon I was alive and well, so?"

Chase broke eye contact. "I needed to get your statement and thought you might want to be spared the police interrogation routine. Plus, I didn't think it wise for Shannon to come to your rescue alone."

His emphasis on the word alone cut into her.

He locked eyes with her. "And I felt certain you'd want to press charges."

"I don't. I told you that. I got my information." She pivoted back around to stare out the front windshield.

Shannon gasped. "The DNA?"

"Yeah, he gave it to me."

"Where is it?" Chase's eyes searched around her.

"I left it at the cabin. It felt like another trap. I'd already been snared once."

His trained demeanor evaporated. The wrinkles on his brow increased and his eyes became warm. "He didn't physically harm you in any way? Honest?"

She pressed three fingers on his arm. "No, none of them did."

He audibly sighed his relief.

Maybe he did care. Bailey glanced at Shannon who winked in the rearview mirror.

They rode in silence for several minutes. The buildings of San Antonio loomed in the purplish distance. As she pulled off the highway onto the road that headed to their once-small town, Shannon sang out, "Home sweet home."

"I want to soak in a hot bubble bath for at least an hour." Bailey laid her head against the window.

"After you do, please call me. We need to talk."

Bailey swiveled to face him and saw his expression held a serious edge.

"What about? I told you I don't want to file a complaint."

He sighed and leaned toward her. "I get that. Though I don't approve and I seriously hope you will reconsider."

She started to open her mouth to object, but he placed his finger on her lips, indicating her to hush. "I may have some other news for you."

She sat upright. "Tell me."

He gently tugged her hair. "After you no longer smell like a campfire."

Bailey stared at him. Don't do it. Don't... her heart twitched.

He did it. The wink.

Chapter 31

Chase had ruined her desire to soak. What information did he have to share with her? Her mind bounced like a pinball against the levers. With a groan, she slid down into the water and soaked her hair in the vanilla scented bubbles. She had to find out today or she'd be pacing a rut in the carpet.

Bailey blew dry her hair, applied a touch of eye makeup, and pulled on fresh jeans and a soft, downy sweater. Then she dialed Chase's cell phone number.

"That didn't take long."

"Can you tell me over the phone? Or do you need to come by?" In general, good news could be shared by voice, text or any other way. Usually, people wanted to deliver bad news in person.

"Are you decent? Because I'm sitting in your parking lot."

"Seriously?"

He chuckled. "I knew you couldn't wait. You are an information junkie, Bailey Matteson."

"Guilty as charged."

She heard his car door close. "I'm on my way. Unless you need more time…"

"My hand is already on the front door knob waiting for your knock."

His laugh echoed through her speaker. Within a minute the tapping of knuckles sounded on the door.

Bailey reached to jerk it open then hesitated. The last time she thought she knew who stood there had proved disastrous. She rose on tiptoe to peek through the peephole.

An eyeball glared back at her, and she squealed.

His voice came through the metal. "It's Chase. I promise."

She sucked in her breath and yanked the entry open. "Ha. ha."

Chase walked in. "Glad to see you checked. You passed the test." He swiveled his torso. "Where do you want me?"

She folded her arms. "Cocky, aren't we?"

His cheeks blushed. "I, um I meant—"

"I know." She flashed him a snarky grin. "Two points for me. Since we seem to keep slipping back into the who last razzed who game." She motioned for him to sit in the living room. He took the side chair.

"We do seem to keep doing it, don't we? Maybe it's our thing? Normally I am a pretty serious, cut and dry type of guy. Ask any of my colleagues."

"Or one of your dates?" Bailey winked at him this time.

He dipped his finger on his tongue and made a slash mark in the air.

She eased onto the sofa and curled her legs under her. "Okay, Mr. Cut and Dry. You said you had information pertaining to my case."

He eyed her as he pulled his cell phone from his pocket. "Yes, ma'am. Actually, it is what I don't have that I wanted to share. While you were running around collecting DNA samples, I let my fingers do the walking and put in some calls." He punched up his notes.

"And...?"

He set his phone aside. "Before I tell you, there is something else I must say, Bailey. I have blurred the lines, again. For that, I apologize. You are my client first and foremost, and my interest, above all else, is in your safety. That's my job. I've let my personal feelings get in the way."

She blinked. A small part—no, a pretty large part—of her liked that she had him flustered for a change, but she had no idea what she'd done to put him in such a state. She tilted her head as he stood and paced.

"I'm a police officer, and we are trained to remain neutral. Treat every citizen the same no matter how they look, act, or smell. Trouble is, Bailey Matteson..." His Adam's apple bobbed. "... you look and smell amazing."

She pressed her hand to her cheek to thwart the blush she knew appeared on it. "Thank you?"

He returned to his chair. "Look, I'll be honest. I don't have that much information to share with you. I only wanted to make sure you were all right. Sometimes it takes a while for it all to soak in."

"No pun intended?" She motioned to the bathroom down the hall.

He rolled his eyes. Then he scooted forward in his chair and clasped both of his hands. "I, um, do have one more question."

"Yes?"

He took in a swallow. "I, um, I know you said you are still getting over losing your fiancé several years ago, and that you haven't dated anyone since then. Unless you count the fiasco with me last spring, which I hope you won't."

"So…?" Why did he want to talk about Jacob? He started to perturb her.

"Huh?"

"You were saying?"

"Right. Yes. So, perhaps, um, I mean, it might be time to, I mean after this case is closed…"

Bailey leaned back and laughed. In a Southern drawl that mimicked Scarlet O'Hara, she fanned herself. "Why Detective Montgomery, I do declare. Are you asking me out on a date?"

He cocked his head. "And not doing a great job at it. I'd understand if you turned me down."

She felt the familiar coldness grip her heart. The you-don't-want-to-be-hurt-ever-again warning bell clanked against her chest wall. She gazed into his eyes and saw sincerity and schoolboy nervousness. Her smile faded. The man deserved to know the truth.

"I really like you. You get me, possibly because of how we were raised. You are also moral, have a deep faith and are Southern gentlemen, all of which are a rarity these days. And you do make me laugh, which I appreciate because it does calm my anxieties."

"Thank you. I try. But…?"

"But, honestly, the thought of dating again freaks me out."

His shoulder slumped, which told Bailey she'd wounded his male pride. She wanted to reach across and stroke his arm but refrained thinking it might encourage him again. "Chase. I'm sorry. It's not personal, trust me."

"Very well. I understand."

"I hope you do." She felt her heart twist. "Look. I cherish you as a life-long friend and confidante. If I sent wrong signals by playing the damsel in distress…"

He held up his hand. "We may banter, but you have never, ever played games, which by the way, is to me a rarity these days. Most girls, in my experience, seem to come with an agenda."

"I could say that it works both ways. But, I've never thought it of you either."

His cheeks became ruddy. He shifted in the chair.

"Well, Bailey Matteson, I do have an agenda, which is to make sure you are not a damsel in distress again. So, back to the matter at hand." He retrieved his phone and scrolled through his notes.

A relief lifted from her chest. The room took on a freshness as if a window had been opened and a lot of stale air had escaped. She hoped he felt the same.

He spoke, still focusing on his phone screen. "Everywhere I searched, every rock I peeked under, I expected to find a clue linking the Archer family. None existed. Now we know why. I don't think either A.A. or his dad broke in here, stole your laptop, trashed the place, or hurt Bower."

"You are sure?"

"Yes, I am. Which means we are back to square one."

"Then why did he kidnap me?'

"So, you admit it." He eyed her like a school teacher catching a student cheating.

"I never denied it. I simply do not wish to pursue it."

"Right. To answer your question, you kicked him in the shin, so to speak. And then threatened to tell everyone in order to embarrass him if he didn't do what you asked. Seriously, Bailey. How did you think he'd react?"

He had a point.

He scoffed and pocketed his phone.

Wait, he gave up awfully quickly. A thought flashed across her brain, one she didn't want to think. Was Chase Montgomery in the Archer back pocket, too?

"You are not pursuing this case now?"

"I told you, I do have another suspicion. Though I am not sure where it will lead at this point. So, it's on the back burner as far as I am concerned."

She searched his face for deception. If he hid it, he did it well. And she'd always known him to be upfront about things. She decided she'd been silly to even consider it.

"But, what should I do about my Aunt Edwina? They have muddied her name. She has a right…"

"Which she never chose to exercise. Nor did Edwin. You have to ask yourself why, Bailey. Or you could simply ask her next month when you see her."

"Yeah, about that. She won't respond to me or Mom now, so I think she changed her mind. And if we do go, Uncle Elliot wants to tag along, so…"

"So, you don't need me."

Did a smidgen of hurt show in his face? Bailey held out her hands. "It seems Elliott and Edwina were tight as kids. She understood him when the other brothers only teased him. He truly misses her."

Chase's facial muscles relaxed. "I hope you all get to go, then. I'll pray for safe travel and a good reunion. And, happy birthday by the way. That's coming up, too, isn't it?"

His comment warmed her on the inside. He truly was a decent guy. "Thanks. It is. But with all the reunion planning, I don't want a big deal made of it. Thirty-one is sort of a non-event anyway."

"No social gathering, then? Or a soiree on the lawn

with stringed orchestra?"

She rolled her eyes. "Absolutely not."

They sat in silence for a few minutes. Then Bailey gazed into his eyes. "Did you have anything else to tell me?"

"Not yet." He pocketed his phone. "I want to get more facts first. It wouldn't be fair to you to…" He stopped. "If and when I have something more solid, then I'll contact you."

He rose and extended his hand for her to shake.

She stood and gave him hers. Then she laid her other hand on top of his. "I'd like to be casual friends, if that's all right?"

"Define casual."

"Go to dinner, see a movie or concert, jog together."

A smirk grew on his lips. "Tennis at the club?"

"Oh, please no. Tongues would wag."

He chuckled. "True. Our mothers would start planning when to have the engagement party there."

They let out a mutual groan.

Chase strolled to her door. "I want you to do me a favor, though. And I am serious about asking it."

She leaned a shoulder against the wall. "Okay?"

"Let me do the snooping. Give me a month or so. You plan your family get-together, but no more delving into the past. Especially about the wreck."

"You think the accident is the catalyst, don't you? Even if you agree A.A.'s almost admittance is false."

He pointed his finger at her nose. "No comment. I'll keep an extra patrol around your complex for a few weeks just in case, but I'm confident if you stop meddling the threats will stop."

She opened her mouth to object, then closed it. "Right."

"Even so, bolt your door. Small town or not, you are a single woman living alone. And the big city is encroaching, which means the crime scum seeps in with it."

"Yes, officer."

With a head nod, he left.

She flipped the bolt. Safe and secure. No one allowed inside.

Same as her heart.

February fourteenth arrived. She, Jessica, and Shannon shared sparkling grape juice, a heart-shaped box of chocolates, and a sappy romantic classic on DVD for Valentine's. Jayden had sent Shannon a dozen red roses, and two extra.

"'One for each of her friends who keep her from getting lonely.' That's what his note read." She held up the card.

"What else did it say, Shan?" Jessica wiggled her eyebrows as she sniffed the bloom at the end of the long stem. "We want to live vicariously."

"Forget it."

"Nothing from Chase, Bailey? Not a single rose or even a candy bar?" They both turned to her for an answer.

She knitted her brow. "Why would there be?"

Shannon groaned. "Because the guy is into you, knucklehead."

"He's simply a friend. That's all. And I haven't heard from him in ten days, so there."

Jessica nudged Shannon. "She's counting the days."

Bailey shoved her hands to her hips. "I am not. Start up the movie and hush."

No way was she letting on about her mild disappointment that she didn't at least get a text. She had almost sent him one but decided that might falsely encourage him. Instead, she posted a general one on Instagram and sent e-cards to her new relatives, including one to Edwina's hotel email.

Two days later, when she checked her email after work, she found an e postcard in her inbox It showed the skyline of Amarillo on the front. She opened it on her phone and read as she climbed the stairs to her floor.

Quit trying to contact me. Tell my sister the same. I cut off all communication for a reason. EJH

She propped against the stairwell wall and read it again. Why?

Ugh. She dragged herself up the stairs. Elliott would be so disappointed. So would her mom. Though initially against the whole idea, lately, it came up in each conversation. Sure, Edwina danced to a different beat, and yes, perhaps her gypsy lifestyle had been frowned upon by her blueblood family, but...

Bailey crouched on the top of the stairs and put her chin in her hands. She respected Edwina's wishes, but something told her the refusal to be part of the family went deeper. There was something she didn't want to be revealed. But what?

Chapter 32

That Sunday after dinner, Bailey retrieved the postcard and showed it to her mom.

"Doesn't surprise me." Her mother handed it back to her without expression. But Bailey saw her jaw twitch.

"I still think we should go."

Her mother wiped the counter in tight circles. "I can't understand why. She'll only refuse to see us, and we will have driven all that way for nothing. Forget it."

"But, Mom."

She spun around. "No."

Bailey rocked back. She hadn't heard that tone since she'd asked to stay out all night after prom her sophomore year—except when her mother scolded the dog for piddling on her rugs. If she'd had a tail, Bailey might have tucked it under.

Her mother sighed and leaned against the granite top.

"Honey, think of Elliott. You and I can stand disappointment, but he would be devastated. It would be cruel."

Bailey traced her finger over one of the stone's embedded patterns. "You're right. Sorry. I am being selfish."

"Yes, you are." She dried her hands. "I appreciate your wanting to reunite us all, but four out of five isn't bad, my dear." She walked closer and cupped her hands under Bailey's chin. "I hope you aren't setting your expectations too high."

"I'm afraid I am. I want it to be a like a family reunion on steroids."

Her mother laughed. "Let's settle for mildly cheerful and no one getting drunk."

"Oh, Mom."

They walked arm-in-arm through the dining room. "By the way, Mom. Can I borrow the albums again? I thought it might be fun to pick a few pictures and blow them up so we can place them around the yard on sticks, sort of like for sale signs the realtors use. And I want to glue some to gold leaves and hang them from the live oaks. Get it? Family tree?"

"Cute idea, Bailey. Can I help with the cost?"

"Not at all. I can do it all on my computer and printer."

Her mother clucked. "What an age we live in. Of course, you may have them. Just be careful not to spill anything on them."

Bailey huffed into her bangs. "I'm not ten anymore."

"I know. Pity." Her mom shrugged and walked into the den for their video chat with Travis and clan.

As well as being her birthday, mid-March meant a month until yearly and quarterly taxes were due. For an accountant with a successful fast food joint, that translated into late nights, little sleep, and eating all the wrong things. Especially when friends she hadn't heard from in months kept calling her for advice as they filled in their forms.

Perhaps aborting the excursion to Amarillo had been a good thing. Each night as Bailey dragged up the stairs and unlocked her door, the photo albums beckoned. Her brain refused to stare at anything other than the inside of her eyelids. May tenth lay eight weeks away. Plenty of time.

She had seen Chase at church one time. He waved from across the meeting hall as Marsha Eastwood nestled her hand in the crook of his elbow while she chatted with a group of people.

"Guess they are an item?" Jessica nudged her with her elbow.

"I don't see it, do you, Bailey?" Shannon crinkled her nose. "Marsha is too… flighty."

Bailey swatted Shannon's arm. "Shh. Be nice."

She ignored the twinge of jealousy in her heart. He had made no effort to contact her since the night in her apartment when he stumbled over how to ask her out. And she'd body-slammed his ego into the rug like a professional wrestler.

Then he basically slammed the door on her delving into Edwina and Edwin's claim to the Archer fortune. Little wonder he hadn't called. She sighed. "Guess his leads led nowhere."

"What?" Jessica leaned in to hear over the din of conversations in the crowded room.

"Nothing. I feel like Chinese. Anyone want to join me?"

"Aren't you going to your parents' for Sunday dinner?" Shannon joined the conversation.

"Not today. Mom has a pounding headache. Seasonal allergies I think. She and Dad left the service early."

"Ah, I'm sorry." Jessica pouted. "Sure. Chinese sounds super."

By the time Bailey got home, the clock read a little after three. Already? Wow, could the three of them chat when they got together. She felt blessed to have such good friends. Sunday meant a day of rest, no working on taxes, hers or anyone else's.

Bailey made a mug of hot tea in the microwave and settled at the dinette table. Maybe a walk down memory lane would be a good, mindless way to spend the afternoon. She scooted the top album toward her. As she flipped through the pages, she marked the pages of baby and family Christmas photos with paper clips as potential candidates for enlarging and gluing to the golden leaves. When she had twelve of them ranging from 1942 to 1953, the span of the siblings' births, she stopped and removed the snapshots, leaving a sticky note in each place. She traipsed into the bedroom, placing them one by one on the copier. After all had been scanned in, she returned to the table and her laptop, expanding and cropping, enhancing and photoshopping them to the way she wanted. Then she hit print.

As they slid onto the out tray, she picked up each and smiled. Perfect. Both Eugene and Edmond's wives had emailed early childhood pictures of their kids and grandchildren, so she printed those. Twenty-two pictures in all to dangle from the live oak. Eight she scanned to a thumb drive to take to the office supply store to be blown up into a yard sign size.

Would that be enough? Perhaps it would be fun to have a few of their teen years. She started flipping through one of the other albums, giggling at the hairstyles and clothes. She found prom pictures of Edmond and Eugene. Then she turned the pages to 1968.

She pulled out a picture of her mom standing on the stairs in a long formal dress and corsage on her wrist. Her face lit with joy and her smile dazzled for the camera. Bailey ran her finger over it. "Mom, you look gorgeous and happy."

But wait a minute. In 1968, her mother would have been in college then, so not a prom night. She glanced at the date. April 15. Of course, Fiesta week in San Antonio and the Queen's Ball.

Three weeks before her grandparent's demise and her mother had no clue of the tragedy that would tear her family apart. Eerie. The fact Bailey knew what her mother in the photo didn't know chilled Bailey's bones.

She shuddered. So much for her traipse back in time.

She slipped the photo back in its slot. As she did, something caught her attention.

Wait. Shadowed in the background, another figure stood further up on the stairs. She squinted. Edwina. Had to be. Wow.

Bailey slipped it back out and scanned it to her computer, then enlarged it. Yes. Her aunt stood several steps higher in the stairwell in a halter top and cut-offs, and she had an awful scowl on her face.

Bailey sat back in her chair. Bad blood even back then? Or jealousy because she couldn't go? It must have been when she had returned with Edwin as a toddler. She swatted it away. Not important. Think about the reunion. Not Edwina who refused to show up. Some things were not fixable.

She put the photo back in the album. Perhaps there were more of her mom. She turned the page and gasped.

Her mother stood in the same outfit, her arm linked with a tall guy with curly black hair. A chill raced through Bailey as she peered closer. The photo was discolored with age and a bit out of focus, but she recognized the goofy smile on the boy's face.

"Of my heavens. That's Mr. Hanson."

The room swirled as if she rode a carnival ride. No way.

She rose to pace. Had to be some other guy. Someone resembling the weird old man in her choir.

She slumped back into her chair, closed the album, and rubbed her temples. Enough for one night. She stacked the albums and put the flash drive in her pocketbook to take to the photo lab.

But that night she tossed and turned. The image of the young man who escorted her mother to the ball wouldn't fade out of her mind. She had to find out who he was.

The next morning, she called on her Bluetooth as she wound her way to work. Her father answered the phone.

"Morning, Dad. I have a weird question."

"Oh? Did you want to speak to your mother? She's in the kitchen."

"No, you can answer it. When did you and mom start seeing each other? In college, right?"

"We started dating the spring of her senior year. In 1972."

"But didn't you go to the same high school?"

He drew out the answer and then paused for a moment. "Though we went to the same high school, our paths never really crossed. I was two years ahead of her."

"That's what I recalled. Was Mr. Hanson in your class?"

"Hanson? Oh, Albert Hanson who sings in the choir? I believe he was in the class above me. Why?"

"Thank you."

"Bailey, why did you call this early on a Monday morning to ask that?"

"Nothing, Dad. Going through the old photo albums and I noticed a picture of a guy who looked like him."

"Why in heaven's name do you keep dredging up the past? You have your mother in a tizzy. You should be concentrating on your future."

"Dad?" Rarely had she heard such sternness in his tone.

"I mean it, Bailey. You need to give this whole blasted thing up. I have half a mind to cancel the reunion."

"That's not fair." She set her teeth.

"Bailey, you are bordering on sounding like a whiny child. Don't push it."

He hung up.

She stared at her screen for a minute. What got his goat? Bailey shrugged. He probably worried about her. If the roles reversed and her grown daughter had called that early, she also might have mildly panicked and become irritated, too.

Even so, her heart ached that she'd unwittingly upset him. She couldn't recall the last time they'd ever had words.

As she waited for the traffic light to change, she shook it off. But as Bailey turned into the office parking lot, she couldn't help but think perhaps there was more to the whole Edwina-Emily thing than she'd been told. Why did Edwina scowl on the stairs three weeks prior to the accident? Had communications been severed for some reason other than their parents' deaths?

How many skeletons did her family closet hide?

Chapter 33

Bailey had to rush from work to make the Bible study on time. Now she wondered why.

They spent the whole time haggling over the passage in Matthew 19 about divorce, which made Jessica squirm in her chair, even though her husband had the adulterous affair and filed. Still, Bailey felt sorry for her.

As they walked out, she nudged Jess. "Rough discussion. Sorry."

"It's okay. I've asked the same questions. Can I remarry? Would I be committing adultery if I did? I mean we weren't married before God, only the county clerk staff, but still…"

Shannon joined them. "Have you talked to Pastor about it?"

"No, I guess I should. Perhaps deep down it's why I

don't want to date."

Bailey rolled her eyes. "That and the dating pool is rather scummy."

"Speaking of…" Shannon halted. "I heard through the grapevine that the Marsha-Chase thing ended rather abruptly."

Jessica chuckled. "I heard no 'thing' existed, except in Marsha's and her mother's scheming heads."

Bailey lifted her hand. "Enough. Chase Montgomery's love life is none of my concern, and gossip is a sin."

She stomped off, huffing through her nose. She got in her car and jammed her fist into the steering wheel. What was going on? First, the dad displeasure scene threatening to cancel the reunion, and now her two friends were focusing on Chase as if he were a prize at a carnival. Why did she care about it enough to explode anyway? She, nor any of her family, had emotional outbursts before this begetting bug bit her. Now, the very mention of his name set her off. She never should have contacted him in the first place. Argh.

Enough of this genealogy stuff. All it brought on was heartache and trouble. Why, oh, why did she ever want to get into it, to begin with?

With a shaky sigh, Bailey turned the ignition and peeled out of the parking lot.

She decided she needed a break from all the stress she'd brought on herself and her family. For two days she didn't respond to texts, emails, or phone messages except to say, *Very busy, tax season. Talk later, in a few days.*

What about choir? From Shannon's phone.

Need to skip this week. Sorry. I'm fine. Don't worry.

She'd see Jessica and Shannon when they all went out to eat for her birthday that Saturday. The last thing she needed was knight-errand Chase to beat down her door because Shannon panicked again. Well, to be fair, the last time could have turned out differently if A.A. hadn't been so chivalrous.

After some grueling days at work, she vegged out on computer games, rented movies, and watched old TV shows. Anything to keep from thinking about her family secrets, most of which she had yet to unveil, which irked her each time she thought about it. Why did her parents insist on sheltering her from the truth? She'd be thirty-one this week. Well, celebrating her birthday over the family Sunday dinner, followed by a video chat with Travis should make it a less tense time. She made herself a promise not to mention the reunion or Edwina, or who that weird guy in the photo fifty years ago happened to be. Her mother most likely wouldn't recall. Her father said these things were all socially orchestrated anyway. Bailey had to strain her brain to remember the names of her high school prom dates, come to think of it. They'd all been last minutes ask outs.

Enough. She scolded her brain and clicked through the selection to choose an old Audrey Hepburn movie. Popcorn bowl on her lap, she slithered down into the sofa, alone in the darkened room with only the glow of the TV screen. Bower curled up next to her.

A bang came on her door. She jumped, spilling half of the snack on the rug. She tiptoed over the puffy kernels and peered through the peephole. "Yes?"

"Special delivery."

"At seven o'clock at night?"

The guy shuffled his feet and held up the package with the carrier logo on it. "Stomach flu's hit. We are short-handed."

Four in her office were out with it. Sounded legit, but so had the pizza guy. She kept her eye peeled to the tiny circle in the door. "Can you show me some identification?"

The guy's head rolled slightly backward. "You gotta be kidding me, lady. Look, I got a package here for Bailey Matteson." He held it for her to see through the peephole. She recognized her Aunt Susan's penmanship, her father's sister, on the return address. Then he set it down and reached into his back pocket, pulling out a wallet and holding it to the glass. "Here's my license." He replaced it and pulled his jacket open. "And my name tag."

She squinted to read them. The names matched.

"We good?"

"Yes, sorry." She opened the door a tad but kept the chain bolt on. "Can't be too careful these days."

"Uh, huh." The delivery man sighed and slid his device through the narrow opening. "Sign here please."

Bailey scrawled her signature over the electronic reader. If anyone could decipher it the CIA ought to hire them.

He flipped it around, stared at it, and nodded. He handed the express letter through to her. "Here, have a good evening."

She mumbled a thank you and closed the door, bolting the second lock. Just in case.

She turned it over, pulled the tab and lifted out a manila envelope. On the front, she saw a note in the familiar elderly script.

Your mother said you were planning a family reunion and collecting old photos. I always considered you as family—well, because you are—and didn't want Chester to feel left out. So here are some from his youth. Love, Aunt Susan.

Ahh. Nice. She lifted the fastener with her fingernail and pulled out four photos wrapped in tissue paper. The first, her dad's baby picture, faded to more brown than black and white. She recognized the smile, even though toothless.

The next showed him in a cowboy outfit. Perhaps for Halloween? She guessed his age to be about six.

A third one depicted him with glasses and a lanky half-boy, half-man figure. Obviously early teens. His short, black hair curled over one eye, slick and shiny as was the

327

style in the late 1950s. No doubt his attempt to look like Elvis.

She sat on the couch and pulled out the fourth one.

There her father stood. Tall, lanky, black curly hair, but slicked back. He wore a tuxedo. His smile reached his cheekbones. His hands crossed over his chest in a cocky stance.

He rested his hip against the hood of a white car. The date stamp read April 1968. In faded ink, her great aunt had penned: *Ready for Fiesta in fancy car.*

Fiesta party? Bailey's brain swirled like cotton candy on a stick. She took it over to the dinette table and took out the photo of her mom and her date. In the background stood a white car. No.

Bailey dashed down the hall. She rooted in her desk for the magnifying glass she'd purchased a few months back, brought it back to the table, and stared through it. There stood her dad by a big white automobile. A girl stood near the front passenger side, though Bailey couldn't make out the face. Not her mom, though. Too tall. She glanced back and forth between the two pictures. No doubt about it.

The same car. The date stamps matched, too. Had to be the same Fiesta ball.

She sat back, her hand to her chest. Her father not only knew Hanson, he had double dated with him. And with her mom! Why had he lied to her? Chester Matteson revered truth and honesty above all else. It's what made him so successful in business.

Bailey felt the anger bubbling up from her. Mattesons keep their promises. Mattesons are trustworthy. "You drummed it into me from the time I could walk. And now I find you are not any of those things?"

She brushed the photos off the table and grabbed her hair at the scalp in her hands. Her chest heaved and her brain spun. She prayed for clarity, and logic to filter into her mind, shoving her emotions back into her objective, investigative mode—the same way she pushed her arms through a sweater and drew it around her when she felt a chill.

After a few moments, her breathing calmed.

Before her birthday, she and her father definitely had to have a conversation. But not tonight. She bent to retrieve the photos and place them in the folder to be photocopied.

Yet even when she resumed the old movie, her eyes didn't see it. They still concentrated on the photo and her father in it. He had the stance of a young man who knew where he wanted to go in life and had planned how to get there. The charming grin that still melted her mother's heart, as well as Bailey's, gleamed at her through the decades gone by. Oh, Dad. How could you?

Then she took her attention off her dad and onto the white vehicle. Wait a minute. Why did a white car strike a chord? Something she'd read?

She grabbed her laptop, scrolled through her history, and pulled up the search she had done on Pontiac GTO Coupes. Why had she? Think.

Of course. Because of an article she'd seen in the San Marcos paper in 1968. She printed the picture of the car and then scrolled to find the article. There. She opened the file and scanned through it.

The clerk described him as a young five-foot-ten Caucasian with dark curly hair, slicked back. He wore new blue jeans and a blue and white striped, button-down, long sleeve shirt. He also wore a white crew-cut tee-shirt under the other shirt. He may have had a pock scar on his forehead. He drove away in a white '65 Pontiac GTO Coupe SS.

Police state the headlight glass at the scene and scraped paint left on the car carrying the Holstons could have been from a similar make and model reported by AAA Rental as possibly stolen. An all-points bulletin had been filed on the suspect. If you think you have seen this man...

She glanced at the one in the photo, and the one she'd printed out from her computer search. Identical.

She read the description very slowly once again. Five-foot-ten, young, dark curly hair slicked back. Pontiac GTO.

Oh, Lord. Please, no. Had she seen that man every day growing up?

Tears fuzzed her vision as she punched in Shannon's phone number.

Shannon answered on the second ring.

"Sh... Shannon?" Her friend's name barely left her mouth, it shook so hard.

"Are you all right?"

"No." Bailey shuddered and gulped. "Please come over. Now."

"Okay. On my way."

A minute after she hung up, Shannon's telltale knock banged on her door.

Bailey opened it, saw her best friend, and beckoned her inside.

Chapter 34

"It has to be a coincidence. Let me see that laptop."

Bailey brought it to her and placed it on the coffee table, along with the photos from her Aunt Susan. Shannon sat cross-legged on the couch and did a new search as Bailey looked on.

Shannon bobbed her head. "I thought so. See. GTO's were one of the most popular cars among young men in the 1960's." She pointed to the screen with her forefinger. "Says so right here. And white is a common color, even today. It is purely circumstantial."

"Then why did he lie about not knowing Hanson back then? There he is… with mom, as her Fiesta double date. Next to my dad and another girl in his fancy, white GTO." Bailey tapped the photo with force.

"Okay. That is weird. But seriously. Your mom had to

know the description of the car that killed her parents a few weeks later. Obviously, no alarms went off. You think she'd have dated and married your father if he wrecked into them?"

Bailey dabbed her nose with the facial tissue. "No. But dad told me they never took stock in these setup dates. Maybe she didn't connect the dots, even when they dated years later."

"Why would he even date her and marry her, girl?"

"Guilt? Vow to take care of her since her parents couldn't?"

"Wait, let me see that article about the accident."

She handed Shannon her laptop and maximized the screen again.

Shannon tapped the monitor. "There. Look what it says. The car *may* have been a stolen rental, girl. And the guy had a pockmark on his forehead. Your dad doesn't, right?"

Bailey let out an elongated breath. "No, of course not. Duh." She smacked her forehead. "I'm sorry I had you dash over here for nothing."

Shannon handed back the laptop. "Girlfriend, you have been wound up as tight as a child's spinning top. What is going on?"

"I don't know. My life seemed so uncomplicated before we got into that Bible study."

"You mean before you became ga-ga over the begats."

"Yeah." She popped the kink from her neck. "I keep

seeing skeletons dangling from the family closet. Secrets, as if we lived in an ancient English manor. Am I going nuts?"

"A little. Digging up all the unhappiness of the past has gotten to you." She gently shoved her shoulder against Bailey and looked at the pictures again. "I admit Mr. Hanson always gives me the creeps. And it does resemble him. But to think your mom dated him, even socially? Ugh."

"Tell me. But this is a small town where everyone knows everyone else, even if we are on the edge of San Antonio."

"You have no idea how long he's lived here, though. I mean you don't recall him being here when you grew up, right?"

"No. Or that grumpy Mr. Garcia. You're right. I am totally out there. Sorry."

She swiveled to face Bailey. "It was nice of your aunt to send these. You're doing a good thing getting most of your family back together. At least for one day. Enjoy it."

"I guess."

A knock tapped on her door.

Shannon's cheeks turned a deep rose. "Um, that would be Chase."

Bailey leaped to her feet. "What?"

"I'm sorry. I thought you'd been attacked again or something." She lifted her shoulders to her ears. "So, I called."

Bailey stomped to the door, saw his face in the peephole, and swung it open. "Hi."

Chase's eyes scanned her. "You aren't bleeding, I see."

"No, only in my heart. Come on in." She pointed to the living room. She squelched a fleeting idea to dash to the bathroom and repair her makeup or change out of her grub clothes. Chase might get the wrong idea, like she cared how she appeared in his presence.

Shannon moved to the side chair and motioned for him to sit on the couch.

He took a seat and spread out the photos on the coffee table as Bailey stood by, her arms hugging her torso.

His jaw moved. He turned to Bailey. "You know, huh?"

"Know what?" Bailey glared into his eyes.

He scratched his eyebrow. "I think you had better sit down."

Instead, she pressed her feet into the carpet and locked her knees.

"Suit yourself. No, on second thought this is not the time or place. I'll be right back."

Chase rose and left her apartment, his cell phone cocked to his ear.

Bailey opened her mouth to speak then twirled to face Shannon, who lifted her hands out to the sides, motioning she hadn't a clue. Bailey ran her hand through her hair and walked to the window. She pulled the blinds down with her fingers and craned her head. Chase stood underneath the window near his car in the parking lot. His head bent down, he crossed his long legs as he leaned on the hood of his car, the cell phone still pressed to his ear. Then he straightened up and pocketed it. With a glance up at her window, he headed to her stairwell.

"He's coming back up."

She scuttled to the couch and sat down, her hands in her lap. His knuckles tapped on the door, and he entered. His expression oozed authority. "Okay, Bailey. Come with me."

"Where?"

"I'll tell you on the way. Shannon, I think it would be best if you didn't join us."

They exchanged glances.

Shannon shifted her gaze down to her hands in compliance. "I think I understand why."

"Well, I don't." Bailey shoved her fist to her hips. "What is going on?"

"It'll all become clear in a while. Now please, do as I say and come with me."

"Go on, Bailey." Shannon rose and grabbed Bailey's hand to help her up. "Go with him. I'll lock up."

"All right. I'll go. Let me freshen up first." Her words came out tersely, but she didn't care. Honestly, she'd rather they all go away and leave her alone. Shove the skeletons back deep into the closet. Sweep the family dirt under the rug where it belonged.

337

She took her time, mostly because her hand kept shaking the mascara wand. Hair brushed and facial smudges erased, she emerged with a quick head bob and grabbed her bag. Threading it onto her shoulder, she turned to Chase. "Let's go."

He held the front door open for her. She mouthed a "thank you" to him more than spoke the words. When they arrived at his car, he punched the fob and pulled the handle to the passenger side door.

She slid in without comment. He closed it, rounded the back bumper, and opened the driver side. As he clicked his safety belt, he turned to face her. "Bailey, I'm sorry you found out the way you did, but I want you to withhold judgment for the next hour until you hear all the facts, understand?"

"Found out what? Are you telling me my father's car caused my grandparents to flip in the bar ditch? The article said it was a rental."

"Bailey. Please don't ask me anything else until we get there."

"Where?"

"To learn the truth about the other lead. Now sit quietly."

She sighed and turned to view out her window. They rode in silence to where she assumed would be his office. On low volume, voices over a police radio chatted numbered codes and locations. She guessed he listened to it.

They turned down a side street but then took the accelerator lane entrance onto the highway. Did he know a shortcut? Bailey read the illuminated sign hanging over their lane. "Wait. Isn't this the way—"

"We're headed west, to your parents' house."

She spun to face him, as the seat belt dug into her chest. "Why, for heaven's sake?"

"Okay, I'll tell you. Though I'd prefer you heard it from the horse's mouth." He flicked on his blinker. "When I first met your dad the day after the break-in, you know… when I came to re-interview you at their home?"

"Yes."

"Something about the expression on his face and a hidden tone in his voice perplexed me. When the Arthur angle didn't seem to match up, I began digging into your dad's past. I thought maybe he knew something. Then my friend at San Marcus APD sent me the report, on the sly."

"You read the clerk's testimony."

Chase's eyes darted in her direction then returned to view the expressway lanes ahead of them. "How did you know about that?"

"I had found it, though it took a while."

"When? I thought you promised…"

She touched his arm. "Calm down. I went to the newspaper archives in San Antonio last winter and found they also kept actual copies of the surrounding towns' chronicles, including ours on microfiche. So, I read the weekly newspapers from May 1968. On the back page of the one from San Marcos, the story continued, even though it never said so on the front page where the story began. Somehow the rest of the article never got entered online. So I scanned it and saved it to my laptop."

"And that part contained the bit about the clerk's description of the car."

"Yes, and the man, which sounded a lot like Dad. When I saw the old pictures his aunt sent tonight and recognized the car…" She gulped and flipped her head to stare once more out the side window. "I panicked and call Shannon. She calmed me down again and showed me that the police report said it was a rental."

"Your father had rented it for the Fiesta and college year-end party season since he drove a clunker." Chase pulled into the drive and killed the engine.

Bailey felt cold, even though outside the March evening temperatures hovered in the sixties. "What are you telling me?"

"I'm telling you it wasn't your father in the car that night. Someone else took that rental car. Let him explain, all right?"

She blinked back the dampness that gathered in her eyes. "You're certain?"

"Yes."

Bailey's mouth dropped. "Then who?"

"You'll find out soon enough."

"Tell me."

"It's not mine to tell." He shot her an authoritative

glare. The kind reserved for principals or courtroom judges. It evaporated any defiance bubbling up into her chest.

Chase rounded the car and opened her door. He gave her his hand to help her out, then closed the door and pressed his palms into her shoulders, bending to meet her eye to eye. "Your father is expecting us. Please, be quiet and let him speak. This is going to be difficult for you both."

Her father greeted them at the door. His face appeared drawn and pale. The mumbled greeting instead of his usual confident buoyancy puzzled her. Shuffling his feet, he led the way. "Let's go into the den."

"Where is Mom?"

"In her room. Most likely crying." He stopped and turned to face them. "I already told her. She never knew either." His eyes focused on Bailey and narrowed. "Frankly, I'd hoped to keep it that way."

Bailey cast her gaze down. Did he blame her for partially uncovering the family secrets?

Chase clasped his hand on Chester Edward's shoulder. "The truth shall set you free."

A momentary glimmer lit in her dad's eyes. "You didn't bring the handcuffs then, huh?"

"No, sir. Not into your home."

What? Handcuffs!

Chapter 35

Bailey's mouth flew open, but no words emerged.

The two men broke eye contact. Her father motioned for Bailey to enter the room first.

She curled up on the couch, her legs tucked underneath her to the side. Instinctively she drew a throw pillow to her chest. She wished for a crackling log burning in the fireplace. Even though spring weather warmed the night air, a chill settled over her. Like the time she entered the house, oh so many months ago after her parents had argued about the fiftieth anniversary of his high school reunion. Did this have anything to do with that?

The two men gazed at each other as they each took a winged chair and sat.

"What does she know?" Her dad addressed Chase.

"Your sister sent her photos of you. Childhood milestones. One showed you in front of the white GTO."

Her father's eyes darted in Bailey's direction. "And

you put two and two together."

Bailey tucked her legs further under her. "I didn't want to add it up, actually."

His shoulders buckled as he clasped his hands to the arms of the chair. "Bailey. I didn't kill your grandparents."

Bailey scrunched her forehead. "Who, then?"

"My roommate, my freshman year in college."

Bailey's ears filled with a swooshing sound. Had she heard correctly? "Excuse me? Your… what?"

"Roommate. Charles Stubbs. Kinda a loner, but from a good family in Seguin."

"I don't get it. The picture Aunt Susan sent is of you with the tux standing by the car. And another guy, who looked an awful bit like Mr. Hanson, by the way, stood by the same car with my mother in a photo from her mother's albums." She spit out the last words with disgust.

"Yes. I'll get to that, Charles may have well been my shadow that year in college. Shy and scared to be in such a sea of people, he stayed in the background and I dragged him through the seasons' events on my coattails in an effort to get him to shake from his shell. Quite honestly, I am not sure many people in the social circles remembered him at all."

"So, you two went to the Fiesta balls. That's when you escorted Mom?"

"Back then, as I have told you, a social coordinator arranged the escorts for the debutantes. The time-honored, old society way of doing things. Kept the young ladies from coupling up with one guy. Gave everyone a fair shot at the pickings."

"So you said. It still sounds gross and archaic." She scrunched her nose.

Chase chuckled. "It does remind you of a livestock auction."

"In a ballroom for the arena, yes." Her father gazed into the empty fire grate. "We all mingled. I barely danced with her. Neither did Charles or Albert Hanson. Your mother was quite a looker. Still is. Her card filled in no time."

"Albert Hanson dated her, too. That *was* him in the photos."

"That night, he did, Bailey. As you said, the whole thing bordered on archaic. A farce none of us took seriously. But the social circles clung to tradition back then, and if you wanted your reputation and name to remain solid, you played along."

"Same in my era, too, to some extent, Mr. Matteson." Chase snapped his fingers. "Wait. Bailey, you never made your debut, did you?"

"Nope. Went to grad school instead. Convinced Dad it was money better spent."

"I knew you were smart." He tapped his forehead and, yes gave her his infamous wink. She let it affect her momentarily then blinked and returned her attention to her dad.

"What really happened, Daddy?"

Her calling him that caused his facial muscles to soften. "Charles went into a tailspin when he saw Edwina shopping one day. Fell head over heels. He stalked her and tried to get her to go out with him, even though everyone knew she had a child by then. He didn't care."

"His actions obviously spoke volumes." Chase crossed his legs.

"Yes, and I never picked up on it." Her father glanced away.

"How did Mr. Hanson play into this?"

Her father returned his attention to her. "Hanson was Charles' best friend. When it came up that he had been assigned to escort your mom, Charles asked him to sneak him in to see Edwina. All he wanted to do was talk to her and convince her to go out with him. Hanson agreed to the plan, and they set it up. I rented the car for our double date so to speak. Hanson's and mine. Charles rode in the trunk and snuck around to the side of the house where her bedroom window stood while Hanson rang the doorbell for your mother."

"And you went along with it?"

"I didn't know he hid in the trunk until he crawled out. But, I didn't try to stop him either. I did excuse myself from my date sitting in the passenger seat and followed him, though."

"Did Edwina see him?"

"Imagine her surprise when he climbed up the trellis to her window. Edwina wouldn't have anything to do with him. She still wanted to hook Arthur, I guess. She became really, really mad. Her yelling brought her father around to the side."

"So, he and my grandfather got into it?"

"Your grandfather threatened to call the police. Charles yelled even more, and so he whacked Charles with the butt of his shotgun. Broke two of Charles' teeth."

"How horrid. What happened next?"

"Charles ran off. I backed away and dashed back to the car, pretending I'd not seen a thing."

"That explains Edwina's scowling in the photo. Did Mom have a clue?"

"I'm sure she did, but she didn't know we knew. She apologized for holding us up saying they'd had a family issue that needed settling. I don't think your mom knew about the scheme until Hanson confessed on the way to the ball. Probably why she ignored both of us the rest of the evening."

"When Hanson and I got back to the dorm, Charles sat there on the stoop with white hate in his eyes and a blood stains on his shirt. He'd been drinking."

Her father took in a deep breath.

"I guess Charles stewed in his juices and got more and more angry?"

"Yes, Chase. And it didn't stop with that night. He brewed for several days, would yell at a drop of the hat, and slammed drawers a lot. He also skipped classes and drank more."

"You're saying he ran my grandparents down on purpose? Acted out of revenge?"

"That's right, Bailey. He was convinced Edwina's father had tainted her view of him. Better than realizing Edwina rejected him. His fragile ego wouldn't let him go there I guess." Her father's eyes shimmered in the low light of the lamp. "He stole the GTO from me the day before I was to return it to the rental company."

"And drove under the influence, right, Mr. Matteson?"

Her dad nodded. "Yes. Guess he picked up a coed on the way or something. We will never know who she was or what happened to her. The police found him three days later in a field about a mile and a half from the scene. The buzzards led them to him."

That last sentence made Bailey shudder. "You mean he died?"

"Internal injuries. He bled to death, only all inside." Chase informed Bailey in a flat tone.

Bailey felt her stomach flip. She hugged the pillow tighter. "What a horrid fate, no matter what he'd done."

"Coroner stated it probably took hours, but Charles's blood alcohol levels were so high, he assumed he passed out during most of it."

Bailey shook her head, hand to her heart. "I guess there is some mercy in that."

"I hope you show me mercy for hiding the truth so long, daughter. And your mother, too." His voice wobbled.

"Oh, Daddy." She rushed over to her father's chair,

knelt at his feet, and hugged his knees as she laid her head upon them.

"I am so, so sorry." Her father stroked her hair as he did when she was a child. He kept talking, though now in almost a matter-of-fact manner, as if reciting the facts from a book. "Your mother and her siblings never learned the description of the car, only that the suspect died later that night."

"So, they considered the matter resolved."

"Yes. The chief of police in San Marcos was an old fraternity buddy of my father's. For my sake, he kept the story from the papers and called in favors to remove my name from any of the court documents, since the car had been stolen. He figured I'd suffered enough losing my dad, then my mom. And the police decided Charles' family had suffered enough losing their son. They closed the case." He lifted her by the chin. "My attorney paid for the rental car out of my inheritance. And for a new car for your mother's family."

She wiped her eyes and brought his hand to her lips. "The pieces all fit now."

"It wasn't until several years later that I formally met your mother at a party. I decided I needed to tell her what I knew about her parents' death. But I couldn't get up the gumption. I asked her to a picnic where we could discuss the matter in private, but that never happened. We hit it off, and the right time never came. The more we dated, the harder it became for me to confess about Charles. When I knew I loved her, well, I guess I feared the truth might ruin our chances."

Bailey rocked back on her feet. "Edwina knew, didn't she?"

"Yes. Charles wrote her a note. Let her know he wanted to get even with her dad. I don't think he meant to kill them, only ram their car." Chester's voice quivered again. "It all went wrong, so very, very wrong." A single tear escaped down his cheek.

She tucked her arms around him and bent her head to his. In the background, she heard Chase's footsteps leave the room. She appreciated his sensitivity.

Lifting away from the hug, Bailey ventured to learn more. "One thing I don't get, Dad. Why does Mr. Hanson hate me?"

"You resemble Edwina as well as your mom. Didn't you know that? You've studied her photos enough."

"I guess I didn't think about it."

"Well, I imagine seeing you brought back bad memories. Charles was his—how do you say it now? BFF?"

She chuckled. Ten years ago, maybe. "One more question. Who did you take to that Fiesta ball? The picture appeared too fuzzy to tell."

"I took Mary Francis Boyd." His face lightened.

Bailey let out a nervous laugh. "Chase's mother?"

"She wasn't at the time. As I said, it was all arranged." He glanced away and then puffed through his cheeks.

"There is something else I need to tell you, Bailey."

The quiver in his voice sent prickly ice up her arms. "Daddy?"

"Hanson hired the goon to trash your apartment with money I lent him. Mr. Garcia made the contact."

Her own father? Her world spun out of kilter. "You knew what he planned to do?"

He blinked, then focused somewhere else in the room, not on her face. "Yes. I did."

Bailey's ears filled with her fast-pulsed heartbeats, as if blocking her from hearing more. The question squeaked through her tonsils. "To hurt Bower?"

He shook his head. "I didn't authorize that. I only wanted him to snatch your laptop, and to make it appear as if it had been a robbery."

Her father turned his head to gaze into her eyes, his now red-rimmed. "When I heard what he'd done to your poor pet I became so angry I asked for the money back."

He reached for her, but she recoiled.

"Daddy, how could you?"

"I wanted you to back off. That's all. I was afraid if the truth came out it would destroy all of us. I told myself I did it to protect you and your mother, but the truth is I really did it to shield me. Oh, Bailey, I am so, so sorry."

"That's why you paid the vet bills."

"Honey, I'd have done that anyway. I know how much that cat means to you. I swear I would never, ever agree to anything to hurt him, or you."

351

She swallowed back tears from forming. "And the other threats?"

He sniffled and gave her a slow head bob in response as he gazed into the fibers of the rug. "Hanson told me he arranged them through Garcia once Garcia discovered you continued your research. And I went along with it." He held up a finger. "But with strict instructions not to harm you or anyone else in any way."

She clenched her teeth to keep her emotions in check while her brain tried to assimilate this information. "How did they know?"

"Believe it or not, Garcia is quite the computer nerd. Has a Master's degree in computer engineering and kept up with the technology. He knew how to hack into your phone."

"Wait a minute." She held up her hands. "You're saying Mr. Garcia tapped my phone?"

"Yes, and I gave him your mother's. No one stole it." He still refused to meet her eyes. His hands started to shake. "I confessed it all to Chase several weeks ago. If you want me arrested, I'd understand."

She felt as if something had punched her in her windpipe. The other lead. Not sure where it would head. I'll let you know. Chase knew. Why didn't he tell her? She answered her own question. It would devastate her and he knew it.

The man did care for her. He'd crossed the line.

She turned back to her father, who sat before her,

hunched over as if he'd turned ninety-five before her eyes. No longer the invincible, powerful man she'd always counted upon.

Never had she seen her father so weak, so out of control. It unhinged her. Her heart melted and all the anger spilled silently onto the Oriental rug.

"Of course, I am not going to press charges, though I have half a mind to have him arrest Mr. Garcia and Mr. Hanson."

He raised his head. "Which will implicate me, my dear. And you have every right to do so."

Again she felt trapped between wanting justice and what her heart told her she should do. A very hard and painful lesson. One God insisted on teaching her.

She had a choice. Forgive and rebuild her relationship with her father, or let her emotions carry her down the path of distrust and bitterness.

She closed her eyes. No, there had been way too much of that in her family the last fifty years. She had to break the tradition once and for all. Right here. Right now.

She opened her eyes and took his hands. "Daddy, I love you. I am so sorry I drudged up all this unhappiness." She reached in to kiss his cheek, and then rocked back and raised herself to stand. "I better go see about Mom."

Her father gave her a weak smile. "Good girl."

When Bailey came back downstairs, Chase sat at the bottom fiddling with his phone.

"Where's Dad?"

"He went to bed. In one of the guest rooms is my guess." He stood and met her eyes since she'd halted a few steps above him. "How's your mom?"

"She'll live. She doesn't blame Dad. She only wishes he'd never kept the secret from her. Makes her wonder what else he's never told her. I reminded her of the time she told me that sometimes in marriage you have to withhold the truth. She's evidently done it too, so she can't fault him too much."

Chase nodded without inquiring if Bailey knew what they were. Very un-detective like, but she appreciated it. He glanced up the stairs. "Think they'll be all right?"

Bailey clutched her waist. "Eventually. They have a strong marriage"

He smiled tenderly and took her hands, unwinding them from her middle. "And, how are you?"

"Surprisingly all right."

He grinned. "Hungry?"

"Starved."

"Cheeseburger or pancakes?"

"Pancakes with a mound of butter and a gallon of syrup." She laughed. "And you're buying, Detective Montgomery."

Chase offered her his elbow. "Wouldn't have it any other way, Ms. Matteson."

Chapter 36

On the way to the Pancake House, Bailey sent one more text to Edwina. *Mom knows. So do I. It's okay. Please come.*

She enjoyed Chase's company. He acted like an old friend. They laughed, talked, and he didn't chide her once about the calories she downed. Not that he would.

He drove her home and walked her to her door. "It's almost eleven. Will Shannon be up pacing the floor?"

"Possibly. I'll text her." She clicked her fingernails over the keyboard. "There. I told her I am fine, and I'd tell her everything over my birthday dinner tomorrow. Jess, too."

"Is it well?"

"Yes, I think so."

He leaned against the wall next to her jamb. "You are an amazing lady."

She scrunched her face. "Am I?"

"Most definitely." He took her keys, opened her front door, and peered inside. "No boogie men. Your castle is secure, my lady."

She curtsied. Before she entered she turned back to him. "Chase, Dad told me he put out the money for Hansen and Garcia to hire the man who trashed my apartment and hurt Bower. And the other times, too."

He sucked in a breath. "I hoped he would."

"Why didn't you tell me?" She pressed her spine into the door jamb.

"It wrenched your father's heart to know what that hired thug did to Bower." He rested his hands on her shoulders. "I figured eventually he'd come clean, so I kept dropping hints that I'd figured it out."

"I recall the stealthy glances between the two of you."

Chase nodded. "He called me a few weeks ago and told me. But of course, he had no actual contact with the jerk. In fact, none of them did. It was all arranged through a cousin of Garcia's. That's how those things usually work." He gazed into her eyes. "The pizza incident and message for Shannon were courtesy of them also. Same purpose. This time with the stipulation no law, property or living thing would be harmed."

"And the message on my phone, the one left on Edwin's car,"

"No one stole your mother's phone."

"He told me. Why did they persist?"

He clucked his tongue. "To get you to stop prying into

the past, obviously. I figured they were behind those events, but there wasn't a thing I could do about it. Then your dad somehow got enough information a week ago which has allowed us to track the thugs down."

"The other lead."

"Yes. We arrested them four days ago"

"Does Dad know that?"

"Yes. I told him when I called and said I was bringing you over. I'd hoped he'd get the hint and work up the gumption to confess it to you."

"I can't believe he, Garcia and Hanson planned it all." It came out as a statement, a reality she gulped down in an attempt to digest it. "I didn't even know they knew one another, other than attending the same church."

"You sure you're okay?"

"I will be. Are you going to arrest Dad?"

"Only if you press charges."

"I wouldn't do it for A.A."

"To protect your family."

"Right. I won't, now, for the same reason."

A smile spread across Chase's mouth. "Don't tell anyone I said so, but I'm glad."

She stepped from his reach and yanked her keys from the deadbolt. "As far as I'm concerned, the case is solved, Detective. I don't want to think about it anymore."

"Then it's closed. I'll file my report in the morning." He pushed off. "Sparing all the details that occurred before 2017 and keeping certain names anonymous to protect the informant."

"Hey. Thanks." She extended her hand for him to shake. She hoped he didn't bend to kiss it, even if he had acted as her chivalrous knight a few times.

He didn't. He gave her fingers a firm, yet tender squeeze. "Take care of yourself, Bailey Matteson. Happy birthday."

"This is goodbye, then?"

"Oh, I'll be around if ever you need me, ma'am." He gestured as if he donned a cowboy hat, tipping its rim to her. "Or want to eat pancakes without telling your girlfriends."

Don't do it. Don't do it.

He did.

The wink.

Okay. Yes, the man made her heart flutter. Maybe she needed to rethink things.

But not now. She had too much else going on in her life.

She winked back. "I'd like that. After the reunion, to which I hope you'll come."

He grinned even more. "Wouldn't miss it."

"Good."

He turned to leave. As he headed down the hallway, he called back. "Bolt your door."

May tenth drew near and Bailey scurried to make sure everything looked perfect. Shannon and Jessica pitched in with the leaf-making. They, along with Travis' wife, Liza, helped Bailey hang them on the tree limbs the day before the event.

"Almost feels like Christmas." Jessica giggled.

"Maybe it almost is." Bailey glanced at the outdoor lights strung around the pool area.

Shannon hugged her. "You are giving your family a huge present, girl."

"Yes, if only Edwina would come. That would be the bow on top." She held up the picture on the leaf of Edwina peering into her mom's cradle.

"Put it on. You can never have one leaf too many on a tree." She nudged her shoulder. "Even a family one. Still time to pray on it, girlfriend."

Jessica huffed out a long sigh. "Shannon's being wise again."

They all laughed until tears formed.

That night Jessica and Shannon stayed at the Matteson home, chatting and watching Disney movies with Travis' girls until Bailey's mom told them to all go to bed.

The day of the reunion, everyone showed up on time, except one.

Bailey sighed under her breath. "Still time to pray."

Then Jessica left suddenly. Bailey and Shannon assumed that for Jessica, seeing so many family members together plucked a heart string too hard for her. Though she had a great adopted family, Bailey guessed it didn't seem the same.

Bailey's mom pulled her to the side. "Chin up. You are the hostess. Muddle through."

"You're right. I'll go see her tomorrow."

As Bailey set out more ice for the drinks, Chase caught her eye. He pointed with his head and winked.

Bailey followed his gesture and then gasped.

Edwina came around to the backyard, dressed conservatively with a minimal amount of makeup.

When Elliott saw her, he ran and hugged her.

Emily Matteson wandered over with tears glimmering under her mascara and gave her sister a hug.

Soon Edmond and Eugene joined them and they all shook hands.

Then Bailey came over, fighting tears of joy. She extended her hand in the Matteson hostess style. "Hello, Edwina. Thank you for coming."

Edwina's nervousness slid off her like a shell of ice. She took Bailey's hand in both of hers. "Thank you for inviting me."

They both broke out in the same wide smile.

Edwina and Edwin stood off from each other at first, but as the evening progressed, Bailey noticed they slid off together to sit on one of the benches at the back of the garden.

"A mother and son talk?" Her mother laced her arm through Bailey's.

"I hope so. A long overdue one."

"Hmm. And all your doing." She lightly pinched her daughter's cheek. "I am proud of you."

Bailey squeezed her mother's hand. "Are you all right, Mom? Really?"

"I think so. It's as if a giant tension has been released. I think I always knew your dad had a secret. Perhaps that is why I had a few of my own. I was wrong, Bailey. Marriage shouldn't have any."

Her mother, admitting she was wrong? Bailey tried hard not to react. She peered at the reflection of the stringed lights in the swimming pool. "Charles was a sad person, wasn't he? A truly tortured soul."

"Yes. I'm surprised your dad ever befriended him."

"Have you forgiven him, Mom?"

She smiled. "Your father? Of course. He has suffered enough. Think of the burden he's carried all these years. It would've undone a weaker man, you know."

"Yes, I do. Which is why I have forgiven him also."

"Good." Her mother patted her hand. "He loves us both dearly."

Her dad's laughter sailing over the barbeque pit made them both turn. He flipped hamburgers as he chatted with Edmond's two sons and Joaquin, Edwin's son, no doubt sharing some male tale. Eugene and Edmond's wives sat on lawn chairs talking with Maria. The younger crowd perched on the retaining wall, all staring at their cell phones and occasionally sharing screens.

Bailey rested her head on her mom's shoulder. Warmth flowed through her as she focused on the golden leaves, with the family pictures pasted to them, fluttering in the oak trees. They reflected the lights around the pool area, dancing and mingling on the water's surface. Edwina's fluttered in the center, where it belonged.

A perfect metaphor to describe these newly-discovered kin. Love shimmered and bounced off every one of them, reflecting the rediscovery of what it means to be a family. A lesson Bailey had learned, too.

Hopefully, given time, they'd all sink deeper into a relationship with each other. As she gazed at each of her relatives, Bailey breathed a satisfied sigh and thanked God that she'd been begotten into this group of unique and interesting people.

She pondered. How long had it been since her dad's side of the family had a reunion? Too long.

She'd write Aunt Susan in the morning about organizing one.

Dupree-Holston Family Tree

Reymont and Claire, nee Jartain, Dupree

- ❖ Juliana   m. Jason McDaniel (d. 1941)
- ❖ **Mary Beth**   m. Edgar Holston
  - ➢ **Edmond**   m. Betsy Adams
    - **Taylor**
    - **Michael**   m. Ann Kinsley
      - ○ **Madison**
      - ○ **Leah**
  - ➢ **Edgar Eugene**   m. Julia Jordan (d. 1984)
                          m. Autumn Simpson
    - **Robert**
  - ➢ **Edwina**   m. Arthur Archer
    - **Edwin Arthur**   m. Maria Sanchez
      - ○ **Angelina**
      - ○ **Joaquin**
  - ➢ **Emily**   m. Chester Matteson
    - **Travis**   m. Liza McDaniel
      - ○ **Lily**
      - ○ **Tanya**
    - **Bailey**
  - ➢ **Elliot**
- ❖ Agnes

Acknowledgments

I'd like to thank Marji Laine Clubine for encouraging me to write the Relatively Seeking Mysteries, and her daughter for coming up with the wonderfully creative title for this series.

I believe when God taps on my shoulder several times in a short period, I need to perk up my ears to the direction He is leading me.

I never delved into my family's genealogy but my brother has for decades. At a recent family gathering, he began to discuss the lives of our maternal relatives who had long since passed on and it tickled my interest. While leading a women's retreat, I stayed with a woman who is neck deep in ancestry research and spent several hours explaining the processes to me. At a book club lecture a few weeks later, another woman approached me about possibly writing a series on genealogy. On the hour drive home, I kept mulling it over in my head until it began to solidify. By the time I pulled into my apartment complex, I had two of the three book synopses plotted.

But, in retrospect, the journey toward writing this series began a long time ago…

I am blessed to have a real hand-drawn "family tree" from 1916. It shows my patriarch and matriarch from the 1300's England on my father's side as the trunk, and ends with my paternal grandmother as one of the last branches. As I stood on tiptoes as a young child tracing the branches of that tree behind the framed glass, I envisioned who these folks were and what they looked like. Perhaps, in part, that yellowed with age depiction became a catalyst for me becoming a fiction writer.

I wrote suspense and romance, until my older sister challenged me to write the genre I personally love— mystery. From middle school on I have always loved reading or watching a good whodunit. That was four years ago.

Having finished one cozy mystery series, I felt a deep void as to what to write next. It is similar to the day after you send your child off to college. Then God opened this new door for me to become contracted to write this second cozy mystery series, and I've so enjoyed plotting the winding path from the crime to the culprit. I hope you enjoyed the trek along with me, as portrayed through the life of Bailey Matteson and her kinfolk.

And, I trust you will enjoy the second and third novels in the series, Fallen Leaf and Leaf Me Alone to be released in 2019 and 2020.

Thanks,

Julie B Cosgrove

About the Author

Besides being a professional speaker, freelance writer, and an award-winning author of sixteen books, including the Bunco Biddies Mysteries and the Relatively Seeking Mysteries, Julie B Cosgrove is a digital missionary as on staff with Power to Change (formerly Cru Canada). Julie works for The Life Project assisting 26 plus volunteer writers produce free daily devotionals as well as meaningful testimonies and articles which lead people to seek confidential spiritual mentors to assist them with the issues they face. She also has a blog with readership in 51 countries, Where Did You Find God Today.com.

Julie believes in writing vividly visualized, real-life literature with believable characters who try to live out their faith in their daily lives. After all, that is what she is trying to do. Being a missionary herself, she is active in her church's mission and ministry council as well as an international women's ministry called the Daughters of the Holy Cross. She has a passion for leading women into a deeper relationship with God and with each other as sisters in Christ.

A native Texan herself, Julie writes about her state and its people. She was raised in the Hill Country and San Antonio, raised her child in the Austin area, and now as a widow, lives in Fort Worth.

Coming soon from Julie

Fallen Leaf: Book 2
Jessica knows she was adopted and searches for her birth parents' identities so she can trace her family history. Bailey and Jessica, her close friends and fellow genealogy buffs, decide to help. When they uncover something scandalous about her familial past ... and present, someone else will do what they can to keep the girls quiet.

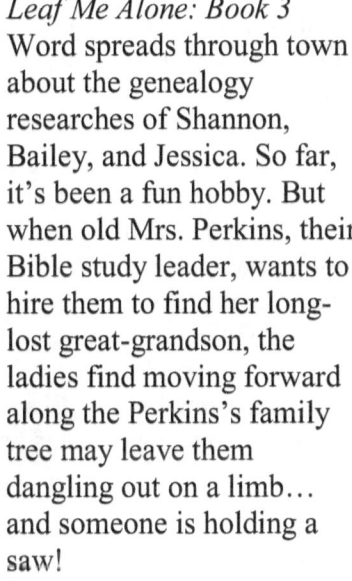

Leaf Me Alone: Book 3
Word spreads through town about the genealogy researches of Shannon, Bailey, and Jessica. So far, it's been a fun hobby. But when old Mrs. Perkins, their Bible study leader, wants to hire them to find her long-lost great-grandson, the ladies find moving forward along the Perkins's family tree may leave them dangling out on a limb... and someone is holding a saw!

Mystery and Suspense from WIP

Amy Juliana Emerson might be a cultured debutante, but she's doing her best to follow her mom's rebellious footsteps. Her desperate attempt to escape her father's control, however, comes at a time when she might find that she's playing into the hands of the enemy.

Someone wants to complete the final assignment of a murdered hit man.

Her dad's gone, her diner's closing, and her car's in the lake. Cat McPherson has nothing left to lose ... except her life. And a madman, bent on revenge, is determined to take that, as well.

How can a small-town girl survive when ultimate power wants her dead?

Find both of these mysteries at Amazon.

Thank you
for reading our books!

Look for other books
published by

P

Pursued Books
an imprint of

W

Write Integrity Press
www.WriteIntegrity.com

www.ingramcontent.com/pod-product-compliance
Lightning Source LLC
Chambersburg PA
CBHW020517260626
47156CB00006B/2036